TWISTED LIVES

MEL SHERRATT

CHAPTER ONE

Monday

The October day was pretty calm as Detective Inspector Allie Shenton drove along Hanley Road towards Smallthorne roundabouts, blue lights flashing and sirens wailing. There was a cloudless sky with a light breeze, and a temperature that wouldn't go amiss in late summer. Even considering the circumstances, Allie was glad to be out of a stuffy office to enjoy the fresh air.

It wouldn't be for long, though.

It was lunchtime in the city of Stoke-on-Trent, and the roads were fairly steady. Allie negotiated the traffic to get to her destination as quickly as she could. Two members of the public, a man and a woman, had been found dead in a house, and she was on her way to investigate. Detective Sergeant Perry Wright and Detective Constable Frankie Higgins were with her too.

A call had come in from a distraught female who, according to the control room, hadn't stopped screaming all the way through it. Allie didn't want to think about what she must have seen to make her react that way, but she knew from experience, seeing one body was bad enough, never mind two. And stumbling on them would be a horrific ordeal. She hoped the girl wasn't alone at the property.

'Is there anything you know happening in the vicinity?' she said, manoeuvring through a tight space - a loading lorry parked half on the pavement and half on the road.

'Only the usual.' Perry shook his head. 'Nothing's really happened since Billy Whitmore's murder.'

Seven months ago in the north of the city, Billy Whitmore had been found at the back of a disused pub with fatal stab wounds. The Red Lion was on the next street to where he'd lived on the Limekiln Estate.

They'd caught his murderer shortly afterwards, but since then, the estate had been going into a freefall, a turf war between two groups of young males getting more violent week by week. Billy Whitmore had been a drug dealer, and people were still fighting to take over his patch.

Allie took another corner sharply. 'I haven't been to a murder-suicide in years.'

'I don't think I've ever been to one.' Perry held on for dear life in the passenger seat. 'It's probably some idiot who's killed his wife and then turned on himself because he can't live with a prison sentence.'

'Don't be stereotypical!' Allie turned towards him quickly to show she was joking, only to find him grinning. They were well aware in their line of work that there were assaults and violence aimed at, and on, all sexes and genders. There were no exceptions.

A few minutes later, Allie turned into Neville Street, switching off the blues and twos. Like many streets on the Limekiln Estate, it consisted mostly of semi-detached properties owned by a housing association and the local city council. Occasionally, the odd one was rented by a dodgy landlord. It was narrow for the amount of traffic that flowed through it, an unfortunate shortcut from one main road to another.

Ahead, an ambulance, emergency lights flashing, stood outside the house they needed, number four. She parked, and they went over to the property, noticing nothing unusual. At the moment, it seemed most of the residents of Neville Street were going about their daily business unaware of what was going on. But not for long. A woman leaned on a gate at the top of her path, a phone to her ear. Across the other side, a young woman watching from the doorstep, a child on a tricycle racing around the front garden.

Allie would give it fifteen minutes for people to start arriving for a gander. It wouldn't take long for the place to flood with crowds of onlookers as well as their emergency vehicles.

The garden of number four had been butchered; an attempt had been made to make it seem half-decent before the winter set in. At least someone was making an effort, even if the cuttings were in a pile that would go up in seconds if someone threw a lit match to it.

Flicking on latex gloves and shoe covers for now, she knocked on the door. 'Hello, Police.'

A uniformed officer appeared in the hallway, wearing gloves too. He was tall, early-twenties, with receding brown hair and a menacing demeanour. Friendly with it, she assumed, by the concern in his eyes.

'DI Shenton,' she informed him. 'Can you give me an update, please?'

'PC Shanahan, Ma'am. One IC1 female, late teens, and one IC1 male, approximately mid-thirties, both deceased on my arrival. I was walking past when I heard screaming. There are three females in the kitchen. None of them were able to tell me much more than we know.'

That wouldn't be unusual, Allie mused. Not if they'd witnessed the murders. They would most likely be in shock, even if they'd been involved and were trying to cover their tracks. She had to think of every eventuality.

The first thing to do was to split the three women up, talk to them separately, and under no circumstances treat them as anything other than victims for now.

'Okay, PC – what's your first name?'

'Callum, Ma'am.'

'Can you watch the front door, Callum, see that no one gets in or out until the team get here?'

'Yes, Ma'am.' He didn't move. 'I couldn't help them. They look as if they've been dead for a while.'

Allie motioned with her head to Frankie.

'Come on, fella.' Frankie manoeuvred Callum outside. 'Let's set up a first point of call. Have you done one before?'

Allie blew out a deep breath and went inside the house. In the kitchen, the crying had subsided, a faint murmuring taking its place. In the living room, there was nothing anyone could do for the victims.

At a glance, Allie could tell that life had been extinct for a few hours.

CHAPTER TWO

Memories of the first dead body Allie found in her rookie days came flooding back to her. A man in his seventies had suffered a heart attack after some kids had been throwing things at his windows. The kids had been terrorising him for months, and as the final straw came, he'd run out swinging a bat around and then collapsed in the garden.

Allie had arrived as he was going into cardiac arrest, the kids in question sitting on the wall across the road watching everything that had gone on. Of course, no one could be held responsible, despite witnesses coming forward to say the lads had been harassing him. It had been traumatic at the time, especially with no one being charged for his death.

She looked down at her feet. Both victims were fully clothed. The woman was unfamiliar to her, but she knew the man very well. His name was Davy Lewis. He was known to be involved with one of her long-term nemeses, Kenny Webb, who oversaw the running of six branches of Car Wash City, rumoured to be drug fronts. The Organised Crime Unit were hard at work gathering together the evidence needed to convict him, and many others who were involved.

The bodies were grey, dried blood congealed around a gash on the female's temple and the male's abdomen. Apart from the head injury, the woman seemed uninjured anywhere else. She was no more than a teenager really. A small table had been overturned, with blood and hair on a corner of it, the contents of a full ashtray and a lighter on the rug.

Davy Lewis seemed to have a stab wound to his stomach, his white T-shirt covered in the blood that had spilled out through its tear. There was bruising around an eye, which was easy to see on his grey-tinged skin.

Their blood had started to pool due to the amount of time they'd been dead. Allie took time to nosy around the room now. It was sparse, a settee and an armchair in grey Dralon that had seen better days. A flatpack bookcase and TV stand. A few knick-knacks, a photo of the deceased and another girl in a frame. A card for a recent birthday on the window sill.

The carpet was cord, threadbare in places. But it was all clean, mostly tidy, and smelled fresh with the hint of vanilla from the plug-in air freshener.

What on earth was the girl doing with Davy Lewis? Was this one of his pick-up points and he'd come off worse for it? Had she stabbed him first, and he'd counterattacked her, then died from his own injuries as he'd watched her do the same?

Had anyone else seen what had happened at the time? Or had the women in the kitchen been the first people to stumble across the two bodies, like they were saying?

'I hate to say it, but what comes around goes around,' Perry said.

Allie had almost forgotten he was there. Neither of them had moved much, wanting to leave the scene as secure as possible. Once she'd spoken to the three girls, she'd get a forensic suit on.

'Hmm.' She sighed. 'I wonder who he pissed off today.'

'I've checked upstairs. There's no one else here. I'm going to grab a suit.'

'Thanks. I'll be with you in a minute.'

She rang DC Sam Markham, giving her an update that she could pass on to the control room. 'Can I leave it in your capable hands to get the rest of the people required here?' she finished.

'On it, boss.'

Allie went to talk to the girls. She pushed down the handle on the kitchen door. The female nearest to her screamed, and Allie put up a hand to reassure her.

'Staffordshire Police,' she explained, seeing them huddled around a table piled with used mugs. The kitchen was as sparse as the living room, white units and a black worktop that was covered in detritus. A sad-looking spider plant sat on the window sill.

Allie didn't recognise any of the girls, but they clearly knew each other well. None of them seemed older than twenty. By their clothing, they'd been out clubbing the night before.

'Are any of you hurt?' she asked.

They all shook their heads.

'Did any of you see what happened?'

'No.' The girl nearest to them found her voice. 'There's just us. Janey is missing, though.'

'Janey?'

'Janey Webster. She's Chantelle's friend. She's been here for about four weeks now, but her mum lives in Harrington Street.'

'Is Chantelle the name of your friend in the living room?'

The girl nodded.

'Has she been in touch with any of you today?'

Shaking heads again.

The girl swallowed. 'Are they both... dead?'

'Yes, I'm so sorry.'

All three girls burst into tears.

Allie gave them a moment before speaking again. 'I need you to stay in the kitchen, is that clear? There will be an officer here in a moment who will take care of you.'

She was about to go outside to find Frankie when Perry came back in. The paramedics had arrived, declaring life extinct.

'Dave Barnett is on his way,' he told her, glancing again at the bodies on the floor. 'There's no knife I can see anywhere, so it's not looking like murder-suicide.'

'I agree. It's possible the girl, Chantelle Bishop is her name, stabbed Davy Lewis in self-defence and then he continued to beat her until he himself collapsed, but I think she'd have more bruising than that if so.' Allie pointed to the wound in Davy's abdomen. 'The knife has gone in deep, and in the right place to cause maximum harm.'

'Even if it was here, if Davy had killed her and then panicked, I'm not so sure he would have been able to stab himself like that.'

'Davy is a coward. He would have run before killing himself. I definitely think it's a double murder rather than a murder-suicide.' She pointed to the body of Davy Lewis. 'One killer here. Whether purposely or by accident will be determined by the evidence. The other killer is on the loose. We need to chat to the *friendly* landlord as soon as possible.'

'That's going to be interesting.'

Allie had emphasised the word friendly on purpose. Number four Neville Street was an address they were familiar with. It had been written in one of two notebooks they'd found on dead drug dealers over the past few months.

The owner of the property was Kenny Webb, and he was a lot higher up the chain than Davy Lewis.

CHAPTER THREE

Allie left an officer in the kitchen with the girls while she dressed in forensic gear, and caught up with Senior CSI, Dave Barnett, who had just arrived. She then went upstairs. She was curious as to why there were several females residing at the property and one dead man known to them as a trouble-maker. Davy Lewis was a loan shark, and he also did a bit of dealing. So that was two angles they needed to check.

Upstairs, the front bedrooms had two single beds in apiece. There were women's clothes and shoes scattered everywhere, make-up on sets of drawers. The smell of perfume and deodorant made a pleasant change from the stench of a lot of places she visited during her work.

Frankie was in the back bedroom, the box room with a single mattress on the floor. There was no pillow or bottom sheet, a duvet thrown back as if someone had slept there, though.

Frankie was scrolling through a number of photos on an iPad. He glanced her way.

'I think there's another girl staying here. I found this

shoved under the mattress with the name Janey written inside it.' He handed Allie a notebook.

'Makes sense. I've just been told she could have been with Chantelle last night. Is there anything of use written in it?'

'I've only skimmed it so far, but it seems to be mainly lists of shopping or toiletries. It does mention a meeting with Milo.'

'Hmm. There's only one Milo around here.' She rolled her eyes.

Milo Barker worked at the Longton branch of Car Wash City and, along with Davy Lewis, was known to be involved with Kenny Webb's extracurricular duties, too.

'I wonder if she was here, perhaps saw the incident?' Frankie went on. 'She might even have gone to help the female and then stabbed Davy Lewis in fear of him turning on her after she'd seen what he'd done.'

'That's a good theory.'

'There's also four beds and this mattress, which suggests the girls downstairs are staying here, too.'

'Yes, I noticed.' She pursed her lips. 'This place will have so many fingerprints, it's going to take some time to sort out.'

'Allie?'

The voice was coming from DCI Jenny Brindley. Allie turned around to see her coming up the stairs. Dressed in a forensic suit, she almost seemed like a ghost appearing in the dim light of the landing.

When she'd heard there were two suspicious deaths in the same property, Allie had been expecting Jenny to visit the crime scene. Jenny would want to be there from the beginning of something like this.

'What a mess,' Jenny said. 'Thoughts?'

'It's looking like two separate murders in my opinion, Ma'am,' she said. 'Although, the female victim *could* have stabbed the male first and he lashed out, knocking her over and hitting her head as she went down. Alternatively, Davy Lewis could have pushed her, then someone else knifed him in retaliation. Either way, we haven't found a murder weapon in the house.'

'Which obviously means a third party took it or hid it.'

'Yes, Ma'am. There'll be a thorough search as soon as we are able.'

'What does Dave think?'

'He suspects the same as me but obviously won't commit to the notion fully until he has the forensic evidence to back it up.'

'Who lives here?' Jenny stepped aside for a forensic photographer to come into the property.

'Four females, all under the age of twenty. Another one is missing. She's been staying here for about a month, but she lives on the estate. We're going to visit her home address to see if she was here or not last night. One of the girls said she was staying over. She could be a key witness who's run from the scene, frightened of repercussions. Our female victim is the same age, too. Chantelle Bishop. The girls pay rent and share the house. It isn't up to much, a little sparse but mostly clean. The house belongs to Kenny Webb.'

Jenny sighed. 'And none of them saw anything?'

'They went out last night, didn't get home until midday. I think they're too scared to talk anyway.'

'Sounds convenient. Can you bring them in for questioning?'

'Already on it, Ma'am. I'll task Perry with it while I go and tell the deceased's families the news.'

Allie followed Jenny back downstairs, moving carefully through the living room. Metal plates had been put down for them to step onto. The place was buzzing with people going about their business. Dave Barnett gave her a nod in acknowledgement. She let him get on with his job.

Jenny's phone rang, and she went outside for a moment. Allie turned her attention to the two bodies at her feet. Photographs were still being taken, and it would be a few hours before either body would be moved. Before that, no doubt Dave had a lot of things to swab and sample for analysis.

Back in the kitchen, Allie explained to the girls what would be happening next. She wanted to ask more questions – they seemed as if they knew each other, perhaps friends, or even associates, who were working together – but she didn't want them to say too much while they were in a group.

At least the house didn't seem as if it was a home for immigrants looking for a fresh start that would turn into a disaster for them. Stoke-on-Trent was far away from any port, but she wouldn't put it past traffickers to get a way around that.

Afterwards, Allie went to find Perry. 'Can you organise three vehicles to collect the women? They need to be taken to the station separately.'

Behind her, Dave shouted her name, and she went over to him.

'I thought you might like to see this. It was in the male victim's pocket.' He held up a notebook in his gloved hand. 'It's similar to the other two we've found over the past few months.'

Allie took it from him and had a quick flick through it. Pages and pages of names, dates, and amounts of monies owed or paid. It was indeed the same as the two they'd come into contact with recently. One had been inside the flat of the deceased twenty-three-year-old Carlton Stewart, and the other in Billy Whitmore's pocket on the night he'd died.

'I'll photograph a few pages until we can get it back from you,' she said. 'Sam can then go through them in detail. Hopefully, this one will give us more information to cross-reference with the first two.'

CHAPTER FOUR

Andrew Dale sat in the small canteen at work, eating his cheese and tomato sandwiches. His mum had made them for him that morning. She'd also put a packet of plain crisps and a chocolate biscuit in his tuck box, too. Yesterday, she'd made him a huge Sunday lunch, and there had been apple crumble and custard for pudding. Andrew had ended up eating two bowls of that. Then he'd fallen asleep on the settee for an hour. It had been good to feel so relaxed.

Andrew had stayed at his mum's house since finishing work on Friday evening. It was better than being with that idiot, Milo, and his bunch of lunatic friends. Andrew hated them with a passion he hadn't known was possible. It wasn't fair what they were doing to him, but he didn't want to say anything to them. He wouldn't dare retaliate.

Milo and his friends had all but trashed Andrew's flat over the past few weeks. After Billy died, and then Carlton, Milo started to come round more and more. At first, Andrew had kept his head down, but as things picked up again, Milo began to think the flat was his. He stayed over, sleeping on the settee, pushing Andrew into his bedroom at about nine o'clock when the other lads joined him.

They'd hit him if he hadn't brought food in for them all, even when he didn't have enough money. The bills had to be paid, and they were using so much electricity to play games on his TV. Andrew had to give Davy Lewis most of his wages now, so he wasn't left with much.

It wasn't his fault they bullied him. That's what Grace, the policewoman, had told him. Andrew liked Grace, but when someone had seen her with him, they'd told Milo. Andrew had been threatened that if he met her again, they would beat him up. So he'd ignored her calls since.

The sense of fear was still with him. But the joy of not having anyone hit him, shout and swear at him, and then make him stay in his room all night, had been worth the risk that weekend.

Milo had punched him in the stomach on Thursday night. He didn't have a reason for doing that, and it was the first time it had really hurt. Andrew was used to slaps around the head, but a fist was a lot to deal with, especially as he'd done nothing wrong. So, on Friday morning, he'd packed a bag and gone to his mum's straight after work. But he couldn't stay with her for long, in case they started coming round to her home too. It was bad enough what he'd had to put up with.

He needed a plan, and this was where he was stuck. He had no one to turn to, no one to help. If he told anyone what had been going on, he'd be in trouble for his part in it. He knew what they had him doing was wrong, but he had no choice.

What was he going to do?

'Are you okay, Andrew?' Cathy, his supervisor, asked him. 'You look as if you're miles away. Is there something on your mind?'

'No, I'm fine,' Andrew fibbed, not wanting to bring attention to himself. If he said one word here, it might get back to Milo. He would tell Kenny, and then he'd be in even more trouble.

'That's good to know.' She sat across from him, other people piling in for the second break.

Andrew glanced at the clock and realised he should be back at work now. The first break had finished five minutes ago.

'Don't rush off. I have some news for you.' Cathy smiled. 'You remember when you first started here a year ago and you were put on a probationary period?'

Andrew nodded. Getting the job here was the best thing that had happened to him. He'd been worrying about his placement ending for quite some time now.

'I just wanted to let you know that, as of the end of this month, you're no longer a temporary member of staff, you're a permanent one. That is, if you'd like to stay with us?'

Andrew beamed. 'I would like to stay. I like it very much.'

'Great, that's settled then. I'll send you a letter so that you have it in writing. Congratulations, you've worked so hard to achieve this.'

'Thank you.'

'Now, you'd better get back to work or else Mrs Mellor will be onto you.' She smiled again. 'I know she has a soft spot for you, though. Because you work hard.'

Andrew smiled again. Then he stood and left the canteen. His prayers had been answered. He'd got a permanent job. It meant a little more money, too. If Kenny didn't find out, he'd be able to keep the extra dosh he earned.

For once, he was happy. Things were looking up. If he could just get rid of Milo and his gang, he'd feel much better. But for now, the job being permanent would have to do. It was the first job offer he'd had since leaving school. Here he could be himself, not different. He didn't stand out here. He was one of them.

Maybe it *was* time to move out of his flat. He'd taken the placement there because it was within walking distance of his mum's house. Now he had to spend money on bus fare to get to and from Redmond Street.

He would speak to his mum and see what she had to say. If it wasn't going to be dangerous for her, then he'd stay there for good.

He had a plan at last.

CHAPTER FIVE

Allie took Frankie with her to tell Davy Lewis's mum the bad news. She parked outside the family home on the Seddon Estate. Allie knew Carol Lewis, having had many run-ins with her when she'd been out on the beat.

'This is going to be so much worse than a normal visit,' she said with a grimace. 'No matter how much Carol Lewis gets on our nerves, and Davy when he was alive, she's lost a son in a violent crime. She might go wild, so brace yourself.'

'Will do, boss. Have you known her for long?'

'A fair few years. She has – had – three sons. Davy is the youngest one. The other two are in prison, and Carol has blamed everyone but them, and herself, for their behaviour.'

They walked up the path, a familiar one to her. She'd only been there a few months ago, when Davy had been caught on security footage at The Wheatsheaf pub just before the murder of local man, Kit Harper. It turned out he had nothing to do with that crime, although there had been something dodgy going on between him and Kenny Webb that she could never quite figure out.

She knocked on the door, but there was no answer. After

trying again, she peered through the large window into the living room.

'She's asleep on the settee.' Allie banged hard on the glass, ensuring Carol heard her. She pressed her warrant card to the window and then moved back to the door.

'She might be hungover or even drunk,' she warned Frankie.

Carol appeared a few seconds later, running a hand through her greying hair. She was like her son in some respects, the telltale signs of alcohol abuse ravishing her body rather than drugs. She was in her early fifties, but she seemed much older with wrinkled skin, sagging eyes, and patches of psoriasis over her cheeks.

'What do you want?' she muttered.

'Can we come in for a moment, please?' Allie stepped inside regardless. 'This is DC Higgins. Frankie. Have you met before?'

As Frankie introduced himself, Allie went into the living room, and they followed her, Carol bustling in at the rear.

Allie swallowed quickly when the smell of cat assaulted her nostrils. She looked around, spotting a pet tower in the corner. Two green eyes of a tabby stared back at her, the cat curled up and not in the slightest bit interested in them.

'What's going on?' Carol wanted to know.

Allie gave a faint smile. 'I have bad news, Carol. Do you mind sitting down?'

'No, I want to know.' Carol shook her head. 'Is it Davy? Please say it isn't.'

Allie pointed to the chair, but Carol shook her head.

'I'm afraid he's been killed. I'm so sorry for your loss.'

Carol's legs buckled. Allie leaned forward and caught her arm to stop her from falling. Now she got her to sit.

'We found him this morning, in a house in Neville Street,'

Allie went on. 'I have to tell you there was a young woman with him who has been killed, too.'

'What happened to them?'

'We're not exactly sure of the circumstances yet, as to why they were both deceased on our arrival.'

'So when you say killed, you mean they were *murdered?*'

'Like I say, we can't be sure until we have further details. Forensic investigators are at the scene, and we have officers going house-to-house to see if anyone saw or heard anything. Is there someone who I can call to come and sit with you?'

'I want to know more. You have to tell me!'

'I'm sorry, but—'

'Tell me,' Carol wailed.

Allie glanced at Frankie. 'Make some tea, please.'

He nodded and went through to the kitchen.

'I can't tell you anything else because *I'm* not sure what's happened,' Allie explained. 'When I know, you'll be the first to find out. Can I ask, does the name Chantelle Bishop mean anything to you?'

Carol shook her head. 'Is she the dead girl?'

'She hasn't been formally identified yet, but we believe so.'

'How did she die?'

'We're still determining that, but she does have a head injury.'

'Davy wouldn't do that.'

'I'm not saying he would,' Allie stressed.

'I know him, I'm his mother,' Carol went on as if she hadn't heard her. Then she paused. 'How did he die?'

'We believe it was a knife wound, although he does have bruising around one of his eyes. Like I say, we're still figuring out what happened. The evidence will take time to come back to us, but we will find out everything.'

Carol wiped at her eyes. 'I don't want you blaming Davy

for this. He would never do that... kill someone. I know he's had his moments but he's not violent.'

Allie thought differently. Her feelings about Davy ran deeper than his mother's. She knew he was more than capable of dishing out the violent attack on Chantelle Bishop. But until she had the evidence to that effect, she wouldn't say.

'Has anything changed in his life recently?' she asked next.

'He's been happier lately,' Carol said. 'He's been seeing Lily Barker. She seems nice, although she's practically half his age.'

Allie knew that name. Lily was Milo Barker's sister.

Carol sniffed. 'He's been round her flat a lot lately, staying over. I was hoping I might get rid of him after he's been here since birth. That doesn't seem funny now.' She looked at Allie. 'Someone needs to tell Lily what's happened.'

'We can help with that. Do you have an address?'

'Seventeen Hereford Street, Tunstall. On the Limekiln Estate.'

Allie noted it down.

'Later today, Davy will be taken to the mortuary. Will you be okay to identify him? It's most likely going to be late this evening or first thing in the morning.'

'You said it was him!' Carol stood. 'Now you're telling me you're not sure?'

'It *is* him, Carol,' Allie said gently, knowing the woman wanted desperately to believe her son was still alive. 'But we need to have someone formally say so, too.'

Carol sat down with a bump again. It was part of Allie's job to see people's pain, but it never got any easier. The sorrow in the woman's eyes was almost unbearable.

Frankie came in with three mugs, a sugar canister, and a plastic bottle half full of milk all balanced on a tray.

'I wasn't sure how you took it.' Frankie put it on the

coffee table. A magazine flopped to the floor, and he stooped to pick it up.

Allie smiled at him when he handed her a mug. He'd made it purposely, to put Carol at ease. But she wouldn't be taking more than a polite sip. The tray was manky enough.

'I don't want tea!' Carol cried. 'I want my son. Davy can't be dead. He can't.'

CHAPTER SIX

Allie and Frankie left Carol Lewis in the house. Allie didn't want to leave her alone, but Carol was adamant she'd be fine. Besides, Allie was waiting to hear who would be the family liaison officer allocated to work with her team and both families. She hoped it would be PC Joy. She'd enjoyed working with Rachel this year.

They were in the car again when her phone rang. It was DC Markham.

'I've found out more about our victim,' Sam said. 'Chantelle Bishop was nineteen. She had previous. Two charges of shoplifting and one of possession of a class A drug. The address we have for her next of kin is on the Limekiln Estate.'

'Thanks, I'll go there now.' Allie noted it down. 'See if we can shed some light on what's going on in that house, and if they know of Davy Lewis.' She disconnected the call and updated Frankie. 'Belt on, fella. Brace yourself to do another death knock.'

The drive to the estate took them about fifteen minutes through the early afternoon traffic. They pulled up outside an

ex-council property with a sweeping drive and a double
garage. The windows and doors had been replaced to make it
more individual, and the garden, even so late in the year, was
a riot of red and yellows.

The front door was opened within a few seconds, this
time by a man in his forties wearing a Royal Mail uniform.

'Mr Bishop?' Allie introduced herself and Frankie. The
man was joined by a woman who was similar to Chantelle in
looks. She had long blonde hair and the deepest of blue eyes.

Allie's heart went out to them both, and a feeling of déjà
vu came over her as they went inside to inform another
family that a part of them was gone forever.

'Was it drugs?' the man asked afterwards.

'Why do you always think the worst, Phil?' The woman's
bottom lip trembled. 'She's dead, does it matter now?'

'Yes, it does,' he insisted. 'The police will want to know
everything leading up to her death, and I'm not going to
spare them any details.'

The woman burst into tears and disappeared from the room.

'I'm sorry about that,' he said. 'We've been having trouble
with Chantelle for a couple of years now, and Jess can't take it
in. How our loving daughter turned into a monster.' His eyes
watered. 'How did she die?'

'At the moment, we're working everything out as it's not
exactly cut and dried,' Allie said. 'But we believe there was a
fight between her and a man. Either she fell and hit her head
on the corner of a coffee table, or someone caused the
injuries to her and then she fell.'

'You mean he beat her to death?' Phil gritted his teeth.

'No, that's not what happened. If it's any consolation, she
wouldn't have known much about it.'

'I told her not to get involved with him,' he went on.

'Who?' Allie queried.

'Davy Lewis. Is it him that's dead, too?'

Seeing as Carol Lewis had been informed of her son's death, Allie decided to tell him a little detail.

'Yes, he died at the scene. His next of kin have been informed, but there's still to be a formal identification.'

'We told her to keep away from him,' Jess said, coming back to stand in the doorway. Her arms were wrapped around herself for comfort. 'He ruined her life, turned her into a monster, and now... now, he's killed her.'

'We can't be certain of that yet, Mrs Bishop,' Allie appeased. 'Can you tell me when you last saw Chantelle?'

'About a month ago,' Phil replied when Jess said nothing. 'She was living at home then, but after a particularly late night and an attitude problem, I told her to sling her hook.' He wrung his hands together. 'I wasn't sure she would listen to me. But the next morning, she left a note to say she'd moved out and wasn't coming back.' He shook his head. 'If I hadn't turfed her out, she'd still be here.'

As he wept, his wife came to his side.

'It's not your fault, Phil. Chantelle made her own rules, and we were never privy to them.' Jess looked at Allie and Frankie in turn. 'Chantelle was hanging around with Davy Lewis before she moved out of here. I collected her a couple of times from another house, and he was there. She was always wasted when she came out. Broke my heart to see her like that, but I was just glad to get her home. She'd often be asleep or out of it by the time we got back.'

Allie spotted a family photo on the sideboard. Chantelle was about ten, flanked by her parents either side, a huge smile on her face. Happier times, Allie mused, when Chantelle was a child, enjoying herself with the simple pleasures in life. Now, probably a decade later, and that child had turned into an addict who'd done anything to get her next fix. In some ways, it was a blessing that no one ever knew what could be just around the corner.

'Did you ever go inside?' Allie asked.

Jess shook her head. 'I knocked on the door once, when Chantelle didn't appear after I'd been there over ten minutes. Davy answered and told me she was busy. When I said doing what, he laughed. He was about to close the door, but Chantelle appeared and shot outside. He didn't seem pleased, but he let her go. When I asked her what was going on, she told me to mind my own business. A couple of days later, she had the row with her dad and that was that. So, no, sorry, I never went inside.'

'Can you give me that address, please?' It could be a lead, if it was different from the one they had found Chantelle at.

'Number nineteen Coral Avenue.'

It was an address in the notebook they'd found on Billy Whitmore. Allie glanced surreptitiously at Frankie. He'd only stopped writing for a fraction of a second before continuing with his notes.

Allie ran through the same formalities she had previously done with Carol Lewis and left them to it. Once outside again, she blew out her breath. A young lad came flying past on a motorbike, flooring the thing to make maximum noise. She waited for peace to come back before she spoke.

'I'm going to arrange for the same family liaison officer to help both families,' she told Frankie. 'Sometimes I love this job for its sense of purpose and justice. But to get to that, we have to go through so many emotions, don't we? I feel drained after that. Are you okay?'

'Yes, ta, boss. I'm good.'

She slapped his back playfully. 'You don't have to hold it in, you know. It's hard what we do, and it can get to us all.'

'Oh, I totally agree. You know I can cry if someone pulls a puppy's tail.'

Last month, Allie had seen Frankie in tears after finding a litter of West Highland terriers that had been mistreated. So much so that she'd been certain one would end up in the Higgins household as a treasured family pet. But he'd surprised her by resisting.

She grinned. 'Yes, you're definitely not afraid to show it.'

They got into the car and settled in the seats. Allie drove off the estate and headed to Hanley, where their base was in Bethesda Street.

'Thoughts, Frankie?' she asked as she stopped at traffic lights.

'Chantelle sounds like she would give Davy Lewis a run for his money, but she was definitely scared of something going on at that address.' Frankie took out a stick of chewing gum, unwrapped it, and folded it into his mouth. 'He was way too old for her.'

'At least double her age.'

'Maybe she didn't fall for his charming advances, and he tried to force himself on her.'

'I wouldn't put it past the scrote to do that.'

'Well, perhaps she gave as good as she got and overpowered Davy.' He paused. 'But as to who killed him? I have no idea.'

'It's a good job we're part of a crack team working on it, then, isn't it? One who won't stop until we find all the answers.' Allie smiled. 'Right, another stop and then it's back to the station.'

CHAPTER SEVEN

Perry and Sam were talking to the three girls found in the kitchen at Neville Street. Perry spoke to Dani Mountford while Sam spoke to Leah Brady. As Perry was the first to finish, he went to see Natalie Rigby, the third girl.

In the soft interview room, Natalie was sitting on the sofa, a cold mug of tea in front of her, black smudges under her eyes and a finger to her mouth as she chewed on a nail.

'Hi, Natalie.' Perry introduced himself and sat across from her. 'There's nothing to worry about. I just need to ask you a few questions.'

'When can I go home?' she replied, her right foot tapping incessantly. 'I've been here for ages.'

'Sorry to keep you waiting so long, but it's been really busy as you can imagine.' Perry smiled. 'Would you like more tea or a bite to eat? We can get you some sandwiches and a drink?'

She shook her head. 'I just want to go home.'

'I'm afraid that won't be possible for a while. The house is a crime scene, and we'll be gathering evidence for quite some time yet.'

'I don't mean back to that...' Natalie shuddered. 'I mean, home to Birmingham. I'd rather be with my olds than live through that again.'

Perry wondered if this was a way out for a troubled teen who had got herself messed up in something she hadn't seen coming. She might give them more details than the two local girls, especially if she was leaving.

'Can you tell me what happened this morning, from when you got up, or got in?' he asked.

'We'd been out to Flynn's Nightclub.'

'That's you, Dani, and Leah?'

She nodded. 'Then we stayed at a friend's house.'

'Who was your friend?'

'Sarah Mitchell. She lives in a flat in Regent Road. We all got back together at twelve.'

'Didn't Chantelle want to go with you?'

'No, she was tired.'

'Was she in on her own?'

'Yes. She was in the living room when we left. I asked if she was okay. She'd been a bit low lately. But she said she was fine and looking forward to watching TV.'

'She wasn't expecting company?'

'She said Janey might pop round.'

'Janey Webster?'

'Yes.'

'So you arrived back at midday?'

'Yes. We were laughing at something as we went into the room. I don't even know what about now.' Natalie pointed to the floor in front of her. 'I saw them first and I-I screamed. They were just lying there. Dead. That's when we called you.'

Perry took a few details down quickly.

'Who made the call?' he wanted to confirm.

'Dani did.'

That was what Dani Mountford had told him, too.

'Did anything happen yesterday that might have led to this?' he continued.

'Not that I know of.'

'How did you meet those girls?'

'They were on a night out in my neck of the woods, at a wine bar near to where I used to live. I was fed up at home. I hate my stepdad. He can be a real bastard at times.' She sniffed. 'I got chatting to them. They were telling me how much they enjoyed having their own place. Dani gave me her phone number and told me to call her anytime I needed someone to talk to. But she started messaging me, and I got to know her. She seemed nice.'

'So you weren't forced to come here?'

'No. I was having a rough time, and Dani said I could stay with her for a while.'

'And when you got here?'

'I didn't have any money, so she said I could work for him.'

'Him?' Perry glanced up.

'Davy.' Natalie caught his eye. 'Can I go now?'

'And you really want to go to Birmingham?' Perry asked. 'It's not because someone might be after you here?'

'I'm never going back to Neville Street.' Natalie shuddered, tears forming. 'It was horrible, really.'

'Why was that?'

Natalie didn't want to say too much, he could tell. So she surprised him when she spoke out.

'It was fun at first, but after a while you realise what a hovel it is. Lots of young lads turning up whenever they felt like, people coming and going all the time. I was scared to go to sleep some nights, in case someone came into my room.'

'Can you give me any names of the frequent visitors?'

Natalie shook her head vehemently.

'Okay.' Perry nodded. 'I'll arrange for you to stay somewhere for the next couple of nights, and then we can get you back to Birmingham.'

'I still need to pay back what I owe.'

Perry bristled. 'Doing what?'

'Dropping off things and collecting them around the city.'

His relief that it was for nothing of a sexual nature was palpable, but he tried to hide it. The girl didn't seem to be troubled by anything other than wanting to go home.

'Who were you working for?'

'Davy Lewis.'

'Anyone else?'

Natalie shook her head.

Perry sighed inwardly. It was the easiest option for her, blame the dead man. No one could question her story.

'You'll stay in Stoke while we check things out?' he added.

He thought she might protest, but she seemed relieved as she agreed.

Natalie clammed up then, no matter how much Perry tried to keep her talking. Physically she seemed all right, but emotionally, she seemed done in, drained of all fight.

He was glad she'd be going back to Birmingham soon. He had a feeling that this little episode would change her life for the better. She clearly hadn't enjoyed living in Neville Street, and she could easily have been dragged into the drug scene culture and wanted more. Hopefully, going home may enable her to forget the past few weeks and move on.

Perry left her with an officer who would take her and her friends to a hotel. His gut feeling told him they weren't lying. He didn't think they were suspects. They wouldn't be under police protection as such, able to come and go as they pleased. The girls, for now, would be treated as witnesses.

He only hoped the three of them could either look after themselves or wouldn't go back to where the danger was. The force couldn't watch over them all. Not with a double murder to solve.

And a killer still on the loose.

CHAPTER EIGHT

Allie and Frankie arrived back at the station just as Perry had completed his chat with Natalie Rigby. Sam was still in with Leah Brady. Allie wondered if they'd found out more about what had happened in the living room. Unless, of course, one of them had attacked Davy Lewis, and none of them were willing to speak out about it.

For purposes of elimination, all three had been processed, knowing their fingerprints would be present at the scene. From this, they'd been able to establish that two of them were known to them already. Dani Mountford had been charged with shoplifting; Leah Brady had received a caution for the same. Neither girl had been in trouble for the past six months, though.

'The third girl, Natalie Rigby, isn't known to us,' Perry finished telling them. 'She's from Birmingham.'

'Let me grab a brew and we can catch up. Anyone got any biscuits to tide me over? My emergency chocolate supply is depleted.'

'Oh, the horror!' Perry joked.

Desk drawers were opened and, within seconds, she had a pick of several choices.

Following on, Perry updated them with what he'd learned from Dani Mountford, which, he concluded, was nothing extra than Natalie had told him.

'Do you think they're telling the truth?' Allie queried. 'They were out, and not part of?'

'Yes, I believe them.' Perry nodded. 'I think they stumbled upon it today. I can't imagine what they were thinking when they saw the bodies on the floor. From what Dani and Natalie have said, I have a feeling they're more scared of someone coming back to do them harm, rather than the fact their friend had been murdered.'

'Safety in numbers, perhaps?' Allie spotted Sam walking towards them. 'Any luck with Leah Brady?'

'Not really.' Sam sat down at her desk. 'Away from the other girls, she was wary of saying anything she shouldn't.'

'Can we check out their story about what time they arrived and left Flynn's Nightclub? Frankie, can you get the CCTV and then pass it to Sam to analyse?'

'Yes, boss.' He took notes.

'Do we think she saw what happened?' Allie bit into a chocolate digestive, wiping crumbs from her shirt as it broke in two.

'No, although forensics and time of death will make certain.' Sam turned to Perry. 'Did you get anything from your two?'

'I came to the same conclusion as you. Extremely frustrating.'

'But we have a good team who can sort this out.' Allie glanced around the room. 'Yes, I'm looking at you guys.'

'Apart from this young whippersnapper here.' Perry smirked.

'*This* one here may only be twenty-eight to you pushing

fifty, but he's going to be brilliant chatting to the younger people,' Allie said pointedly.

'Thanks for the vote of confidence, boss!' Frankie grinned.

'We'll have to speak to so many youngsters that I'm sure you'll know half of them from your beat. I'm going to have a word with Jenny about bringing DS Grace Allendale to work with us, if she's not too busy on something else.'

'She won't want to miss an opportunity to be with the gang again.' Frankie rubbed his hands together in glee. 'And at least I might not be stuck with the old man all the time, then.'

Perry feigned hurt before shooting Frankie the finger.

'Did you see that, boss?' Frankie shook his head in jest.

'Super grass,' Perry went on.

'Okay, kids, we've had a break for fun.' Allie smiled. 'Let's crack on with what we have so far and plan what to do next. Firstly, I called to see Janey Webster's mum on the way back to the station. Janey has been staying with Chantelle for about four weeks now. Her mum says she's a good kid, but she's been concerned about her hanging around with Chantelle and the girls in the house. She tried to talk sense into Janey, but she says all she got was backlash, and more than her usual stroppy behaviour. Janey hasn't been in touch with her mum since last night. She said she'd ask around and get in touch when she comes home.'

Their conversation turned to the three notebooks Sam had been cross-referencing earlier. 'Working through the pages you sent me images of, I've come up with several potential houses that could be being used for the teenagers who we suspect are working the county lines,' she said. 'Plus a few things appearing in each book that I'm going to look into further.'

Allie didn't like it at all. There was far too much exploitation of teenagers and young kids, something they might never get a good handle on. If one of them managed to stop, there were several waiting to take their place. Peer pressure, along with promises of gifts, and cash, ensured they were soon lured into a life of crime.

'Someone must know what's going on with these houses. I want them shutting down,' she said. 'Let's speak to as many neighbours as we can. We have two deceased victims, three girls, two most probably recruiting members to the gang for drug runs but aren't willing to talk about that, and a missing girl we do want to talk to.'

'CCTV is coming in from around the vicinity, but there are no cameras on the street itself,' Perry added.

'Thought as much.' Allie sighed. 'Frankie, liaise with any community groups in the area, see if they've had an inkling of something like this about to happen. Maybe there were rumours going round about unrest.'

'Yes, boss.'

'The rest of us can go through the statements and leads from uniform so far. We can pick up anyone we still need to contact in the morning.' She stood up, stretching her arms in the air. 'Let's grab something to eat and then we can crack on. Evidence from the bodies and crime scene won't start coming through until tomorrow, but I don't want this idiot out on the street for any longer than necessary, nor do I want to give him or her the opportunity to do it again. We're trying to clean up the streets, but that doesn't mean taking the crimes behind closed doors.'

CHAPTER NINE

After a busy day at work, Leanne Milton was resting her legs. She snapped a digestive in half and dunked it in her mug of coffee. It was the first time she'd had a minute to herself all day, and she was determined to make the most of it.

She scrolled through the Facebook app on her phone, seeing posts from people she knew and wondering if they were all as happy as they made out. Take Rebecca, for instance. She said she was all loved-up with her husband, and yet Susan, who worked at the newsagents and lived next door to Rebecca, said she often heard them arguing and was certain he was violent towards her.

A post from her friend, Gemma, brought tears to her eyes. She was with Nicky, someone else she knew, who was showing off her baby bump. She was seven months gone now.

She'd known Nicky Harper and Gemma Clarke since junior school, their men, too. They'd all been good mates through the years. That had all gone pear-shaped when Nicky had found out Leanne and Kit had been having an affair.

Even after Kit's death, Scott had no idea about it, and Leanne hoped it would stay that way. Nicky had kept her promise to keep it to herself, yet Leanne had paid the price of her silence by losing both women's friendship. It had been kind of Nicky not to say anything to Scott. Leanne knew it was only to save him the pain of finding out, though. Nicky and Gemma had no loyalty to her anymore.

It had taken Nicky a while to get pregnant, and now she'd have to bring up the baby without Kit around to be a father. Even so, it stung Leanne to know that she couldn't share in her happiness. Never hold the baby, never be involved in their lives again. She was dreading the birth; she wouldn't get to see the part of Kit who was still growing.

With a sigh, she sent her daughter a message.

What time will you be home? I've made a cottage pie for tea, with onion gravy. Your favourite.

The message came back in seconds.

Half an hour! xx

Leanne smiled. Amy loved her food, and at fifteen was at an age where it didn't matter what she ate because she never added weight to her tiny frame. It was good to hear her excited about something. She'd been temperamental lately, even more than the usual teenage blues, Leanne thought. She was really up and down with mood swings.

Leanne had tried to talk to her several times about it but in the end put it down to her age. She could recall lots of times when she'd been like that herself. That small time frame between no longer being a girl and not yet a woman was a minefield. She'd always been falling out with her parents about something or other, pushing boundaries.

Her husband, Scott, arrived home just before Amy was due in. Surprised to see him so early, she checked on the pie and then went to greet him. But the pallor of his skin, and the worry in his eyes, made her stop.

'Are you okay?' she asked, concerned he was ill.

'Not really. Did you hear anything on the news?'

'I heard that two bodies had been found.'

'Davy Lewis was one of them.'

Leanne's eyes widened in disbelief. 'When did it happen?'

'They found him at lunchtime. There's a teenage girl dead, too.'

'That's terrible. Where was it?'

'Neville Street.'

'In one of Kenny's houses?'

He nodded.

Leanne stood wide-eyed. 'Why didn't you call me?'

'I didn't want to worry you until I got home.'

They went through to the kitchen. Leanne sat down at the breakfast bar before her legs gave way. This was too close to home for her. Just like Davy Lewis had until his death, Scott worked for Kenny Webb, but at Car Wash City, the Longton branch. She hated that he'd had no choice in the matter.

'Do you know the girl?' she asked.

'No. She was one of Davy's.' Scott sat, too.

Leanne gnawed her bottom lip. 'What does this mean for you? Does it change anything?'

'I'm not sure. I shouldn't think so, unless they want me to take Davy's place.' He sniggered.

'That's not funny,' she snapped, even though she could tell his laughter was false.

'I know, I'm sorry.' He took her hands in his own. 'It'll be fine, you'll see. Kenny's got me doing enough anyway. I won't have time to get involved in anything else.'

'That had better be true.'

'It will be, I promise.' He leaned forward to kiss her briefly and then stood up. 'Oh, I forgot to mention, I saw Nicky with Gemma yesterday. Nicky's stomach is huge. She can't be far off giving birth now. Have you seen her recently?'

'You know I haven't.'

He paused and then repeated the question he'd been asking over the past few months. 'What really happened with you three? I can't understand why you're not in touch anymore.'

Scott was referring to the friendships she'd just been sad about, having seen the two of them together on Facebook.

'You know we had words. It was over something stupid. I can't even recall what it was now.'

She said the same thing every time he asked. And every time she replied, she could tell he knew she was lying. At least he wasn't pursuing the matter now.

Scott took a quick shower before eating. His mind racing, he thought of his future and what it might be like now that Davy Lewis was out of the picture. He'd never liked Davy, had many a run-in with him over the years, but after Kit had been murdered, Davy had come into Kenny Webb's fold even more.

Scott hadn't liked it, finding it suspicious as he knew Kenny couldn't stand Davy. For months, he'd been trying to figure out why the sudden change. Davy was a troublemaker, a scrote. It didn't fit the bill.

So Davy's death made him suspicious. It couldn't be an accident, and there was no way that girl would have stabbed him before he'd killed her, which is what all the talk was about the deaths.

Scott wouldn't put it past one of Kenny's minions to have taken a knife to Davy. He'd try and do some digging on the sly.

It always paid to watch your back in this game. You never knew when someone would stab you in it. Or in the stomach in Davy's case.

CHAPTER TEN

Allie wanted to visit Lily Barker before their day was over. She took Frankie with her. Lily lived in Jasper Street, one of the nicer places on the Limekiln Estate.

'Have you met Lily before?' Allie asked him.

'I think I might have, when I was in uniform. There was a fight that got out of hand in the old Red Lion pub. Lily was with Milo then. From what I remember, she gave as good as she got with her fists. Luckily, she was directing them at her brother and his friends rather than me.'

'That sounds like Lily. What was the fight about?'

'I can't remember, so probably something and nothing. Too much ale being knocked back. It was a sunny evening.'

It was like groundhog day as Allie knocked on yet another door of a property with an untidy garden. A pile of rubbish at the side of the house was beginning to smell. What was it with people who needed properties yet were never willing to look after them? Thankfully, most of the city's residents were much tidier.

After a hefty knock on the door, Lily answered it with the tiniest of babies in her arms.

She scowled when she saw their warrant cards. 'I thought you'd come about Davy,' she said.

'We have.'

'Then why show your ID? I know who you are.' She rolled her eyes. 'You'd better come in.'

Allie glanced at Frankie as if to say, can you believe the attitude, before stepping inside, narrowly missing a teddy bear's arm under her feet. Children's toys were strewn everywhere.

Lily propped the baby on her chest, collecting a few items up with her spare hand and dumping them behind the armchair.

'I wasn't expecting anyone, so I haven't tidied up,' she muttered.

'That doesn't matter. We won't keep you long,' Allie replied. 'How did you hear about Davy?'

'His mum rang me.'

'We're sorry for your loss.' She took the opportunity to sit down, Frankie doing the same. 'What did Carol tell you?'

'That he was found at Neville Place.'

'When did you last see him?'

'Yesterday morning. He stayed over. He's been doing that a lot lately.'

'So you were a couple?'

'It's complicated.'

'But you were together?'

'On and off.'

Allie nodded her understanding. 'Was he acting strange in any way? Or had anything been bothering him lately?'

'Nothing more than usual. He could be a moody bugger, but he'd been fine.'

'Do you know what he was doing at the address where he was found?'

'What he did was his own business. He gave me money

for the kids, that was good enough for me. None of them are his,' she hastened to add, running a hand over the little boy's head. He'd fallen asleep in her arms. 'I have three in bed, too – well in their bedrooms. I doubt they'll settle until I've shouted up the stairs at least five times. I'm surprised they didn't appear when you arrived. It makes me nervous. I'll have to check on them soon.'

Allie groaned inwardly. Lily wasn't even twenty-five and had so many family responsibilities. Perhaps Davy had been good for her.

'Had he been in any trouble with anyone?' she asked then.

'He had a fight with Milo on Sunday.'

Allie's ears pricked up. 'Did Davy say what it was about?'

'No. Milo gave Davy a black eye. He said his ribs were hurting, too. They were always arguing over something. Pair of idiots.' Lily shook her head. 'Davy always wanted to be top man, and some of the younger men were forever trying to trip him up.'

'About what?'

'Oh, I meant in general,' Lily faltered.

They sat quietly for a moment, giving Lily time to fill the silence, but she didn't.

'Do you know Chantelle Bishop?' Allie went on.

'If he was with that bitch, I'll swing for her.'

Allie raised her eyebrows, the darker side of Lily appearing. The child in Lily's arms snuffled, hands waving for a few seconds, but continued to sleep.

'Do you think there was anything going on between Chantelle and Davy?'

'There'd better not be.' Lily frowned. 'Are you saying she was the dead girl?'

'We believe so.'

'Did she kill him?'

'Why would you say that?'

'No reason. I just wanted to know.'

'It's not clear yet.'

'She's a layabout, that one. Hasn't done a day's work in her life.' Lily tutted. 'Trust her to be involved.'

'Do you know her?'

'Only from the estate. She used to be in and out of people's houses in a shot if she found a window open. Haven't seen her much lately, though, come to think of it.' Lily stopped. 'Neville Street. It's one of his houses, isn't it? Kenny Webb? I hate him with a passion.'

'Oh?' Allie kept her surprise to herself.

'He's always coming around here, lording it up like he owns this place, too.' She threw up a hand. 'Well, he doesn't. The council does. He comes on the pretence of speaking to Davy, but I've seen his eyes wandering. I was hoping he didn't ever want paying in kind, you know?'

'Did he suggest that to you?' Allie sat upright a little more.

'No, but you can tell, can't you? The way they speak to you, suggestively.'

Allie had never heard anything to indicate Kenny curried favours in any way he could. She wondered, was Chantelle Bishop something to Kenny Webb? Had he arrived at the house and interrupted something? Perhaps found Chantelle with Davy? It was certainly another angle to think about and would give Kenny a motive.

'We're after someone called Janey, who lives in the house where Davy was found. Did you know her?'

Lily shook her head.

'Davy never mentioned her to you?'

'Why would he? I was never interested in what he did.'

Just his money. Allie kept that to herself.

Once back in the car, she turned to Frankie. 'Lily seems

very hard. As if no one frightens her, and that she doesn't get emotionally attached easily. What are your thoughts?'

'This is a twisted case, isn't it? I can't keep everything we've found out in my head.'

'It's coming at us from every direction.' She started the engine. 'Before we go back to the nick, let's go and talk to Milo about the fight he had with Davy Lewis.'

CHAPTER ELEVEN

She sat on the train, the bag on her knee as close to her chest as she could get it. Trying not to seem nervous, she ran her sweaty palms over her jeans, hoping not to bring attention to herself.

It was ten past eight. The carriage she was in wasn't full, maybe about twenty people in total, scattered among the seats. Still, she clung on to her handbag rather than place it on the vacant one next to her.

A few minutes from Stoke, she took out her phone and sent Connor a message, telling him what time the train would pull into the station.

She'd finally done her first run. She couldn't believe that she'd been brave enough, even though her mum would kill her if she found out.

The train drew into the station, and she stood up, moving towards the doors. Glancing round, she couldn't see anyone getting off. No one seemed to be watching her. They were all going about their own business. Her heart dropped into her stomach as the doors opened and she headed for the subway.

Her step quickened in her haste to get out. She passed through the barriers and out onto Station Road.

She'd done it.

Connor had said he'd be parked to the right of the North Stafford hotel. A horn beeped, a flash of car lights indicating where he was. Trying to resist waving to him like a silly teenager, she crossed the road. It was raining so she hurried, getting into the passenger seat.

'Everything all right?' he asked.

'I think so.' She patted her handbag. 'I have the money.'

'Was Eddie on time?'

'Yes.'

'Any problems?'

'No. He seems nice.'

She'd actually been terrified when she'd seen him waiting for her. In his mid-forties with a weathered look about him, he seemed a brute of a man. He'd asked her name, and when she'd told him, he'd nodded and said to follow him.

So many things had run through her mind. What if he took the package from her and made off without giving her the money? Would Connor be in trouble? Would she get in bother, too?

Or what if he kidnapped her and sold her to someone who did awful things to her?

She'd almost stopped at that thought.

But the transaction had gone smoothly. Eddie had taken her for a cup of coffee in the station café, and they'd swapped envelopes discreetly. Then she'd caught the next train back to Stoke, the money he'd given to her safely tucked away from prying eyes.

Connor drove away from the station. 'Want to stop for a Maccy D's?'

'No, thanks. I'm good.'

They drove for a minute or so and then turned into a side street and parked up.

'Let's be having it, then.' Connor held out his hand.

She retrieved the envelope from her bag and gave it to him. 'It's all there,' she protested as he began counting it.

'Relax.' He peeled off a few notes. 'I was only getting your fee.'

She grinned. A fee sounded so grown up.

'Remember, you tell no one where you've been, nor what you were doing.'

'I promise.' She sighed inwardly, realising how childish she sounded. 'I won't tell anyone,' she added, although that didn't seem any better.

Connor popped the envelope in the glove compartment and turned to her with a grin. As he leaned across and kissed her, she almost melted in his arms.

She still couldn't believe she had his attention and that he was so nice to her. They hadn't slept together yet. As she was fifteen, he wasn't willing to risk it, even though he said she drove him wild. He told her that all the time. She would do whatever it took to keep him as her own until then. He was hot property among all the girls she knew, but he was hers.

'So now you've popped your cherry with the run, you can do it again,' Connor said. 'We operate every Friday usually, different times but not too late. I'll keep you on the Stoke to Stockport route for now. It's less risky.'

She nodded, glad she'd made a good enough impression for him to ask her again.

With one last kiss, they said goodbye. She had school in the morning. He got her home just after ten o'clock, and she raced indoors. She had to be in by ten, but she couldn't tell him that.

Yet, what a night. It hadn't taken long to do the drop-off,

have a coffee, and get two trains. She could easily fit in other trips of that length.

She pressed a hand to the cash that was tucked away in her pocket. That money had been so easy to earn. She was sure she'd be in this for the long haul when they saw how good she was.

She let herself in the house, closing the door quietly behind her.

'Is that you, love?'

'Yes, it's me, Mum. Sorry I'm a few minutes late. I was waiting for Dani's dad. He's just dropped me off.'

'Where have you been?'

'Just hanging round at her house.' She sat, training her eyes on the TV. A blush appeared on her cheeks, but her mum was too busy watching the news.

A few minutes later, she yawned loudly. 'I'm going to bed. Night.' She kissed her mum.

'Night, love.'

Upstairs, she undressed and got into her pyjamas, then climbed in bed, a huge grin on her face.

She'd got away with it!

She picked up her phone to message Connor only to find he'd beaten her to it.

You did great tonight.

She didn't reply. She wouldn't until the morning. It wouldn't do to be so keen.

But she hadn't been able to resist, and, within a few messages, they had everything worked out for next Friday.

She beamed. Things couldn't have gone any better.

CHAPTER TWELVE

Connor Lightwood smiled to himself. It had been so easy to get the girl under his spell. It didn't hurt that he was a handsome dude and could get any woman he wanted. Well, that was his opinion anyway, and it hadn't failed him yet.

Counting out some notes, he pocketed his own fee, which was twice as much as the girl had got, and then dropped it off at Car Wash City in Longton. Kenny would be pleased he'd got another recruit. Things were looking good. He was determined to make his mark by being indispensable to the man.

On his way home, he called in at the chippy, knowing his mum would always help him to demolish a huge mound of chips with a carton of curry sauce. He felt sorry for her at times, not being able to get out as much as she could without relying on other people. She didn't let her condition, multiple sclerosis, get her down too much, though. She was forever singing and trying to hug him when he waltzed past her.

Connor had lived in Reginald Street all his life, his mum for over twenty years. She always made him laugh telling him about the antics of the neighbours, current and new. Drugged-up Andy from number two who had tried to climb through the privets of number four to get to his front door and got stuck. The couple with the new-born who had a Land Rover pushchair and couldn't get it up and down the steep steps leading to their house without falling out about who could do it better. Nigel Swayne at number thirteen constantly coming home drunk. Debbie threw Nigel out one week, and he was always back the next. His mum took guesses as to how long he would be away for each time.

Yet all Connor wanted was his dad to come home. Derek Lightwood had walked out when Connor was sixteen, and no one had heard from, or seen him, since. It was as if he'd vanished from the face of the earth. His bank account remained untouched. His car had sat on the driveway for six months, before his mum had told Connor to use it. Derek's friends and work colleagues couldn't understand it.

Of course, his mum blamed herself. She said her condition had put a huge amount of strain on their marriage when she'd become so reliant on him, and she didn't blame him for not sticking around.

It had left Connor and his sister to do the work he'd done. They didn't mind, but it wasn't ideal. And Mum was getting worse, although she would never admit to it.

Connor often wondered if his dad had been in trouble and done a runner, though. Derek had always held down a full-time job at the local factory, working shifts which had been tough graft, he'd often said. But he'd been a good man, providing well for his family. Connor had sometimes thought too well, which led him now to believe he'd been working on the side, perhaps doing something similar to himself.

The police had looked into his disappearance for a while, but with no leads, he couldn't blame them for going quiet. And wasn't Connor doing the same, trying to keep his side-line from his mum? It would tear her in two if she ever found out what he was up to.

Without the extra money he brought in, life would be harder. He paid towards a lot of the bills, put food on the table, decent stuff, not supermarket brands all the time, and he treated Mum and his sister to gifts whenever he could. He loved his family. Any girl he introduced to them would have to be special because of that.

Getting in the car after he'd fetched his order, he glanced behind him to see a BMW, its windows tinted so he couldn't see inside. He peered at it again but couldn't see its occupants. But, not giving it another thought, he got in his car and drove away.

It was when he arrived home that he saw it again. It was at the bottom of his road, on the opposite side, engine ticking over. He frowned, wondering who it was; thought about going over but decided against it. He'd have a word with Kenny about it, see if he knew the vehicle.

Then again, it could be someone Kenny knew who'd been told to keep an eye on him. Well, he wouldn't find anything untoward happening. Connor knew when to stay on the right side of things. He knew life could change in an instant if he stepped out of line.

A voice shouted through to him when he opened the front door.

'Is that you, our Connor?' Sandra Lightwood asked.

'Yeah, it's me, Mum.' He pulled his keys from the lock and chucked the bunch on the table. He went into the living room, careful not to trip over the wheelchair that was blocking most of the hall. The council had promised them a better house, with wider doors and facilities to accommodate his mum's condition, but so far, there had been nothing but broken promises. Every year, she deteriorated a little more. It was cruel to see it, but she always kept her spirits up.

'I've brought chips. Are you hungry?'

'I'll have a few, please, lad,' Sandra said, smiling brightly at him. 'You get the rest down you. You're a growing boy. Have you had a good day?'

He nodded. 'It was fine and dandy. Is Claire home?'

'She's gone out with Sonny again. I think she has the hots for him.'

Connor sniggered. 'Good, because any fool can tell he's mad for her. I like him. He'd do her proud.'

Sandra nodded and went back to the TV.

Connor nipped upstairs before he tucked into his food. He left the light off and walked across to his bedroom window. It gave him a great view of the bottom of the street.

The Beamer was gone. His relief was palpable. Maybe it wasn't even the same car he'd seen earlier.

He needed to keep his cool. Paranoia was not a good guise.

CHAPTER THIRTEEN

Riley Abbott went into the house to find her mum, Fiona, on the sofa asleep and her sister nowhere to be seen. It wasn't unusual to find Kelsey out. She often stayed over at her friend, Mallory's, house – not that Riley could understand why. Mallory's family wasn't one of the cleanest, and she wouldn't like to sleep in any of their beds.

She made herself a coffee and sat down on the armchair to take off her trainers.

Fiona stirred, stretched her arms above her head, and yawned. 'Hello, duck.'

'Hi, Mum.'

'I thought I'd wait up for you, but I must have dozed off. What time is it?'

'Just after nine.'

Fiona balked. 'I've missed most of a *Vera* rerun again. Did everything go okay?'

'Yes.'

'That's good. Did you get paid?'

Riley nodded but turned to watch the TV. She didn't want

to talk about her evening. For months she'd resisted joining in with her mother and her drug dealing. But when Fiona had been beaten and threatened after her partner, Billy, had died, Riley was given no choice but to help out as well or risk her mother getting attacked again.

Her sister would have been dragged into things, too, and Riley wanted to keep Kelsey out of it if she could. She was only fifteen, extremely clever at school, and Riley hoped at least one of the Abbott women would get off the estate and do well.

'Have you heard anything else about Davy?' Fiona reached for a cigarette and lit it up. She took a noisy drag.

Riley hated that she still smoked. She'd been trying to get her to quit for years, but the most Fiona had stopped was for a week. She seemed worse than ever now; said she had to do it to calm her nerves.

'My friend, Dani, thinks Davy attacked Chantelle and then someone else killed him.'

'When did she tell you that?'

'This afternoon. She found the bodies when she got home with Leah and Natalie.'

Fiona shuddered. 'I wouldn't have liked to see that. Did they call the police?'

'Yeah. They were all taken to the station to be interviewed.'

'But they didn't do anything, did they?'

'Process of elimination, they were told. They weren't being blamed for it.'

'I should think not. Mind, who knows these days.'

They were silent for a moment.

'Someone else must have killed Davy, Mum,' Riley went on. 'Chantelle might be a mouthy bitch, but I doubt she'd ever had murder in her.'

Fiona shook her head. Neither of them had liked Davy much, but it had shocked them both to hear of his death. Riley avoided him mostly because he didn't mind using his fists on anyone whenever he felt like it.

She'd met Chantelle Bishop on several occasions and hadn't really liked her either. She was a hard bitch, bullying the younger girls. Often, she'd have to be put in her place.

But to think they were both dead was horrible and brought back memories of the time around Billy's death, too. He'd been stabbed and left to die as well. No one deserved that.

'Well, someone must know something,' Fiona remarked, blowing out the last of the smoke from the cigarette. 'I expect we'll find out soon, once the evidence comes in. I must admit, I've been thinking about Billy since I heard. I still can't believe he's gone.'

'Yeah, me neither. Do you want a cuppa?' Riley stood up.

'I could murder one.' Fiona gasped. 'Sorry, terrible choice of words.'

Riley sniggered. While the kettle boiled, she took some of the money she'd earned from her pocket and hid it in the tin at the back of the sink unit. Even though her mum wasn't drinking as much now, she'd been known to snaffle a note here and there and deny it. Riley would shift it in the morning. For now, she wanted it out of sight.

'At least they won't come around here again,' Fiona shouted through to her. 'Although I wouldn't put it past Allie Shenton calling to speak to us.'

'Why?'

'To see if we know anything. Not to see if we're involved.'

'Isn't that the same thing?'

'No, smarty-pants, it isn't.'

Riley had met Allie Shenton several years ago when Fiona had been a victim of domestic violence. Allie had helped them get away from Trevor Ryan and kept an eye on them unofficially. She'd looked after them on more than one occasion now. Kelsey had a soft spot for her, too.

So it wouldn't be wise to cross Allie. Whatever they were doing, they had to keep it to themselves. But Riley also knew that one day that help from Allie wouldn't be offered. They'd be in deep, on their own. She dreaded the day that happened.

Riley rejoined her mum, passing over a mug. 'We don't know anything because we're not involved,' she continued the conversation.

'Allie will take a lot of convincing.'

'So why hasn't she been to see us yet, then?'

'I don't know.' Fiona took a slurp of her tea, wincing at its heat. 'I've been waiting for her to turn up. I think she's building up a case on me. Chipping away, as she does.'

Riley could see how worried her mum was. Fiona had almost been caught earlier in the year because of her fingerprints on the notebook belonging to Billy. Imagine if Allie came snooping around and found out Riley was involved, too. She shuddered. It didn't bear thinking about.

Because Riley had been there, at the house in Neville Street, the night before the murders.

Of course, she wouldn't tell anyone about that, unless she was asked about it. But her fingerprints might show up soon, and then she'd have to explain why. Allie Shenton was going to be so mad with her for getting involved, when she'd clearly warned her not to. She needed to think of an excuse.

But Riley hadn't had a choice, not after what had happened to her mum. Kenny had made it clear that it was either her or Kelsey who would have to work for him now. Her mum wasn't aware, but she was doing a bit of dealing herself, as well as dropping off and collecting. It was small fry, enough to get her in trouble, though. She did it to keep

Kelsey safe. Kelsey had yet to be tainted by the world she was being dragged into.

And as her big sister, with a useless mum and a father who'd deserted them many years ago, Riley would do anything to protect her.

CHAPTER FOURTEEN

Milo Barker hadn't been in touch with Allie since she'd left the card with her contact details. Neither had anyone else, so Allie would try again in the morning. Gossip would come in overnight, she was sure, once the estate rumours began to fly around.

Just then, she received a message from her husband, Mark. It flashed up on the home screen before it disappeared.

It's here! The email!

Her stomach rolling over, she opened it and read it again. This was it. The moment they'd been waiting for.

A few months ago, they'd started the ball rolling to become foster parents. After numerous interviews, training sessions, questions from panels and board members, they were waiting for the final decision to arrive.

They'd asked to be informed via email so they could both be there at the same time, rather than one of them receiving a phone call. Sadly, they'd have to wait a little longer as she was swamped. Allie sent a message back to Mark.

I won't be home for another hour. Sorry!

You can't make me wait that long. Only kidding. Really, I am. I won't open it until you're here, no matter how late.

I'll be home as soon as I can, I promise!!!

Allie reckoned the situation warranted the overuse of the exclamation marks. How exciting for them both. Everything had been on hold until they had the decision. She prayed it would be in their favour, unsure if she'd be able to cope if they were rejected.

Finally, the team had come as far as they could. Visits to the mortuary had been booked for the following morning for both families of the deceased, and a family liaison officer allocated. She'd been pleased to see it was PC Joy. A press conference had been set up to add to the one this evening, and the evidence was coming in slowly but surely.

'Let's call it a day,' she told everyone. 'Get some downtime. It's going to be a long one tomorrow.'

Perry yawned loudly, stretching his arms in the air. 'Sounds good to me. I'm knackered.'

'Can't take the pace,' Frankie muttered, laughing.

Perry picked up a stress ball and lobbed it at him, aiming to miss. Frankie ducked anyway, and the ball flew across the office.

Allie smirked. They left the building together and, after saying their goodnights in the car park, she made her way home. She couldn't wait to open her front door, her head full of what was to come.

Fifteen minutes later, she parked in the drive and went indoors.

'I've opened it,' Mark cried, almost making her jump as he came out to her. 'I couldn't wait.'

'Really?' she said, disbelief in her tone.

'Of course not! I'm surprised you'd doubt me.'

'I didn't.'

'Yeah, right.' He tutted playfully.

Even with everything that had happened today, the pending decision had never been far from Allie's mind, about how their future could change once they'd received it. And now the moment of truth was here, she was almost too scared to find out.

'I've put the champagne on ice,' Mark added. 'I figured if it was a no, we could get hammered anyway. And then we'll appeal.'

'Isn't it me who's usually the cynical one?' She laughed, kissing him before going inside.

Mark's laptop was open on the kitchen island, the mouse hovering over the email.

'Shall I open it or do you want to?' he said.

The excitement in his voice made her giggle. 'You do it.'

He clicked, and they both leaned over to read the words.

Allie got as far as "I'm pleased to inform you that you have been accepted" before Mark pulled her into his arms and twirled her around the room.

'It's a yes!' he cried. 'Ohmigod, Allie, it's a yes.'

Allie hugged him back, his words not sinking in. 'Did it really say that?' she asked.

'It sure did.' Tears poured down Mark's face and he took her own into his hands. 'We're going to make great foster parents.'

Her eyes welled up, too. 'It'll be hard work but–'

'Ah, I wondered how long it would be until Ms Pessimistic showed herself.'

She slapped his arm. 'I was about to say it's going to be fun, too.'

They stood together, grinning and wiping eyes, until Mark raced to the fridge and popped the cork on the champagne. He poured it in two glasses and passed one to her. Then he raised his in the air.

'To us and the new kids.'

'To the new kids on the block!' Allie clinked her drink against his. Her relief was immense. Everything had seemed hopeful as they were completing the paperwork and being interviewed and checked, but you never really knew until the decision was in.

And now it was.

'I wonder when we'll get our first child,' Mark said. 'I hadn't really thought much past the process. What happens if someone needs a bed tonight?'

'We've prepared for this.' Allie pointed to a list on the side of the fridge. For the past few weeks, they'd been adding anything they could think of to it, so they knew what to buy. 'You're still not getting a trampoline, though.'

'That's so unfair!' Mark stuck out his bottom lip.

'Knowing you, you'll come off it and break a leg, and we can't have you out of action now.'

'Okay, I'll settle for a remote-control car.'

Allie smiled. Suddenly her nerves had gone completely. They would come back, especially when they got their first placement, but equally she was sure she and Mark would get better at fostering with each child they looked after. Of course, it would be hard work, perhaps testing them and their marriage to the limit. It would be taxing, but eventually they'd settle into a routine.

'What would you like first?' Mark quizzed her. 'A girl or a boy?'

'I don't care as long as we can help them.' Allie put down her glass and hugged him tightly again. 'I can't bloody wait.'

CHAPTER FIFTEEN

Tuesday

Andrew was on his mid-morning break. When he heard the mention of a familiar name, he put down his coffee mug and paused to listen to the two females in conversation in the corridor

'He was found dead in a house.'

'No way! Where?'

'Neville Street, on the Limekiln Estate.'

'My friend lives a couple of roads from there. You don't expect things like this to happen close by, do you?'

Andrew looked away as the staffroom door opened and Cathy and her friend, Lucy, came in. Cathy smiled at him before continuing the conversation.

'I've never liked Davy Lewis.' Her voice had dropped a little, their backs towards him. 'Do you know him?'

'Not really. I've heard he's a bit of a knob.'

'That's the understatement of the year.' They laughed as the kettle was flicked on. 'Hark at us, talking ill of the dead.'

'I know. I wonder who's killed him. Do you think it was the woman he was with?'

'It could have been, but the list will be long, I expect.'

'If she didn't kill him, then someone else did, and is still out there.'

Lucy shuddered. 'Ugh, I don't want to think about that.'

Andrew's fingers tingled, his breathing getting laboured. Davy Lewis was dead? Had he really been murdered? What would that mean for him? Would he get the blame for it? Sweat broke out on his forehead. He retched, covering his mouth with his hands in case he vomited.

Cathy turned to him. 'Are you okay, Andrew? You've gone as white as a sheet.'

'I don't feel well at all,' he replied.

'Have you eaten this morning?' Lucy fetched him a drink of water.

'Yes, it's porridge day.'

She handed him the glass, urging him to drink. He took a small sip, his throat feeling tight. He hoped she didn't ask him if he was worried about anything as his cheeks would burn if he lied.

Cathy's phone went. After she'd taken the call, she turned back to him.

'Lucy and I have to go, but I won't be more than a few minutes. Why don't you sit here until I get back, see how you feel then?'

He nodded, watching until she'd disappeared. Then he sank his head in his hands.

Davy Lewis was dead.

He wondered how it had happened, and who the woman was who they'd mentioned. However it had happened, a horrid thought entered his head; he hoped it had hurt.

Andrew had never liked Davy. He had always been mean to him. It was another reason why he wanted to move out of his flat. Davy had turned up whenever he felt like it. But he wasn't going to tell anyone at work about it.

Cathy was back in ten minutes. Andrew was still sitting where she'd left him, his coffee untouched.

'Are you feeling any better?' she wanted to know.

'Not really. I still feel sick.' He didn't, but he couldn't stay at work today.

'Do you want to go home? You do seem very pale, and I don't want to let you loose by the machinery. You'll probably feel better again by the morning.'

'Thanks, I will.' Andrew nodded, an idea forming. He could take the opportunity to go home and check his flat. If anyone showed up, he would open the door and run like Forrest Gump so that they wouldn't catch him.

Twenty minutes later, he got off the bus on the Limekiln Estate. He walked past the row of shops that he visited most days. They had become so familiar to him over the years, and he was going to miss popping into some of them.

The Co-op where he shopped every evening. The newsagent's he visited every morning before he went to work. The Wright's Pie Shop that sold delicious pies and cakes that he would treat himself to at the weekend.

As he turned into Redmond Street, he noticed someone coming up the path, away from his flat. He stopped suddenly, his stomach dropping. It was Kenny. He ducked behind a hedge quickly, hoping not to be seen.

He stayed hidden until Kenny drove past in his car a minute later, then he sighed with relief. That had been close. Perhaps he'd be safer going straight to his mum's. He'd tell her he'd been feeling poorly, although he wouldn't say why.

Mum had said he could stay for a while. No one would come looking for him now that Davy had got killed, would they? They'd be lying low, worried who might be next.

Then a thought struck him. Maybe it was one of the boys

who visited his flat who had killed Davy. Milo, for instance? He and Davy were always arguing when they came around. Andrew didn't like it, often covering his ears with his hands while they laid into each other. Sometimes there were fights as well as cross words.

Then there was Connor Lightwood. He'd been hanging around for the past few weeks, but he'd not come as much recently. Andrew didn't like Connor either, although Connor treated him better than Davy or Milo did.

But why had Kenny Webb been in his flat? Should he go and see if he had stored anything in there he could get in trouble for?

A white car came around the corner. Andrew flew behind the hedge again. Kenny's car was white. Had he spotted him earlier? But then he saw it was Mrs Smith from number twelve. It wasn't Kenny. Even so, he didn't feel safe anymore.

With another quick glance up and down the street, Andrew scurried away quickly.

CHAPTER SIXTEEN

Allie's first job that morning had been to meet the families at the mortuary to identify the bodies. Another press release was due out later, uniformed officers resumed house-to-house, and the rest of the team were collating and sifting through information that had come in overnight.

Before going to see DCI Jenny Brindley, Allie wanted to catch up with a few things.

'The three girls' stories check out,' Sam shouted over to her as she came into the main room. 'I have footage of them entering and leaving Flynn's Nightclub at the times they said. Also, the remaining fingerprints are back.' Sam paused. 'There's someone on here you might like to see – or rather not.'

Allie made her way over to Sam's desk and read the email from the computer screen. She groaned when she saw who Sam was referring to.

'What the hell was Riley Abbott doing at the property?' Allie would see if she could pop round on the quiet when she was out that afternoon. She pointed to the ceiling. 'I'm going to have a word with Jenny. I'll be back in fifteen minutes.'

Having rung ahead to see if Jenny was free, Allie went upstairs. In Jenny's office, she brought her up to speed with a few things.

'We also have a tentative lead in Milo Barker,' Allie went on, explaining what she'd learned from Lily Barker. 'His fingerprints are on a long list of many, though.'

'Any other people known to us?'

'A few who've had cautions. One shoplifter. And Riley Abbott.'

'Really?' Jenny tutted.

'I was surprised, too. I hoped she'd stay on the right side of us after all the recent trouble. Lily Barker also mentioned Kenny Webb. She clearly hadn't got much time for him.'

Jenny frowned after she'd updated her about Lily's thoughts. 'Young girls aren't his thing, surely?'

'I don't think so either. Nor do I think they're being used as sex workers. I think they're a benefits scam. Lots of people staying in one house, and he's claiming while taking payments from them all.'

'It's so exploitative and brings back nasty memories of the racket with the Steele family.'

The Steeles were a criminal family who had lived in Stoke until a couple of years ago. One of two brothers, Leon, had been the main ringleader behind a grooming gang, girls and boys, along with his wife, who had shocked them all by being involved. It had turned out to be a hideous case.

'Not to mention awkward for DS Allendale,' Jenny added.

The Steeles were Grace's estranged half-family. She'd been working in their team then, although relocating from Manchester where she had lived from the age of twelve. She hadn't seen any of the family since fleeing her violent father with her mother in the middle of the night. George Steele had been a brute to them, and to his other family, too.

'Speaking of Grace, Ma'am,' Allie said. 'With the amount

of people we need to talk to about these murders, I was wondering if she could join us on this. She has great liaison skills in the community. I think she'd be an asset.'

Jenny paused for thought and then nodded. 'I'll call her now, see if she's available.'

'Thanks. Do you need me for anything? The press conference going out?'

Jenny paused and then shook her head. 'Let me handle it. I'll give you a shout if I change my mind.'

Allie nodded and left the room. Downstairs, the team had gathered in the incident room.

'Welcome to Operation Mitchell.' She pointed to the digital screen where photos of the deceased were on show. 'Let's start with the basics.' She quickly ran through their victims' names and what had happened to them again. 'Some forensics have come back. Minute blood traces on Chantelle Bishop match with Davy Lewis. Looks like he did punch her, causing her to fall and hit her head.

'Then someone either tried to stop him from attacking her again and stabbed him in retaliation or *that* someone was mad about what he'd done and put a knife in him. We'll know more as we go along, but for now we can release to the press that we're after someone else in connection with these murders. It's going to mean a lot more work for us as people speculate. Perry, Frankie, I want you in Neville Street this afternoon.'

Perry and Frankie nodded their understanding.

'There are also several sets of fingerprints around the house,' Allie went on. 'As well as the girls who live there, there seem to be lots belonging to outsiders, too. We need to cross-reference them to see who we have on our system and what they've been up to lately.'

She glanced at the list she'd scribbled down before coming back into the room.

'We're still waiting to talk to Milo Barker. He wasn't at home when I called last night. His mother hasn't seen him since the weekend. I shall be visiting Car Wash City and having a chat with the wonderful Kenny Webb later. We need to locate Milo as soon as possible, to rule him in or out as he'd recently been fighting with Davy Lewis. We also have to find the missing girl, Janey Webster.' Her phone went, and she checked the message. 'That was confirmation Grace Allendale will be joining us. She's on her way.'

'Great stuff,' Frankie said. 'I miss working with her.'

Everyone spoke their agreement.

'Anything on CCTV, Sam?' Allie asked.

'Nothing concrete yet, but I'm still searching. I do have a woman who spotted a white BMW near the scene, though.'

'Interesting, as that matches Kenny Webb's choice of vehicle.'

'I'll let you know once I've spoken to her. I'll try to get footage of it around the surrounding streets if the source is reliable.'

'Cheers.'

'Ma'am.' A uniformed officer came over to them. 'Someone's come forward with information.'

CHAPTER SEVENTEEN

The call had come in from Mr and Mrs Radcliffe, saying they had news about the house Chantelle Bishop had been staying in. Allie decided to visit them.

The address was in Barlaston, on the outskirts of the city. She pulled up outside a pre-war detached house and sat for a moment, wondering what had brought her here. It was certainly a nice change from the places she usually visited.

The property had been tastefully renovated, two large bay windows, stained glass in the front door. A Porsche sat on the cobblestoned drive, next to a Mercedes. A Victorian lamp post stood proudly in the middle of a neat lawn to her right.

The door was answered by a woman in her forties. She was dressed casually in jeans and a jumper, dark hair scraped from her face in a ponytail, with the slightest of make-up to give her a bit of colour. The man behind seemed close to her in age. His grey hair was thinning, and he was wearing fashionable thick-rimmed black glasses.

'Mr and Mrs Radcliffe?' Allie held up her warrant card. 'DI Allie Shenton, Staffordshire Police.'

'Come in, please.'

She was shown into a room so stylish that envy washed over her. Allie was good at making her mark on a room, but this was way out of her league. It looked effortless, and it suited the house precisely.

She sat on the edge of a mauve leather armchair, Mr and Mrs Radcliffe on a yellow settee across from her.

'You have a beautiful home,' she remarked. It was small talk to put the couple at ease, but she really meant it. 'Have you lived here long?'

'Seventeen years. It's all Hannah's touch.' The man smiled faintly. 'She's the one with the flair. I'm Mike, by the way.'

'Thank you. You wanted to see me in connection with the murders of Davy Lewis and Chantelle Bishop?'

'Yes.' Mike cleared his throat. 'Our daughter, Chrissie, went to stay at that house for a few months.'

'Is she here now? May I talk to her?'

'She... she died a month ago. A heroin overdose.'

'I'm so sorry for your loss.' Allie gave a faint sigh but wanted to stay on point. 'And you think that was in direct correlation to Neville Street?'

'Yes, and no, because it's not the only house she stayed at,' Mike said. 'She came back for a while, wanting to give up the drugs. We tried to help her, but in the end we think she couldn't cope. She must have got some when we were at work.'

'When I got home, she was...' Hannah gasped for air. 'I found her unconscious in her bedroom. We rang for an ambulance, but it was too late.' She gulped back a sob. 'She was our only child, our life. Gone at seventeen.'

'I'm so sorry,' Allie said again.

She truly was. She hated how criminals preyed on kids and young people. Chrissie had been no more than a child, at the prime of her life, with so much to look forward to. It was sickening.

'Mr and Mrs Radcliffe, I will do everything I can to bring the people who did this to justice,' she told them.

'It was her own fault,' Hannah said softly.

'You don't really believe that.' Mike shook her head. 'If she hadn't met those girls, she wouldn't have dabbled with drugs, got hooked, and then wanted more.'

'Girls?' Allie probed.

'Dani and Leah.' He sneered. 'They became her best friends overnight. Leeches if you ask me. I thought they were sizing up the house at first, coming back to rob us. But no, they were interested in exploiting Chrissie. We didn't realise until it was too late. Her moods got worse, she started to steal money, and then she lost so much weight. It was as if she didn't care about herself anymore.' He smiled then. 'She had always prided herself in her appearance.'

Hannah reached for his hand and gave it a squeeze. 'It's all so raw for us, Inspector. We only buried her two weeks ago. I still can't go into her room without throwing myself on her bed and sobbing until I fall asleep with exhaustion.'

Allie was at a loss as to what to say next. Although Mr and Mrs Radcliffe had asked to speak to her, sadly, they hadn't anything to say other than what the team already knew. Yet Allie was certain the house in Neville Street was being used to recruit young girls as drug runners by enticing them to use so the gangs could get them addicted. It was a classic ploy – give them free stuff, hook them on it, and then reel them in with a large debt that they'd have to pay back by working for them. A never-ending circle. Once they were in, they were stuck. They could never leave without threats of violence and repercussion for their families.

She needed to find proof this was happening.

'There was one other thing we wanted to tell you, in case the name meant anything to you,' Mike said next. 'Chrissie was picked up one night by a different man. When she came in, I asked her who he was, concerned that he was a lot older than her. He seemed more my age. Chrissie clammed up. She wouldn't even tell us his name, but she slipped up when we were arguing. It was Kenny.'

It had to be Kenny Webb. What had been going on with him and these girls? It was strange that Allie was hearing this now, after knowing him so long and not getting an inkling of it. Was there something he was keeping quiet about?

Like so much that went on in private, if they hadn't found the notebook on Billy Whitmore, which had led them to start looking into the addresses, all this could have gone unnoticed.

'Did you see the make of the vehicle?' she asked him, wanting to be sure.

'It was a BMW, white. I didn't get the registration number. I couldn't see it without bringing attention to myself.'

'Can you describe him for me, please?'

'Stocky with a shaved head. I think he'd be a big build out of the car.'

Yes, that sounded like Kenny.

'Did she go anywhere else, do you know?' Allie asked.

'We found her in another house several times before she died,' Hannah said. 'Number fifteen Lymer Road.'

For a nanosecond, Allie glanced up from the notes she'd been writing. Then she continued, without giving anything away. But she would be checking that out with the Organised Crime Unit as soon as she got back to the station.

Because it was another property on the list that had come from Billy Whitmore's notebook.

CHAPTER EIGHTEEN

Next, Allie went to see Kenny Webb at Car Wash City. She'd thought about taking Frankie with her. Like the many times he'd been with her before, it would be good for him to mingle with the young lads working there, washing and valeting the cars. Sometimes they slipped up with a snippet of gossip, but more likely than not, they kept everything close to their chest.

But this time she wanted to speak to Kenny alone.

Allie and Kenny Webb were the epitome of frenemies. To each other, they were smiley and affable, but they both had an agenda.

Kenny wanted to stay one step ahead of Allie and her team. Allie wanted to put him behind bars.

Allie knew so much about Kenny, and yet she couldn't question him about any of it. It could jeopardise the case that was being built up by the Organised Crime Unit.

Kenny was known to be working for Terry Ryder. He was due out of prison next month, something both her and Kenny would be wary about, too.

Kenny wasn't certain that Ryder hadn't heard he was

working for his arch enemy, Steve Kennedy. Ryder had killed Steve's brother, Phil, and his nephew, Lee, was still banged up for murdering Ryder's friend.

Allie wasn't sure Ryder had forgiven her for putting him behind bars for such a long stretch.

Neither of them were clear which one would win the battle at the end of the day.

It had to be a weird world to live in, she mused, wondering if any of them could be trusted among themselves. Knowing that one day someone could act as if they had your best interests at heart, and the next be selling you short, or even, pointing a gun at your head and pulling the trigger.

The crime rate in Stoke-on-Trent for that kind of violent crime was low. Still, Allie wouldn't step on any toes while a team was working hard to secure convictions. But she would be grateful when she was given the go-ahead to pull Kenny in. To jail him, too.

Kenny was in his office, his back to her as he made coffee from a machine.

'Want one?' He peered at her from over his shoulder while she stood in the doorway. 'I assume you're going to be here long enough.'

'No, thanks.' She glanced around and then sat across the desk from him. The office had been almost emptied since her last visit. 'You've had a clear-out.'

'We're expanding next week.' He pointed to the wall behind her. 'That's coming down, and we're joining the two rooms. I'm taking on more staff. The car wash business is a good one to be in.'

Allie doubted he'd know anything about that side of things, even though he was the overall manager. His staff would be doing the hard work of getting everything fixed and sorted. The car wash franchises were extremely successful, regardless of what went on behind the scenes. There was always a line of cars waiting to be cleaned on the forecourt, and most of their occupants didn't seem the type who would pay to get their cars cleaned just to collect a fix at the same time.

'Business that good?' she queried.

'Booming, even without half of my staff ending up dead.'

'Ah, you've heard about the recent murders.' She nodded in acknowledgement.

'Couldn't really miss them. Everyone's talking about Davy Lewis.'

'And the girl, the one who died?'

Kenny shrugged. 'I'm not with you. She wasn't with Davy. He's seeing Lily—'

'Barker. Yes, I know. But why the girl?'

'Why the girl what?'

'Why was the girl killed?'

'You'll have to ask whoever killed her. Ah, but you can't because he's dead.'

'Don't play games, Kenny. Now isn't the time,' she snapped. 'What's going on with you? Don't you care that Davy is gone? He was one of your foot soldiers, after all.'

'I don't know what you're talking about.' Kenny's expression darkened. 'Davy probably got what he deserved. I expect whoever attacked him did it because of what he'd done to Chantelle. So no, I don't have an ounce of sympathy. Davy was one of those men who didn't care about hitting a woman. I do, I deplore it.'

Allie raised her eyebrows. She was about to say something damning but luckily stopped herself in time. She still didn't have any proof that he'd hit out at Fiona Abbott, Billy Whitmore's partner, at the time of Billy's death.

'Do you own the property?' she went on, already knowing the answer.

'I do. It's rented out.'

'To who?'

'I'd have to check as I have a few, but I think Chantelle was the tenant. I'm not sure why there were so many people staying there, though. I assume Davy knew why. Now I'll never know, but all this has got to be down to him.'

A silence dropped on the room, the noise from the business the only sounds. A radio blasting, lads shouting and laughing above it. A horn beeped on a car.

'I've really come here to talk to Milo,' Allie told a white lie.

'I haven't seen him since the weekend. He hasn't turned up for work this week. And when he does show his face, he'll be getting his marching orders. I don't care for people who let me down.'

'Quite the man, aren't you?' She shook her head. 'Those boys out there must really look up to you. And you love it.'

'What do you want, Detective?' Kenny sat forward and reached for a piece of paper from his in-tray. He began to read the print. 'I'm busy.'

'I want to know what Terry Ryder has planned when he gets out next month.'

'You sound as if you're after an informant?'

'Not unless you'd like to be one.'

Kenny laughed, loud and hearty. 'You have some nerve.'

'I do. Lots of it.'

'Why don't you come and see him, when he's released? I'm sure he'd love to catch up with you.'

She glared at him before getting to her feet. Despite his insinuations, she wasn't going there. It was none of his business.

'You'll let Milo know I want to speak to him when you see him?' she said instead.

'If he shows his face.'

'In the meantime, I'll try his parents. Does he still live at home?'

'I'm not his keeper.'

'But you are his employer and should have his details on file. I'd like to confirm he's still at the same address as I have from our system, Rochford Street?'

He glared, then nodded. 'Yes, he's still there.'

'Thank you. You've been most helpful, as usual.'

She left him, knowing her words would get repeated to Terry verbatim. There would be no warning of if or when Ryder might attack her – in the work sense, hopefully not the physical. Although she would like to ball up a fist and smack him in the face as soon as she set eyes on him again.

Still, one nasty guy at a time. That would do for now.

As soon as Allie had left, Kenny got on the phone to Martin Smith.

'That idiot, Lewis, has led them to Neville Street,' he told him. 'I think we need to start putting our plans into action. Have you had time to speak to the girls who were staying there?'

'I've spoken to Dani on the phone. She says none of them saw anything.'

'That's good. Make sure it stays that way.'

'I didn't know they were all kipping there, to be honest. They'd been there for about a month.'

'I'd told Davy to keep an eye on them, not rip me off. I bet he was charging them rent and keeping it for himself. The lowlife scum.' Kenny paused. 'I don't like the sound of how things are going. The police are too close.'

'You reckon it's going to fall apart again?'

'I think we'd be best to set things up this week rather than next. Especially while there's some heat around Lewis.'

'I agree. Want me to find out what the boss thinks?'

Kenny sniggered. 'I'm the boss.'

The words went unspoken between them in the silence that followed. He and Martin were both aware that things would change drastically when Terry was released. Kenny wasn't looking forward to it: he suspected Martin wouldn't be either. But Martin would most likely be far better off.

'I'll get word to him and see what he says.' Kenny wound up the call. 'In the meantime, let's do what we said. Get it ready as soon as.'

CHAPTER NINETEEN

Allie knew she shouldn't get as involved in hands-on jobs as she did, but it made things more interesting for her. The DCI hadn't had a problem with it so far, so before she stopped by at the Abbott residence, she decided to check out the house the Radcliffes had told her about. It was only a few minutes away by car.

Lymer Road was the main drag on the Bennett Estate. She pulled up outside number fifteen. It seemed like any normal house, an ex-council semi in among properties that were still tenanted. But that was where the similarities ended.

Number fifteen's garden was overgrown, rubbish strewn everywhere and a battered armchair on what used to be a lawn. A pane of glass was missing from the large window, hardboard pushed up against it to stop access.

She knocked on the door, being careful to avoid the vomit that was all over the step. When there was no answer after three attempts, she peered through the living room window.

The place was a tip, a three-piece suite and a TV around a coffee table that was covered in mugs, beer bottles and chocolate wrappers. Floorboards were bare, and not a painting on the walls. No ornaments or photos in frames.

'They shouldn't be allowed to do that,' someone from next door shouted over the fence.

Allie turned to find a woman in her fifties with short blonde hair.

'To do what?' Allie stepped toward her.

'Wreck the place. Be rude when we tell them to be quiet. Make so much noise.'

'Do you know who lives there?'

'Yes, a young woman. Well, she's only a girl really. Late teens, I don't know her name. She lets anyone in. It's like a youth club, kids coming and going every hour of the day and night. Music blasting, doors slamming.' She shook her head. 'I bet there's drugs in there, too. Some of them look wasted when they come out of the house. But it's the noise mostly. It goes on for hours.'

'Have you complained to the owner?'

'He's neither use nor ornament.' The woman harrumphed. 'He comes around once every few weeks. I've spoken to him several times, but all he does is say he'll get them to be quieter. It never changes.'

'What about the council? I'm afraid you need to speak to them about noise nuisance issues.'

'Oh, I thought you were from the housing office. Are you police, then?'

Allie nodded. 'I need access to the property, or details of who goes in and out of it.' She tried the back gate to see if it was open. She couldn't budge it, not even with her shoulder. 'Can you help me with either?'

'I'm out at work most days. You should ask Sheila Rowley, number twelve. She never misses a trick. Want me to ring her, see if she'll come across?'

'Please.' Allie loved a nosy neighbour.

'You might be able to see more from my house.' The woman beckoned to her.

Allie followed her through into the rear garden, thinking it was worth a try. The fence was high, but there was a metal bin store next to it. Allie pointed to it.

'Mind if I climb on this to get over?'

'Be my guest.'

Allie dropped down to the garden in the middle of wet grass up to her shins. She trod carefully through the empty beer cans and cigarette packets. The back door had a dried muddy footprint on it. A window upstairs was on the catch.

'Can you see anything?' the woman next door queried.

Allie ignored her and peered through the window. There were no curtains, so she could see straight into the kitchen. It was a mess in there, too. She'd bet the whole house hummed. Takeaway cartons piled high on the table. Mugs littering the worktops. A packet of biscuits left to go soft. A red hoodie hung over the back of a chair, the designer logo in large white lettering.

'Sheila's here,' the woman shouted over the fence.

Allie climbed back into the garden and was shown into the kitchen.

Sheila was a small, round woman with a pale face. Her hair was scraped into a messy bun, which made it hard to put an age on her, but Allie reckoned she was in her late sixties.

She stuck out a hand when Allie approached her. 'The name's Sheila Rowley. What can I do to help?'

Allie stifled a giggle as she offered her hand. She reminded her of Miss Trunchbull out of the *Matilda* novel that was made into a film. All she wanted now was for her to put her hands on her hips.

'I'm Karen Clarkson, by the way,' the original neighbour said. 'Would you like a cup of tea?'

Allie glanced at her watch. She'd have to be quick, but for some reason she expected it would be worth it.

She smiled. 'That would be lovely, thanks.'

Karen pointed at the table, and she moved to sit down with Sheila.

'Lovely kitchen,' Allie made small talk while she got out her notebook. 'Have you lived here long?'

'Twenty-two years,' Karen replied as she prepared the drinks. 'Bought it off the council and have done a lot to it.'

Allie looked at Sheila.

'I've been here for thirty-one years,' Sheila replied. 'It used to be a nice street when we moved in, then it went down bank for a while. It got better a few years ago, but ever since old Leonard died and the place next door was sold, it's become really rowdy again.'

'Karen mentions you might have information about the house?'

Sheila reached for the biscuit tin as soon as Karen popped it on the table. 'I think the landlord is a man in his forties. Drives a black Ford.'

Allie stopped writing notes for a moment. The model of the car threw her. She was expecting it to be a white BMW as the house belonged to Kenny Webb. She made a mental note to check if Davy Lewis had a vehicle once she was back at the office. Having said that, Davy was only in his thirties. On one of his bad days, she might push him into that age bracket, though.

'This man – does he visit often during the day?' she asked next.

'Two or three times a week, I'd say,' Sheila said. 'Always early evening.'

'Does he have a key to the house?'

'Yes. I think it's disgusting that he can let himself in

whenever he feels like. The tenant has no privacy. It shouldn't be allowed.'

'Although it might stop her from getting up to more than she does,' Karen remarked, bringing their drinks over. 'The girl is nice to your face but the same as the rest of them once your back is turned.' Karen sat next to Sheila, opposite Allie.

'And you say there are lots of visitors?' Allie went on. 'Are they the same ones each week, or different ones?'

'The same. I reckon there are about a dozen of them in total. Probably six each of girls and boys. They're all no older than twenty.'

'How do they get here? Any vehicles they use?'

'One has a clapped-out Fiesta. The rest walk or come on pushbikes.'

Allie drank the rest of her coffee, thanked the women for their help, and then nipped back around to next door. With no answer still, she left a calling card for someone to contact her.

While she walked to her car, she thought about her conversation with the neighbours. Who was the mystery man Sheila Rowley was referring to?

CHAPTER TWENTY

Allie knocked a tad harder on the door of the Abbott's home. She couldn't help her annoyance seeping out. Time and time again she had told Fiona to look after her daughters and not drag them into something they couldn't get out of.

Fiona answered the door, sighing when she saw who it was.

'Is this a social call?' she snapped. 'Because if not, you'd better be quick.'

Fiona was in her late thirties, small but heavily set with brown curly hair and a round face. Allie had never once seen her out of black leggings and oversized jumpers and T-shirts, and today was no exception.

Allie ignored her comments and followed Fiona inside.

'Is Riley around?'

'She's at work, why?'

'I need to talk to her. But first I want to talk to you.'

'What about?'

Allie could tell from Fiona's demeanour that she was worried about what she was going to say. Since her arrival, her eyes had flitted everywhere but Allie's own. Fiona knew something; she'd have to tease it out of her.

'I want to know if you kept your promise to me after Billy died, to sort yourself out and stop dealing drugs,' Allie said. 'To give your girls a better life.'

'I never promised.' Fiona's voice went up an octave.

'We had a conversation about–'

'It's not that easy, you know, to stop doing something. Not when the people I work with are breathing down my neck. I have my own safety to think of, too.'

'Maybe so, but you wouldn't tell me who you were needing to keep safe from. How am I supposed to help if you–'

'I don't need your help.'

Allie held in her temper once again. The woman was so annoying, but equally she could understand her fear in talking to the police. Being thought of as a grass around here would mean even more bother.

'When will Riley be back?' she asked.

'A few minutes. You can wait if you like. I'll make some tea. I *promise* not to lace it with poison.'

Allie smiled. At least Fiona was trying.

A few minutes later, Riley came in, almost stopping in mid-step when she saw Allie sitting on the settee.

'She just wants to talk,' Fiona said, raising a hand. 'I haven't said anything.'

Allie patted the seat beside her. Riley flopped into it.

'Riley, what do you know about Neville Street?'

Riley paled. 'I-I knew Chantelle Bishop. I've been to her house lots of times.'

'Recently?'

'Yes, I stayed over last week.'

'So you know Chantelle well?'

'I wouldn't say that. I'm more Janey's friend.'

'Janey Webster?'

'Yes.'

'I borrowed a dress from her and went round to drop it back at Chantelle's, as she's staying there.'

'When was this?'

'Saturday night.'

Allie noted the details down. 'And did you notice anything different or sense an atmosphere?'

'No, we went to the pub, brought chips on the way home, and I stayed there until about midnight.'

'She wasn't worried about anything?'

'She didn't seem to be.' Riley shook her head. 'We had a good laugh.'

'Just the two of you?'

'Yeah, the other girls were out.'

'Okay, that's good for now. As you can imagine, there are numerous prints found in the house, so we're checking everyone's whereabouts. Most of the people are being brought into the station, but I thought as I know you, I'd come and see you. Where were you on Sunday evening?'

'I was here.'

'That's right, I can vouch for her,' Fiona said. 'I was here, too.'

'All evening?'

'Yes, we watched a film. *Top Gun* was on – the original. Some people think it's better than the *Maverick* one, but I haven't seen that.'

Allie looked at Riley, who didn't seem to be in any way fazed by what her mum had said. Normally, if anyone was lying on the hoof, she could see right through it. It didn't seem to be the case here, but she'd check the TV schedule when she got back if she could.

'I must ask you again,' she said. 'Are you telling me everything you know, Riley?'

'Yes.'

'Because I can't help you if you're keeping–'

'It's true!' Riley sat upright, her hands in her lap. 'I still can't believe she was killed by that... that lunatic.'

'We can't be certain that's what happened yet,' Allie cautioned.

'I still hate Davy Lewis with a passion.'

Allie couldn't let that remark go. 'Why's that?'

'You know. He was a nasty bastard. He was charging all those girls rent to live in that shithole. I doubt Kenny knew about that.'

'How do *you* know that?'

'Janey told me.'

Allie had heard enough for now, except for one more thing.

'How's Kelsey doing?'

'Absolutely fine.' Fiona's tone was defensive. 'She's at school.'

'Any problems I need to know about?'

'You're not the boss of me,' she muttered, reaching for a cigarette. 'My family is doing fine.'

Allie stood up, knowing she was getting nowhere. 'I'll leave you for now, but I may want to speak to you again in the coming days. I assume you're not going away, Riley?'

Riley shook her head.

Allie saw herself out, annoyed at the thought of the women being under the power of Kenny Webb. That man was the bane of her life, let alone theirs. If only she could take him down before he was able to do any more harm in the city.

As soon as Allie had gone, Fiona rounded on her daughter.

'Are you sure you're telling *me* everything?' she asked.

'Because if anything has been going on, I need to know right now.'

Riley's cheeks coloured, but still she said nothing.

Fiona sighed. 'I don't want you getting into trouble, duck, that's all.'

'Like you're so innocent,' Riley muttered. 'You've been working for Kenny, too, when you said you wouldn't.'

'That's as may be, but I do it because I don't have any choice.'

Riley looked at the floor.

'He's going to ruin the whole bloody family!' Fiona reiterated.

'We won't let him, Mum. He won't be around here forever, will he?'

'Who knows with him. He's always out for what he can get. But just remember, we're doing this to keep Kelsey out of it.'

'From where I'm sitting, I feel very much like I don't have a choice. If I don't do the runs, he'll make Kelsey do them.' Riley burst into tears. 'I hate it, Mum, I really do. I have to take stuff on a train to Crewe and then meet someone there, swap it for cash, and bring it back.'

Fiona moved to sit next to her daughter and drew her into her arms. 'What a mess we're in. I'll have to think what to do as we can't continue like this. I don't want you to get in trouble with the police.'

Riley felt safe in her mum's arms for a minute, loved even. It was the only time she'd had any affection from anyone recently. After her boyfriend, Carlton, had been murdered eight months ago, she hadn't wanted to date anyone else. They were all a useless bunch of pricks on this estate.

'I think we should talk to Kenny,' Fiona said quietly.

'It's too dangerous.' Riley changed the subject. 'What's for tea? I'm starving.'

Fiona gave up, knowing that Riley wasn't listening anymore. Maybe she was trying to sort things out her own way, and by not telling her everything she was putting a brave face on. But she hated seeing her girl embroiled in such a difficult situation.

If only Fiona hadn't met Billy Whitmore, none of this would have happened. It was all his bloody fault for getting killed.

CHAPTER TWENTY-ONE

Leanne was home from work after leaving early that afternoon with a bad headache. She hadn't been able to settle into anything anyway, not since hearing about Davy Lewis.

All she could think about was Scott. She hated herself for not having the guts to persuade him to move out of Stoke. But equally she knew what would happen if she didn't let him continue with his job. Kenny had made it perfectly clear what he'd do if she didn't abide by his warning. She hadn't liked it, but what could she do? She couldn't put herself, nor her family, in danger.

When Kit Harper had been murdered five months ago and brought the police to their door, she'd been about to try and persuade Scott to give up his job and go back to his scrap metal business. But she'd had a visit from Kenny. He'd warned her that there would be consequences if she didn't let Scott continue to work for him. She'd been frightened to do anything different ever since.

Hearing the news about Davy Lewis and Chantelle Bishop, she'd immediately wondered if Kenny had something to do with the murders. Leanne wished she had someone to talk to about it, but there was no one close now. Instead, it had to fester inside her, worrying her all the time.

And even though she and Kit had been having an affair, so he wasn't hers to miss, it didn't stop her longing for him. Kit had been a huge part of her life for so many years. She recalled the way he used to make her smile; the way he'd wink at her when no one was looking.

The moments they'd met in secret, enjoying each other before going back to their other halves whilst trying to keep a lid on the guilt. The occasions they'd almost been caught.

The times they'd got together and then stopped, started again and stopped, trying to keep their love at bay. Theirs had gone past an affair, but they were both reluctant to break up marriages, and friendships that had been made in nursery schools. They'd been a close-knit group.

Having said that, as those friends had disappeared from her life now, it had brought her and Scott closer together. Without them, they'd been drawn shoulder to shoulder again. She hadn't mentioned Kenny's threats to Scott, and she might be between a rock and a hard place, but their marriage was working better. They were a team again.

So forgive her for worrying about what Kenny Webb was up to, and if he'd had anything to do with the murders. Because as she well knew, things could change in an instant. Leanne's life now revolved around worrying about Scott getting caught because of what he was doing, and him going to prison, leaving her and Amy completely on their own.

Scott had texted to say he'd be home around six. He'd been given an early night. Scott barely got home before nine each evening. There was always some meeting or other, some drop-off or collection he was waiting for.

Leanne would be pleased to have him back early, though.

Every morning he left the house, she kept thinking that it might be the day he wouldn't come back at all. Of course, Scott knew what he did came with a penalty if he was caught, but that didn't appease her. He reassured her, often, that he hadn't been in trouble with the law yet.

Yet.

That one little word had such a big meaning. He'd been close to the wire several times. After he'd been delivering drugs and collecting cash one night, he'd come home the following evening and told her the car he was in before being dropped off had been stopped by the police with the gear in the boot. The driver had been sent down for two years. Thankfully, he hadn't mentioned Scott had been with him.

Another time, the police had been round to search their home after a tip-off. They hadn't found anything as there was nothing to find. But it had caused a huge row between them. Scott had insisted he'd been set up. Neither of them trusted Kenny Webb, so it was a huge possibility.

Had Scott been put on the police radar again? Leanne didn't want officers calling at her home. What would the neighbours think? And Amy, they had to keep everything from her.

She couldn't bear thinking about him going to prison and having to fend for herself. Even though she hated how he got it, they relied on his extra money. Her wage alone wouldn't be enough, and even then, she and Amy would have to look over their shoulders for the rest of their lives. Once in with Kenny Webb, you didn't escape his clutches, even if you'd gone to prison.

Which left Leanne in the difficult predicament of needing Kenny Webb and hating him at the same time. They were saving money, as much as they could, and hoped to get out of Stoke in a couple of years. She wanted Amy as far away from those men as possible. She didn't want her girl introduced to drugs and county lines and whatever else went on behind the scenes at Car Wash City. She shuddered at the thought.

So they would keep their heads down and be compliant. Having said that, the day that Kenny Webb got his comeuppance couldn't come soon enough for Leanne. Until then, her life was on hold.

CHAPTER TWENTY-TWO

Allie was driving to the police station late that afternoon when she spotted someone waving for her attention. It was Simon, the crime editor for the local newspaper, *Stoke News*. Married to Grace, Simon was one of her closest friends.

She parked her car and went out to greet him, waiting until the noise from a passing bus had faded a little.

'Hey, what brings you to my side of the road?' Allie smiled.

Stoke News was based on the opposite side of Bethesda Street, just past Hanley Crown Court and the multi-storey car park. It had been quite handy over the years to have an ally in the press situated so close, especially if either of them needed, or were giving, the other information.

Simon glanced around to see if there was anyone in hearing range. 'I have some information on Martin Smith you might be interested in,' he spoke quietly.

'Oh?' A few months ago, Allie had asked him to see what he could find out about Smith. She pointed to the building. 'Want to come in for a cuppa?'

He nodded. 'Yeah, it'll be a little less conspicuous.'

'What are you saying? That people will think you're a snitch. Or that I'll ruin your street cred?

'You ruined that years ago.'

'Get inside!' Allie pushed him gently.

'Actually, I'm here for the press update about the murders. Unless you have anything to tell me beforehand?'

Allie raised her eyebrows in reply. 'Nothing doing, Cole.'

He laughed as he signed in the visitor's book to get a pass.

'Grace was really excited about working with you again, by the way.' He placed the lanyard around his neck.

'It's good to see her. I only wish it was more permanent. I liked having her on my team.'

'I keep telling her to apply for the vacancy you have. She says she's waiting for a while yet.'

'I'd be happy to put a word in for her, when we can release it. I'm sure she'd be fine without any recommendation, though. She has a good reputation.' She buzzed them through the side door. 'So, Martin Smith?'

'I've been keeping an eye on him since we spoke; what he's been up to, where he's been going. That kind of thing.'

'Bloody hell, Simon!' Allie hissed. 'I didn't mean to play a cop when I asked you to find out what you could!'

He held up a hand. 'I just happened to see him one night in Tesco car park, so I followed him.'

Going upstairs now, aware that people might hear them, Allie kept talk to a minimum until they were seated with drinks at a table in the canteen. There were several officers scattered around them, some in uniform, some plain clothes, depending on their roles. Allie recognised a few faces. A dog handler in the far corner waved at her. She smiled, waving back, and then gave her attention to Simon.

'I hope you only followed Martin that one time?' she continued their earlier conversation once they were settled.

'It may have been on a few occasions.'

'For fuck's sake.' She couldn't help but swear at him. 'Don't you know how dangerous that could have been? I'm surprised Grace didn't tear you apart when she found out.' She glared at him. 'You did tell her about your stupidity?' He said nothing, so she continued with a shake of her head. 'When I asked for your help, I meant a paper trail of what you could find out about him.'

'Okay, okay, sorry. I won't do it again. You're still intrigued to know what I found out, though?'

She smirked. 'Go on.'

'He visited Lymer Road, number fifteen.'

Allie frowned, thankfully stopping herself blurting out that she'd been there that afternoon. 'Did you see him with anyone?'

'Not that night. He had a key to get in the front door, though. There was music blaring really loud when he went in, and it was switched off and didn't come on again, not even when he'd stormed out a few minutes later.'

'Did you see who was inside?'

'Not that time.'

'Simon, it isn't safe for you to follow someone, especially linked to Kenny Webb. That's our job.'

'I know, but I don't think he spotted me. Besides, this was a couple of weeks ago now, and I haven't followed him since.'

Allie still wouldn't be surprised if he'd been seen.

'The third time I saw him, he had a young girl in the car with him. He went inside with her and left her there.' Simon took out his phone and showed her a photo. 'That's her. You should ask her what's going on in there, because it can't be legal.'

The girl in the image was the one she had seen in photographs earlier, in the living room of Mike and Hannah Radcliffe.

'I can't. She overdosed last month. Drugs.'

'Shit.' Simon ran a hand through his hair. 'I hope that wasn't my fault.'

'How would it be?'

He shrugged. 'Feeling guilty, I suppose.'

Allie leaned forward. 'So you only saw Martin Smith and a few teenagers hanging around?'

'From what I can see, it's used for kids to congregate. I wondered if it's a base for a cuckoo, though.'

'It might be. I'll check it out. One more thing, what car does Smith drive?'

'A Ford – black Focus. Nice thing. Newish.'

'Thanks.' Allie wasn't going to mention she'd already been to the property, nor that someone had spotted what could be Smith's car there, too. 'I don't suppose you took any more photos that you shouldn't have?'

Simon sniggered. 'A few, but they're mainly of Martin either going in or coming out.'

'Alone?'

'Sometimes with the odd girl, once with a teenage lad.'

'Can you email them to me?'

'Already in draft.' Simon took back his phone, pressed a few buttons, and then pocketed it. He stood up. 'I've sent it to you, but I have to go or else I'll be late for the DCI.'

'I don't have to tell you that our conversation is off the record?' Allie made her point clear.

'Of course you don't.' He addressed her with a mock-stern glare. 'But tell Grace she'd better be home in time for tea this evening. It's her turn to cook.'

Allie couldn't help but laugh, no matter how annoyed she was with him.

Once he was gone, she sat there for a few moments, scrolling through the photos he'd attached to the emails. There were several teens she recognised, no one of real significance. She would get Sam to cross-reference them with the list of names they'd been given with fingerprints found in Neville Street, plus look into Smith's vehicle to see if it was the same as the one spotted in Lymer Road.

Her phone rang. It was DCI Cooper from the Organised Crime Unit.

'Where are you? Can you talk?'

'I'm here, in the canteen.'

'Can you nip in to see me on your way back to your office? I have some intel for you.'

'Sure. I'll be with you in two minutes.'

CHAPTER TWENTY-THREE

Detective Chief Inspector Shaun Cooper was sitting at a desk on the opposite wing of the first floor. A man in his early forties, he wore his red hair short, shaved at the sides, and had a very endearing lisp. Allie had known him, and his family, for more years than she cared to recall. A keen marathon runner, he'd raised thousands of pounds for a charity close to his heart. His little girl, Selina, had caught sepsis when she'd been five. Luckily she'd pulled through, so it was his way of giving back. An impressive row of medals hung around the corners of his computer monitor, several trophies and rosettes to its side.

Shaun glanced up from his screen, smiling as she approached him. 'Allie! Roll up a chair.'

Allie grabbed the one from the next desk and swirled it round to face him. 'What have you got for me?'

'Tell me what you've been up to first, particularly about the houses.'

Since the addresses they were looking into had appeared in the first notebook, found on Billy Whitmore, the OCU had been keeping an eye on them, too. Allie updated him with everything she'd learned over the past two days.

'Interesting,' Shaun replied.

'Your turn.' She sat forward, keen to hear what he wanted to see her about.

'We've received a tip-off about drugs being stored at the Longton branch of Car Wash City. Our team is going in tomorrow morning.'

Allie's eyes widened with excitement. 'Wonderful!'

'Obviously you can't be there, but do you want to be the first to hear?'

'I certainly do.'

'It won't be an early start because the offices don't open until eight. But we want to be there as soon as the doors open.'

Allie nodded. 'It'll be great to finally get closer.'

'Believe me, there is *so* much going on that I can't share yet. This may be something and nothing, or it may lead us to everything.' He lowered his voice. 'I need you to keep Kenny Webb out of the station. Hang tight and just question him about anything that comes up for now. Don't bring him in.'

Allie frowned and was about to ask why when Shaun continued.

'The tip-off has the potential to put us back for months. It's why we're acting on it. We suspect something is happening elsewhere at the same time, but that's all I can tell you for now.'

Allie nodded, sensing his urgency. She trusted Shaun having known him for so long.

'And the tip-off?' she queried. 'Where did that come from?'

'Someone rang the hotline, about two hours ago.'

'Reliable?'

'Wouldn't give their name. We'll try and locate the

number. Like I say, if we don't follow it up, it will seem suspicious, but we could have done without it.'

'Cheers, Shaun.' Allie stood up, stretching out her back. 'I'll update the team. Keep me in the loop until tomorrow, too?'

'With pleasure.'

She grinned, knowing the satisfaction they would both get if things went to plan. Drugs were only a part of it, but even stopping a tiny piece of what was happening would be a start, especially after so long of not being able to act on anything they'd found out.

Finally getting back to her team, she spotted a familiar face sitting at the spare desk opposite Frankie.

'Grace!' she cried, going to her. 'So good to have you on board.'

'So great to be back.' Grace stood, and they hugged each other.

The two women could almost be mistaken for sisters as they were so alike. Both had long dark hair with blunt fringes, both were slim and five feet four in stature. Both had huge hearts but ambition to bring anyone down they deemed necessary.

Allie glanced at Frankie who was beaming, clearly glad to see Grace, too. He and Grace had worked well together, and Frankie had been lost for a while when she'd transferred to another team. Luckily, he'd now found his place without her, and she was pleased about that.

'I've just seen Simon. He said not to be late as it's your turn to cook.'

'Our in-joke.' Grace laughed. 'He doesn't need an opportunity to take over in the kitchen, he's always doing it. He mothers me, and I love it, and he makes the most amazing flatbreads.'

'He does,' Allie concurred, having tasted them several times.

'I must admit to being pretty pissed off with him when he told me he'd been following Martin Smith.' Grace kept her voice low, so their conversation wouldn't be overheard.

'Ah.' So he had told her.

'He's an idiot, Allie. I don't think he thought for one minute of the danger he'd put himself in. I gave him a right roasting – told him to leave the policing to us.'

'Good for you.' She smiled to alleviate Grace's embarrassment and then surveyed the room to see most of the team were in. 'Okay, everyone. Let's have a catch-up.'

Allie ran through what she had learned that day. 'Are any of the addresses familiar to you, Grace?' she asked afterwards.

Grace nodded. 'We've had several complaints about Lymer Road and a couple about Neville Street. I arranged a nightly patrol for a week, a couple of months ago, PCSOs to walk past, but there's been nothing recently. I'll check in with the residents around the streets concerned.'

'Thanks.' Allie nodded. 'I have intel that Martin Smith may have been visiting Lymer Road, too, although that will need checking up.'

'Intriguing,' Perry remarked. 'I've always had a feeling he was more involved than he's been letting on. No one *just* works for Kenny Webb without being bent.' He paused. 'Do we think the girls are being groomed for sex?'

'There's nothing to suggest it, but we will definitely be looking into that.' Allie couldn't then hide her excitement. 'Also, the OCU are raiding Car Wash City, Longton, first thing in the morning.'

There was a cheer around the room.

Allie grinned. 'Good things come to those that wait. Let's hope the tip-off is a goer.'

'There are a few more forensics back,' Sam addressed the

room. 'Sets of prints from three known troublemakers. I've actioned them, but they need to be passed over.'

'I can do them, if you like?' Frankie offered, before Allie had time to reply.

Allie nodded. 'There are three addresses that are referenced in each book, too. Neville Street, Lymer Road, and Coral Avenue. Still not sure what the amounts by the side of each name are for. I suspect they will be linked to supplying, owing money or rent, or outstanding payments for loans.'

'I'll try and wheedle some of that out, too,' Frankie added.

'Excellent, thanks.' Allie spoke to the team again. 'In the meantime, unless anything comes in, it's all hands to the computers as we ensure we get to everything. Book as many things as you can in for tomorrow. There's also the press conference that,' she checked her watch, 'went out ten minutes ago. Let's get ready for the calls to come rolling in. Hopefully there will be some leads within the dodgy ones.'

CHAPTER TWENTY-FOUR

Outside the North Stafford Hotel, Connor was feeling on top of the world. His biggest rival had been taken out, and he was ready to step into his boots. All he had to do was continue to prove himself and keep that dickhead, Milo, from taking over like he usually did.

The problem was, how? Milo Barker was stronger than him and had given him many a beating over the years. He couldn't go up against him with his fists, so he'd have to use his charm and intelligence to outwit him.

Connor wanted to be top dog. He had what it took to be a face around Stoke, no matter what Milo said about him. And all Milo wanted to do was hang around that poxy flat with that pillock, Andrew, anyway. Sure, it was somewhere to doss when it was cold and raining, but to Connor, it seemed childish to watch TV all night or play stupid video games. This was a man's world, and he wanted in on it all.

He'd already decided he was going to make himself indispensable to Kenny while he worked out who had killed Davy and Chantelle. It wasn't going to be easy, though. Davy had been a thorn in a lot of people's sides. Connor reckoned there'd have been a queue of people who wanted to do it.

But Chantelle was a mystery. Who would want to kill her? Had she got in the way? Had she known too much? Had someone close to the two of them taken her out of the equation just because they could?

It was a shame. From what he'd seen of Chantelle, she'd been pretty hot. Not that she'd given him the time of day. She'd called him boy - stuck up bitch. She was the same age as him.

A young blonde appeared from Stoke Station, and he flashed the car's headlights, laughing as she ran across to him with a huge smile. These girls were so easy to keep keen.

'Hey.' He grinned when she got into the passenger seat. 'Everything go okay?'

'Yes.' She nodded. 'It was a doddle.'

He started the engine and pulled out into the road. A few streets away, he parked up again, counted out her cash, and passed it to her.

'Don't spend it all at once,' he told her with a smirk.

Then he kissed her. Connor liked to keep them sweet. He wouldn't sleep with any of the runners, not even if they were fit, or his type, or even his age. She would be ripe for someone soon, but not for him. He would never put pleasure before business. And a fifteen-year-old girl wasn't his style anyway.

On the way to drop her off in Longton, he noticed lights on at the back of Car Wash City. He thought about texting Kenny but then decided to take a look himself. He wanted to know what was going on. Knowledge was power in his game.

Once he was on his own again, he went back to the depot. The same light was on as he drove past. He parked further down the street, dimming the headlights so he wouldn't be seen, and peered out, hoping to catch a glimpse of who was inside. But it was too far for him to recognise the person in the window.

Something was going on, though. They'd all been sent home on time that day, and it had seemed strange to him. So why would someone then come back?

He started the car again and drove slowly around the surrounding streets to see if he could see any familiar vehicles. Nothing.

In frustration, he banged on the steering wheel. Whoever it was must have either walked in, been dropped off, or their car was around the rear of the building out of sight. It didn't bode well.

He went back to the spot he'd vacated and watched the building for a while. Yet even though the light stayed on and the figure moved around, ten minutes later, no one had come in or out.

With curiosity piqued, he drove away. He would go in late tomorrow, saying his mum had taken a fall or something, just in case. He'd never trusted Kenny Webb, despite working for him, and he was going to tell Terry Ryder as much as he knew about the man once he was out of prison. Who he was working with, who he was double-crossing. About him being pally with Martin Smith.

He wasn't sure if Ryder was aware of all this, but it wouldn't hurt to keep it under his hat in case he needed it for future reference.

CHAPTER TWENTY-FIVE

At home, Kenny was sitting in his study waiting for a phone call. It gave him time to do some thinking, since he wasn't sure if things were running away with him. He was worried about Terry Ryder coming out of prison soon and what might happen to him then.

It could go one of two ways. Either Ryder thanked him for keeping the firm going while he'd been away, because he'd done an excellent job of it, even if he said so himself. Or he would be angry at how Kenny had worked with Steve Kennedy before technically switching sides and coming to work for him.

Maybe Terry would be two-faced, with a view to getting him back at a later date, trying to fool him into trusting him. But he'd never do that. He'd make Terry think that way if necessary, though.

Everything Kenny did was about the money. He wasn't loyal to anyone, nor would he be. He was out for what he could get, before he got too old to mess around at this game. Then he'd cut his losses and go quiet.

But for now he'd better watch his back once the big man

got out of his cell. Or even better, move out of Stoke-on-Trent for a while. Things could get very messy for him.

Then again, he wondered if being inside for so long had mellowed Terry. After an eleven-year stretch, he'd be in his fifties now. Surely he must have calmed down a little. If Kenny was in Terry's situation, he'd be keeping his head down, rather than risk going inside again. Perhaps Terry was more tolerant now, enough to finish completely and take his money and run. Kenny very much hoped that would be the way he played it.

His phone rang, the call he'd been waiting for. It was Martin.

'All sorted?' he asked.

'Yes. We can keep the branch closed once the police have gone. Perhaps a week or two, say it was bad press. Or reopen as soon as possible. The choice is yours.'

'Meanwhile, the police will get a little of what they want. They must have been dying to raid something for ages.'

'Exactly.' There was a pause down the line and then Martin spoke again. 'I'm thinking of moving on, to Manchester.'

'Any reason?'

'I want out before I'm in too deep.'

'Is Terry paying you to leave?'

'No. I'm just getting a little old for this game now.'

'You're retiring?' Kenny chuckled. 'I didn't think you had it in you to stick around this long, to be fair.'

'Seeing the police so close by, and handling all those drugs last night, let's just say I came to my senses.'

'Can't say I blame you. We all have to stop sometime.'

'What about you? Will you be sticking around?'

'Stoke is my home.' Kenny wasn't giving him anymore than that in case he was fishing for information. 'I'll wait to see what Terry wants me to do first. When are you leaving?'

'At the weekend, probably.'

They spoke a little more, finally ending the call. But all the time, Kenny sensed something was wrong. Why would Martin leave at the weekend before Terry came back? It didn't make sense not to see things through.

And why did he have the feeling that he shouldn't trust Martin now? Maybe his plans to leave should be brought forward.

'Mark?' Allie shouted up the stairs when she finally got home that night.

'I'm awake and up for a hot chocolate if you're offering.'

'Give me ten minutes and I'll be with you.' She chuckled to herself.

After a shower, she went back downstairs to make the drinks. As the kettle boiled, a knot of excitement tensed in her stomach. Tomorrow was going to be a huge day for everyone if their source was reliable. At the moment, she had the same niggles as Shaun. No one had ever rung anonymously about Car Wash City, and she hoped it wasn't a set-up to make them look stupid.

She took the drinks upstairs with her, handing a mug to Mark and placing hers on the cabinet. Once he'd put his down, too, as well as his Kindle, she snuggled in beside him for a moment.

'What are you reading?' she asked, relishing the feel of his arms around her.

'Ian Rankin. Want to read it afterwards?'

She laughed. 'I'll pass, thanks.' Reading police procedurals was like a busman's holiday, watching cop shows on the TV, too. 'Is it good?'

'Isn't it always? I'm trying to read it slowly so that it doesn't end too soon, and yet I can't help but turn the pages, so to speak. What have you been up to? Any good leads on your double murder?'

'The usual at this stage. We're checking and talking to people, waiting for the evidence.'

They moved apart while they sat up to drink their hot chocolate. Allie sipped it, grateful for the sugar boost it was giving her. No doubt she wouldn't get much sleep tonight. She was too excited about the day ahead.

'I have an early start in the morning,' she told him after a few minutes.

'How much earlier than usual?'

'An hour, perhaps.'

He took the mug from her and put it with his own. 'Then let's sleep.'

'Not sure I'll be able to.'

Mark turned out the lamp and pulled her under the covers. 'I'm sure I can do something that will help with that.'

Allie giggled like a teenager. It would certainly help her switch off for a while.

CHAPTER TWENTY-SIX

Perry's wife, Lisa, was in bed when he got home. He checked on Alfie before closing the house down for the night. His boy was lying on his front, a foot popping out from beneath the duvet. He chuckled, thinking that if Alfie knew, he would move it quickly under the covers for fear of the monsters beneath the bed dragging him away. Funnily enough, Perry still did the same thing now with his arms, even though his fiends were more real in his day job than in his home at night.

Lisa was snoring gently as he slipped into bed, trying not to wake her. She was a lark – early to bed, up early in the morning – so he always let her sleep.

He lay in the dark, thinking of the day ahead. It would be interesting to see if the tip-off they'd received was a good one. If it wasn't, it would alert Kenny Webb and his team that they were on to them, and that wouldn't help at all. Still, if the tip-off was right, they could be on to a winner.

It would also mean that someone was out to get Kenny, perhaps even Terry Ryder himself.

Perry reckoned no one would be looking forward to Ryder's release, either police or in the criminal world. He and

Allie were taking bets as to who he'd come after first. Kenny Webb had double-crossed him; Steve Kennedy had, too, among many. Perhaps even Martin Smith. The jury was out on him at the moment.

On the other hand, they thought Steve Kennedy might come after Ryder. And then there were the car washes themselves. Perry had been chatting to DCI Cooper earlier after bumping into him in the corridor. The Organised Crime Unit had surveillance on a lot of Ryder's employees. They would be watching every move the man himself made when he came out, to see that he didn't step into the shoes he'd left behind.

It was only one criminal, but Stoke-on-Trent had been the better for Ryder being locked away for so long. People like Kenny Webb were small fry in comparison. Even some of the other families known to them were. Ryder was an entity in his own right. People had killed to work with him.

Ryder would have had a lot of his cronies killed throughout the decades, people who'd gone missing over the years. They'd found some before he'd been locked up in 2011, but no doubt there'd be more. Ryder didn't get his hands dirty often, but his team did.

Some of them had lost their lives working to protect him; some, Perry knew, because they'd crossed Ryder. He was a dangerous man, one Perry wouldn't want to be dealing with if he wasn't a detective.

Lisa stirred in her sleep, turning over towards him. Perry took the opportunity to pull her into his arms.

'Hey, you,' she spoke quietly. 'You're back.'

'Hey, you. I am,' he replied.

When she said nothing else, he closed his eyes, wishing sleep would come to him quickly. Tomorrow was going to be a long day. He hoped they'd have a good outcome.

. . .

Simon was up as Grace let herself into the house. She yawned, taking off her coat. Working in the Community Liaison Team, there wasn't much call for late nights, although she was always on hand to be called out like she had been today. Already, she was exhausted.

It had been a pleasant surprise to take a call from DCI Jenny Brindley asking her to join Allie's team for a while. She'd cleared her desk and joined them in no time.

'Hey,' Simon said when she came into the living room to see him sprawled on the settee. 'I've missed you this evening.'

'Fibber. I bet you've had a whale of a time on your own slobbing out and eating more garbage than usual.'

'You know me well.' He grinned, sitting up and swinging his legs to the floor as she reached down to kiss him. 'Enjoy your day?'

Grace beamed, flopping by his side. 'Immensely. I'm only on the periphery, but it's good to get my teeth into something. I hadn't realised how much I'd missed it until I was back.'

'I told Allie that.'

'She mentioned it to me. And she said you were moaning about my cooking!' Grace prodded him in the chest. 'Nasty man.'

She stayed where she was for a few minutes. Really, she wanted to shower and go to bed, but it was nice just to sit and be still.

'Would you go back?' he asked. 'I know it took a lot out of you mentally, but you were good at it.'

Grace was silent for a moment, thinking about the time she'd been a detective sergeant on that team. It had all been marred by the Steele family cases, even though she'd helped to close down a major grooming ring in the city, as well as put a serial killer behind bars. It was tough to work alongside the team knowing she couldn't say who she was because her DI preferred her not to.

And when it had been leaked, she'd had to gain the team's trust again and, even though it hadn't been much fun at the time, it had worked out well eventually.

'Now that Eddie has left Stoke, I think I could be tempted,' she said. 'Would you be okay with it? I mean, you've had me all to yourself most evenings since we got married.'

'Which is why I want you to apply for the job if it comes up. I like having the house to myself in the evenings.'

She thumped him playfully, then stifled a yawn.

He patted her arm twice. 'Come on, you. I might be persuaded to take another shower before we turn in.'

She grinned, suddenly feeling awake again. Thoughts of work could wait until the morning.

CHAPTER TWENTY-SEVEN

Wednesday

'Amy, do you want a lift or not?' Scott shouted up to his daughter. 'It's twenty to eight, and I'm leaving in thirty seconds.'

Amy jogged down the stairs, appearing in her school uniform, her bag over her shoulder. 'I don't know what the rush is. I've got plenty of time.'

'Not if you want a lift.'

'Chill out, Dad. I'm here now.'

Her cheeky grin made him smirk, knowing that she was winding him up rather than being insolent.

'Can I have a fiver for school please, Mum?' Amy asked, squeezing past Leanne in the kitchen. 'I want to go for coffee with Mallory and Kelsey after we finish.'

'That's not money for school, though, is it?'

'We'll be discussing homework.'

Leanne rolled her eyes but reached for her purse, took out a note, and handed it to her. 'What time will you be home?'

'Around half five.' Amy pocketed the money with a smile.

Scott rushed in, grabbing his phone. 'See you later,' he said to Leanne, giving her a quick peck on the cheek and scooting out again. He got in the car and turned on the radio.

Amy sighed. 'Do we have to listen to old people stuff?'

'I'll have you know Elton John's tracks are masterpieces. You should listen to some of the *old people stuff* before dismissing it. What are you up to today? Anything exciting, or just boring lessons?'

'Really boring lessons.' Amy rolled her eyes. 'I can't see the point in any of it at the moment.'

'You're fifteen. You need an education.'

'Says the man who's done all right for himself despite leaving school with barely an exam to his name.'

'Hey, don't knock your old fella.' Scott turned to her quickly while waiting in traffic. 'No, scrap that. You don't want to end up in a dead-end job, so you need good grades to get a leg up.'

Amy's head was in her phone as she scrolled continually down the screen. Scott laughed to himself. At least having her with him was taking his mind off the work he was actually doing. His daughter wouldn't be too proud to know what he was up to.

A few minutes later, he dropped her off outside the school gates.

'Bye, Dad.' She leaned over and kissed his cheek.

'What was that for?' he asked, surprised she would make such a show where her friends might see her.

'Just because I love ya, nothing else.'

'See you later, duck.' Scott sensed he was being buttered up to buy her something. Kids were so expensive these days. They always wanted the best of designer gear. In his day, he'd had to make do with supermarket trainers or fake designer ones from the market.

Car Wash City was only two streets away from Amy's school. He parked his car around the back and, after switching off the alarm, went into the office. Noticing a blue plastic carrier bag on top of his desk, he frowned. That hadn't been there when he'd left the day before.

He peered inside the bag and pulled out its contents. A kilo of white powder was wrapped up in clear plastic and sealed with duct tape. Where had that come from? Kenny was usually particular about things like this being hidden from sight.

A rush of fear ran through him. He didn't like that it was out on display. Kenny wasn't likely to forget he'd put it there, and he always got Scott to move stuff on as soon as he could. Was there a job he'd forgotten about?

A noise made him jump. Shouts rang out around him.

'Police! Stay where you are!'

'Okay, okay!' Scott dropped the bag and put his hands up.

'I'm DCI Cooper.' An officer in plain clothes approached him. 'Scott Milton, I'm arresting you on the suspicion of possession of an illegal substance.'

'It's not mine,' Scott protested as the remainder of the arrest statement was read out to him. It then dawned on him that they knew his name. This was a raid. Who the hell had set it up?

'I need the keys to the safe, please,' DCI Cooper said.'

'I don't have them.'

'Not to worry. We'll take it with us and have it open in no time. It would obviously be in your best interests to help us, but whatever. We'll still have time to search the premises thoroughly. You never know what we might come up with.'

Realising he'd be better playing ball, Scott nodded at the desk.

'They're in the second drawer down.'

'Much obliged.'

Scott quietened as handcuffs were placed around his wrists. Leanne was going to go mad when he got home that night. Even he knew there wasn't enough evidence to send him to prison. Anyone could have been first in the office when they raided that morning. They had to prove the bag and its contents were his.

They'd be after him grassing on someone, though, and he wasn't about to do that. So until he realised what was going on, he'd keep his mouth shut altogether.

'Come on, fella,' the detective said. 'Let's sit you in the car while we search the rest of the place.'

Scott gulped. He was going to be in big trouble if there wasn't anything else found. If there was other stuff, he could say it was planted.

Actually, it *had been* planted. It hadn't been there last night, and no one had mentioned anything about it since.

Then his mind flipped back to Kenny giving them all an early night. Was that to have time to set him up?

He was led out of the unit, his head held down in shame, even though there was no one around to see it. Scott didn't recognise any of the officers, and if he did, he wouldn't trust any of them. They could be getting paid, perhaps by Kenny, or higher up in the chain.

He was screwed, no matter how he looked at it.

CHAPTER TWENTY-EIGHT

Allie was sitting at the spare desk, Grace yet to arrive, so she'd commandeered it until then. It was quarter past eight, and they were waiting to hear about the raid at Car Wash City.

Frankie's stomach rumbled loudly. She and Perry turned to glance at him.

'I had breakfast at six!' he protested. 'I'm hungry again.'

'If it's a successful mission, I'll treat us to bacon and cheese oatcakes,' Allie said. 'Seven for you, I think, Frankie.'

'I'm a growing man.'

'You're a groaning one.' Perry laughed at his joke.

'That is so lame.' Allie rolled her eyes in jest and then became serious. 'While I have you here, there's something I have to tell you.' All eyes fell on her as she lowered her voice and told them what DCI Cooper had said during their conversation the day before. 'I'm not sure of all the details yet. I expect they'll tell me when they're ready. But we can't bring in Kenny Webb or anyone he's associated with until I get the all clear.'

'Sounds like they're ready to strike in a wider sense.' Perry rubbed his hands together in anticipation.

'It does to me, too, but like I say, I haven't been privy to anything other than to try and stay out of their way.'

'I've followed up on all the interviews regarding the fingerprints found in Neville Street,' Frankie spoke to Allie. 'Nothing was forthcoming that we didn't already know.'

'Okay, thanks.' Allie held up a hand as her phone rang.

'One Scott Milton in cuffs,' Shaun said. 'Caught with a kilo of cocaine, although he's categorically denying knowing anything about it, of course. Looks like he was moving it on.'

Allie punched the air.

'My team is doing a search of the building now. We're going to wait a few minutes longer to see if Kenny Webb turns up. Hopefully someone arriving this morning will have called him or sent a message for him to stay out of the way, so we don't have to show our hand. Do you want to sit in with me while I interview Milton?'

'That would be great.'

Allie disconnected the call and updated everyone. 'I'm sure Milton will deny knowing anything about the drugs,' she added. 'While we talk to him, I want to see if we can get inside some of Webb's properties. Unless he gives us permission, we'll need a reason for a warrant. I can't execute any until I have the say-so, but I want it all set up in readiness. We need to search his properties, get prints, and check them against our system. We're also waiting on forensics for a while as they are working on the two murders for us. It's going to take time to comb through everything in Neville Street.

'Right now, although it's not our case, we need to get as much information from Scott Milton as we can. I think this will be our only opportunity. It's just a hunch but, if Scott has been set up like he's alluding to, maybe whoever did that wanted us to find him with those drugs. Maybe they're planning on Scott telling us something? Because I can't understand why someone gave us a tip-off.'

'To make sure we know they've been storing drugs to hand out to deal?' Perry queried.

'I can't even take a bet on how this one will play out. Let's crack on.'

Half an hour later, Allie took a call to say that Scott had arrived and was being booked into custody. She went downstairs to join DCI Cooper, and they discussed their interviewing tactics.

'Does he have a solicitor?' she asked Shaun afterwards.

'Charles Dinnen has turned up.'

'Already? That almost makes me suspicious.'

Charles Dinnen was known for looking after Terry Ryder and his affairs. He would come and see anyone who needed good legal representation, often turning up beforehand, presumably after taking a phone call of an arrest. Allie couldn't figure out why he had been called this time.

'I suspect he's going to go with "no comment" anyway,' Shaun said.

'Well, he'd be wise to, I suppose. We have a ton of evidence gathering before we can take this to the Crown Prosecution Service.'

They joined the accused and his solicitor in interview room three. Four months ago, Allie had warned Scott Milton about the trouble he could find himself in if he continued to work at Car Wash City. And here he was, not having heeded her words. She wasn't best pleased about it, if she was honest. Scott had had the chance to go straight and start again. He'd chosen not to – and she wanted to know why.

But, like the DCI had said earlier, all they got from Milton was "no comment" to everything.

'You don't owe anyone anything, Scott,' Allie said, leaning closer to him.

'No one cares that they're taking you down,' Shaun added. 'You could have denied knowledge of the drugs if your prints weren't all over them, but you were caught handling them. It's as if someone has seen to it that you were caught with them. Do you think that's what happened?'

'No comment,' Scott replied, his eyes everywhere but on them.

'Where did they come from?'

'No comment.'

'Were you taking them to someone?'

'No comment.'

'Were you storing them for someone?'

'No comment.'

Allie sighed inwardly as Shaun terminated the interview. It was evident Scott wasn't going to help himself, and clear from the furtive glances he kept throwing Dinnen's way that he was being careful with what he said.

Once out of the room, she aired her thoughts to Shaun.

'It's a set-up, isn't it? Someone's cleared the place out of anything we might find, left a pile of drugs, and then tipped us off so that Milton gets caught red-handed. It doesn't make sense.'

'Someone's definitely playing with us,' Shaun agreed.

They walked towards the stairs to their offices.

'Not sure why, though,' he added. 'Unless, like I mentioned yesterday, something is happening elsewhere, taking us off that scent.'

'And we're still not bringing Kenny Webb in?'

'No.' Shaun paused. 'But you could go and speak to him on the quiet, casually, in regard to the drugs. Hopefully he'll play ball. I can't risk too much, but we have to make him think we're not onto him.'

'Sure, I'll look forward to it.' Allie nodded. 'There's someone I need to see first and then I'll go straight there.'

CHAPTER TWENTY-NINE

Allie joined the search team who'd been assigned to the Milton's home. She wasn't sure what welcome she'd get from Leanne after arresting Scott that morning. Even so, it must have come as a huge shock to her.

But Allie also wanted to gauge if Leanne knew what was going on or if she was in the dark. It was touch and go as to which one it would be.

A woman with long blonde hair, wearing jeans and a white jumper, answered the door, her eyes widening as she spotted Allie. They had met earlier in the year when Kit Harper had been killed, and a case from twenty years ago had come to light. Back then, Allie had sensed Leanne knew more than she was letting on, but she hadn't been able to entice her to tell her anything. She was hoping today might be better.

'Mrs Milton, these officers have a warrant to search the house, due to your husband's arrest this morning.' Allie held up the piece of paper and glanced at the team behind her.

Without a word, Leanne stepped aside to let them in.

Allie pointed to the one door that led into the kitchen.

'Can we talk?'

'I don't have anything to say to you.'

Undeterred, Allie kept her arm in the air. Finally, Leanne moved into the room.

From her previous case, Allie knew Leanne Milton was thirty-six. Since the last time they'd met, she'd lost weight, making her wonder if she'd been on a health kick or if it had been caused by stress.

'I didn't know what was going on then and I don't know now either,' Leanne cracked. 'Scott's clearly being framed for something he wasn't involved in.'

'He was caught in the act,' Allie replied.

'I know but he... he's not like that.' Leanne lowered her eyes for a moment.

Allie had told the team leader to give her ten minutes until they needed access to the kitchen. The noise coming from other rooms was distracting. It was always intrusive, but a necessity. She closed the door.

Leanne pulled out a chair from underneath the table and sat down. Allie did the same.

'Can you tell me anything about what's been going on?' she asked, trying not to upset Leanne any more than was necessary. One wrong word and she might clam up indefinitely.

Leanne's shoulders sagged, her eyes brimmed with tears, and she sniffed. 'He promised me after...'

Her pause made Allie curious.

'After what, Leanne?'

There was another pause before she spoke again. 'After Kit died.'

'But Kit's death was nothing to do with drugs.'

'Maybe not, but losing him was hard on us all.'

While they spoke, Leanne kept glancing back at the door.

'Is there *anything* you want to tell me?' Allie probed. 'That you think might be in Scott's best interests?'

'What do you mean?' Leanne sat forward. 'Are you saying he could go to prison?'

'It's possible.'

'I need him here.' Leanne gasped. 'And so does Amy, our daughter.'

Allie stared at her, but the woman wouldn't look her in the eye. The wringing of her hands made her certain Leanne was wary of something. Or someone.

A few seconds of silence passed amongst the noise in the other rooms. Allie stood. 'If you don't help yourself, I can't do much for you.'

'You're not doing this for me!' Leanne cried. 'It's your job.'

'Hey!' Allie's tone was sharp. 'You might see me as the enemy in all this, but I'm not. I'll give anyone assistance, guidance, even reassurance if I can. I don't just work to solve the crime. I help victims, too. And I believe you're now caught up in something that could potentially break your family up, tear it apart. Scott could be going to prison, his income stopping. You'll be the sole provider. How easy is that going to be, unless you have someone who'll take care of you in this eventuality?'

'Do you think Kenny Webb's going to swoop in and give me thousands of pounds to tide me over?' Leanne shook her head. 'I'll have to move out of Stoke. It won't be safe for me to stay here without Scott. And Amy needs her father.'

'She does, so *you* need to think very carefully about your future.'

There was a knock at the door, and an officer opened it enough to show his face. 'Ready when you are, Ma'am,' he said.

Before Allie left, she tried one more time, but Leanne refused to co-operate. Even though it annoyed her, she could understand the woman's reticence. There was obviously more going on behind the scenes that she didn't want to get mixed up in.

'Okay. The search team will be here for a while yet,' she finished. 'Although they may be done by the time the school day is out, I suggest you let Amy know so she doesn't come home to find our officers here, going through your belongings.'

'She's going to be so scared. How could you do this to her?'

'How can *I*? This is entirely your own doing.' Allie put a hand up to stop Leanne from protesting further. 'I have nothing to question you about, but if I do find something, I will be back here to arrest you. Do you understand?'

Leanne nodded, tears falling freely now.

'Get yourself sorted. Now is your chance.'

Allie left the house. The search team had found nothing so far, and she hoped it would stay that way, really. Despite both Scott and Leanne Milton choosing to say nothing, this family was in crisis. She only hoped it wouldn't be too late for them to sort it out this time.

She got into her car, had a quick check through her emails and messages that had come in. When she saw nothing urgent, she headed off in the direction of Car Wash City. Time to have another little chat with Kenny Webb.

Leanne grabbed her coat and went to sit in the garden while the officers continued searching through their belongings. It was cold, but she didn't care. She sat on the wooden bench, looking back at the house. She had always thought of it as her sanctuary. Now it seemed like a prison. Something she was desperate to escape from.

Tears welled in her eyes as she glanced up to see someone walking through their bedroom. She'd been told they would make as little mess as possible, but they were going through their personal possessions. She cringed at some of the things they'd find.

Despite Allie Shenton's comment, she wasn't going to tell Amy about the search, not unless the police were still here when she was due to get in from school. The more she could keep away from Amy, the better. She didn't need to know about everything her mum and dad had screwed up.

Leanne had never felt so low, so out of control. Nothing she did would bring this pain to an end. Would their nightmare ever be over?

CHAPTER THIRTY

Allie parked on the empty forecourt of Car Wash City, its doors closed, and equipment stored away. She wondered if there was anyone here, but then she spotted Kenny's car. Now that the search team had gone, it would be just the two of them. Perfect.

Round the back of the building, she found the door unlocked, but this time she knocked. It was one thing to walk in when the business was open, but another to go in unannounced when it was closed.

Kenny's shoulders rose when he spotted her.

'What do you want?' he growled, leaning on the door frame.

'A quick word. Can I come in?'

'You don't usually wait to be asked.' He turned and left.

Allie took this as her cue to follow.

'Not what I was expecting when I turned up for work this morning.' He pointed to some of the mess that he'd yet to tidy.

'I'm sorry about that,' she said. 'But we were acting on a tip-off. Do you have any idea who would have rung this in?'

'Considering the drugs had nothing to do with me, nor Scott, I don't.'

'You think they were planted?'

'I know so, because I didn't bring them in, nor did any of my staff.'

'How can you be so sure?'

'No one would cross me.'

Allie sighed inwardly. There it was again, the big man attitude. She really wished she could knock it out of him one day. His righteousness, the gall of him to think he was untouchable.

'What do you really want? Have you come here to check up on me? See that there aren't another few kilos hanging around? Catch me at it?'

'Not at all.'

Allie gave nothing away as they chatted a little more, but after a few more minutes of trying to get blood out of a stone, she was done. She slapped her hands on her legs and stood up.

'Right then, I'll be off.' She smiled at Kenny.

'And Scott?'

'Oh, he'll be with us for a while yet. We have things we want to ask him.'

She was almost at the door when she felt a hand on her back, and she was pushed into the wall. She turned herself quickly as Kenny grabbed her arm.

'What the hell do you think you're doing?' she cried, trying to shake off his hand.

'You think you're so special, don't you?'

His face was inches from hers, and she could see the anger in his eyes.

'You *think* because you put Terry away that he won't dare come after you once he gets out. Well, I have news for you. He's already put a hit out on you.'

'Oh, please.' She rolled her eyes. 'Tell that to someone who gives a shit.'

'All it will take is one deserted street you walk down, one car you get into at night. One early morning as you leave for work. And it won't just be you he comes after. He'll be coming for Perry, and that Frankie lad you have working in your team. He'll be after their families, your precious Mark, too. He won't stop until he's destroyed you all.'

Allie's breathing was erratic, but she kept her cool. It was all talk, meant to frighten her, especially when he'd mentioned her husband's name and, even though it was doing its job, she wasn't going to show it.

She looked directly at him. 'Take your hand off me or I will arrest you for assaulting a police officer.'

'No witnesses here.' Kenny glared at her, but he released his grip slightly. 'Mark my words, I will come after you if you ever cross me again, never mind Terry.'

'And mark *my* words, *I* will come after you if you so much as lay a finger on me again. I have the strong arm of the law on my side.'

'It will be your word against mine.'

She nodded, her voice cracking with emotion. She cleared her throat before speaking again.

'I wonder which one of us will be believed.'

Kenny stared at her, but she wouldn't drop her eyes. Finally, he stepped away and turned his back on her.

'See yourself out.'

She left. Sure, she could have continued the conversation, but she was glad to get away.

Outside, and away from Kenny's view, she leaned against the wall for a moment to catch her breath. Tears welled in her eyes at the thought of the danger she'd could have been in. Despite her badge, no one was untouchable.

There were only a few times she'd been really scared

during her career. The worst was when she'd been kidnapped by the man who had attacked her sister. He'd been so mad that she'd thought he'd kill her. Luckily, her team had come good and helped her to get away from him.

No one was immune to being scared. For all her bravado, she'd been terrified back there. It had shown her weak points, her vulnerability. Because she couldn't hide behind the law when she was alone. Kenny knew that.

And so did Terry Ryder.

CHAPTER THIRTY-ONE

Charles Dinnen had rung Kenny to say that Scott wanted to talk to him. To the side of Bethesda Police Station, Kenny was in the car park, waiting for him to be released from custody.

His mind was going over the day's events, recalling how Allie Shenton had turned up earlier that morning, and how surprised he'd been. Threatening her hadn't been one of his finest moments, but she wound him up so much.

She really thought she was something, and yet he could have snapped her neck in seconds. He would have taken great pleasure in it, but it would have caused more problems rather than solving them. As much as he couldn't stand her, she was the law. She couldn't be killed, taken somewhere, her body buried never to be seen again. People would miss her, more was the pity.

Over the years, Kenny had killed or disposed of several bodies, their whereabouts unknown. He knew it was dangerous, especially after Terry had been double-crossed by Steve Kennedy after some of his kills. There had been two men in a clean-up crew who were always at the end of the phone.

Unbeknown to Terry, they had buried crucial evidence with every body he'd wanted disposing of. Gloves, clothes, guns, and knives, all with evidence of the kills. When the police had been tipped off about them, Ryder had gone down for a long time because of it. It was no secret he'd probably take revenge on Steve once he was out again.

Now he was in his forties, Kenny didn't like doing his own dirty work. He was getting too old; it was a young guy's game. But he'd kill anyone who tried to kill him.

Which was why he wasn't looking forward to Terry's release from prison next month. There'd been less bloodshed while Terry had been behind bars. He didn't want it to start up again.

For now, however, all he was concerned about was his need to talk to Scott, make sure he'd taken the rap for the drugs, like he was supposed to do.

It had been Martin's idea to test Scott, see if he had what it took to deal with the law. To his knowledge, Scott had never been inside, not even a charge for anything illegal. How he'd got away with it mystified Kenny, considering the dealing he'd been doing for years, and he'd often wondered if he was an informant for the opposition. Still, it had worked well with his plan of keeping the police off their tail while he shifted everything out of the way.

He glanced up as he spotted someone coming towards the car. Scott was jogging across the car park, his face as white as a sheet. He seemed as if he'd aged ten years in a matter of hours. The experience had evidently shocked him. Good.

'What the fuck's going on?' Scott demanded after he'd taken a seat next to Kenny. 'I get to work, and then minutes later, it's raided. Those drugs were out on display. You set me up!'

'Don't exaggerate,' Kenny told him. 'It was a misunderstanding.'

'You said nothing was going down after hours. Was that why you wanted the place closed early? So no one would see you slip back and plant stuff?'

Kenny shot him a dark look. 'I'd be very careful with the accusations, if I were you. Besides, I don't have to tell you everything.'

'It appears you should have told me that.' Scott ran a hand across his chin then made a fist. 'They were waiting for me.'

'I didn't know,' he lied. 'I'm still trying to work out who it was that gave the police the nod.'

They sat in silence, watching the traffic flowing past on Potteries Way.

'Do you have any ideas?' he asked eventually.

'No.' Scott seemed to be calming down now. 'But it was a close call. They bailed me while they do enquiries. They searched my home, too.'

'There wasn't anything there, though?'

'No, and there never will be. I'm not doing that again.' Scott shook his head. 'You have to make this go away.'

'We'll sort it.' Kenny started the car. 'I'll put feelers out. Because not only was someone getting at you, they were after me, too, and I'm not having that.' He pulled away. 'I'll take you to collect your car. Have you had any lunch? Do you want to call for something to eat on the way?'

'No, I just want to get home. I don't have to stay until the end of my shift today, do I?'

'We're closed after the raid.'

Once back at Car Wash City, Kenny waited until Scott had left and then rang Martin.

'The boy came good,' he told him. 'Apparently, he said "no comment" all the way through and is now out on bail.'

'So he isn't the grass?'

'Possibly not. Still might take him out, though, what do

you think?' His remark was meant for reaction, to see what Martin would say.

'I'll leave that one with you.' Martin replied. 'That's not my department.'

Kenny sniggered. That was an understatement. To his knowledge, Martin had never got his hands dirty. Maybe that was something Kenny should be thinking about, especially as no one had found Milo Barker yet. All hell was going to break loose when they did.

Kenny didn't trust Martin, nor Ryder or Steve Kennedy. He wouldn't put it past any of them to set him up to take the wrap for something big that would put him behind bars for a long time. So there were certain things he was going to put into motion before the shit hit the fan. And before Terry Ryder came out of prison.

Over the years, Kenny's enemies had become many, and with men like those two who might come after him, he couldn't look over his shoulder forever. It was time to start making plans of his own.

CHAPTER THIRTY-TWO

Since getting into Kenny's car, Scott had fought to keep his emotions hidden. It was at times like this that he missed Kit, someone he would have confided in. A problem shared had always been a problem halved when Kit was around.

Yet, even though things had gone from bad to worse after his friend's death, Scott's life was falling apart around him more with every passing week, and it seemed there was nothing he could do about it.

It had been a close call that morning. He hadn't enjoyed the hand of the law on his collar. It had terrified him. He wanted out and, even though he wasn't sure he'd get it, he had to try to do something before he ended up inside for a long time. Scott didn't trust Kenny to look after him. If anything, just the opposite.

He'd have to talk to Leanne, think about cashing in what he'd got so far and then moving on. Christ, she was going to kill him when he got home.

But as soon as he stepped into the house, Leanne was in the hall, her face a picture of concern, not anger.

'Are you okay? I've had the police here searching the house. They didn't find anything but I... I was so frightened.'

He removed the key from the door and left the dreadful day outside.

'I was set up,' he told her. 'They were waiting for me to arrive. Someone had planted a bag of drugs, left them on my desk. I'd just peeked inside and pulled them out when I heard shouting and all these officers rushed in.'

Leanne's hand shot to her chest. 'What did the police do?'

'They interviewed me, then bailed me, pending further enquiries.' Scott's face creased up. 'I don't know what to do, Leanne. I'm so fucking scared.'

She ran into his arms, and he clung on to her, comforted by her familiar smell. Since Kit had died, the rough patch they'd been going through had gone. In a bizarre way, it had grounded them again.

But he couldn't live like this anymore. *This* was killing him.

'Do you ever wish we could up sticks and leave?' he spoke softly into her hair.

'Every day.'

Her words shocked him. That she would think the same as he did made him more convinced to do something about it.

'Let's grab a brew.'

They settled in the kitchen, and for the first time in a while, they had a good chat. He told her everything that had been going on. She told him how frightened she was, how she was always glancing over her shoulder, afraid that someone would harm her, or Amy, to get back at him.

'Kenny threatened me,' she told him finally, catching his eye.

'What?' Scott couldn't believe what he was hearing. 'When?'

'Just after you were released from hospital after the hit and run. He came here to see me, making certain I understood that you would work for Car Wash City as long as he told you to, and that I shouldn't interfere.'

'That bastard! Why didn't you tell me?'

'I was petrified that he would hurt you, and I needed you to think I didn't mind you staying on without Kit. Because if you hadn't, the alternative wasn't worth thinking about.' She wiped at tears spilling from her eyes. 'He would have got rid of you somehow. And what happens when that Ryder fella comes out of prison soon? Is he going to be worse than Kenny?'

Scott paled. He hadn't met Terry yet but knew of his history. He wasn't looking forward to working for him. Some men who'd crossed him hadn't been heard of since.

He reached across for her hand and gave it a squeeze. 'We have to move out of Stoke. I can't see any other way out of this.'

'But Kenny would still come after you.'

'Maybe, but I'm not that big a fish. He might leave me alone.' He sighed. 'It's got to be better than living our lives like this.'

'We can't leave until Amy has finished her exams. She has another year at school. It wouldn't be fair to disrupt her now. And besides, there would be a lot to sort out before then.'

'Where would you want to move to?'

'As far away from here as possible.'

'I'll start getting money together, for next summer. I can't stop what I'm doing until we go, so I'll just have to be careful.'

'At least we have a plan.' Leanne touched his face. 'Something to aim for.'

She smiled then, the same one she'd given Scott back when they were in their teens. It made him yearn for the simpler things in life, when they'd had no worries, nor the chance of getting into so much trouble. When they'd had everything to look forward to. He loved her so much and was ashamed of how much he'd risked losing her.

It was time to calm down and get out. Scott only hoped Kenny would let him leave without hurting him. But, after what he'd said to Leanne, Scott wasn't so certain. He couldn't risk losing his family, or his own life. He'd prefer to leave sooner rather than later.

'Scott?'

Leanne had so much fear in her eyes that it almost broke him.

'It would be better to go next summer, but if we have to, if you're in danger, then I'd be out of here like a shot. I'd leave whatever we were doing, and I'd go. I need you to know that.'

Unexpected tears welled in his eyes. All he could do was nod while he squeezed her hands tightly.

And pray that over the next few days, weeks, months, that things didn't go drastically wrong.

After her altercation with Kenny Webb, the rest of Allie's day hadn't gone as well as she'd hoped. As far as she was concerned, it could almost be considered a wipeout with regards to moving forward with Operation Mitchell.

That evening she'd been going through the statements that had come in from the girls staying in Neville Street again. So far, there was nothing to link any of them to what had happened to Davy Lewis.

She lay her head on the desk. Grace was using the spare, so she was in her office. She wasn't surprised to see Perry coming over to her seconds later.

'Everything okay, Al?' he asked.

'I'm at that time in a case where I'm more frustrated than

optimistic,' she replied. 'The evidence coming back for the double murders is so slow, and even though we're eliminating people, we don't have any suspects. I'm tired of information gathering.'

'We'll get there,' he encouraged. 'We always do.'

'Let's hope so.' She yawned, checking the time. 'I don't know about you, but I'm bushed. Let's call it a night and see what tomorrow brings.'

CHAPTER THIRTY-THREE

Thursday

Andrew had been feeling unsettled for a couple of days. He'd scoured *Stoke News* and listened to every radio and TV bulletin he could, but as far as he could see, the police hadn't caught Davy Lewis's killer yet. He was still out there, here in Stoke.

Staying with his mum had been really nice. She had made him porridge for breakfast, sandwiches to take to work, and his favourite meals for his tea. Sometimes he wished he'd never left home. He would have been happy to live with her forever. Last night, he'd talked to her about it. She'd told him she'd only wanted him to have his own independence, but she had missed him, and anytime he wanted to come home permanently, he could.

As he laid in bed, feeling safe and warm and loved, he'd realised it was the best thing all round for him to be there. He didn't want to be frightened living alone in his flat. He hoped Kenny wouldn't get mad with him. But he had to stick up for himself.

That morning, he'd called in work and said he was sick. He didn't like lying to Cathy, but he had to sort things out, and it was better done during the day so he could visit his flat when it might be empty.

Once that was done, he was going to speak to his social worker, stop his tenancy, and get the flat emptied. Some of his furniture wouldn't fit in Mum's house, so he could donate it to charity. His bed was new, his wardrobes were, too. The settee had been his mum's old one, but it was covered in stains now, so that would have to be thrown away. Davy Lewis had been sick on it at least three times.

He wouldn't take his TV. That hadn't been a gift, he realised now. It had been a bribe to keep quiet.

The bus dropped him off close to Redmond Street just after quarter to nine. He'd wanted to come early because at least there would be a few people around. Something was always happening around that time. Children going to school, the odd car coming past as someone went off to work. He'd be able to run and alert someone if the boys were staying at his flat, and if they were mean to him.

Yet, walking towards his flat made him feel sad to be leaving. Until Kenny and his mob had befriended him, he'd liked living here. It was a quiet street now that the pub across from him was closed, and most of the neighbours would stop and chat to him if they saw him.

Andrew knew he was different. He'd fitted in without trying too much, keeping himself to himself, but also stopping to chat to people. Occasionally, he'd go and fetch groceries for some of the elderly residents, if their own families couldn't help. He would never see anyone stuck.

He jogged down the steps to his front door, the bag to collect some more of his stuff slung over his shoulder. He was going to be super speedy. Hopefully no one would visit while he was there. It was too early for them.

The flat downstairs had finally got curtains up at the windows. It had been empty for two months after Mr Barratt had died. Andrew had only seen the new neighbours once. They seemed okay, but it didn't matter whether they were nice or not – he wouldn't be seeing them again. And maybe Milo and his friends would find somewhere else to make a nuisance of themselves now.

He put the key in the door quietly, then left it open in case he had to make a quick exit. He listened for a moment, but there was no sound. He hoped no one would be there. To his knowledge, only Kenny had a key.

Trying to make as little noise as possible, he tiptoed up the steps to his flat. He couldn't hear the TV on, which was a good sign. He sniffed, almost gagging. There was an unfamiliar smell in the air, something he didn't recognise. It became stronger with each step he took.

At the living room door, he paused. A red smear on the door handle caught his eye, and he grimaced. Was that blood? He wondered who had been fighting this time. Milo was always picking on the younger kids.

He pushed the living room door open and stepped inside. The place was a tip. He'd have to clean up before he left, or else he'd be in trouble when he handed in his keys to end the tenancy. He'd been told when he'd signed the agreement that any damage done would be made good by the housing association, and he'd then be charged. But he hadn't created this mess.

He started to cry, his home in ruins. Why had they done that? All he'd ever been was nice to them. They said they were his friends, but they weren't. They were bullies. They were hooligans. They were animals.

In the kitchen, his hand covered his mouth and nose to

stop the dreadful smell assailing his nostrils. A loaf of bread was open on the worktop, slices spilling out and already going mouldy around the edges. The knife used to butter them was by the side. He opened the fridge. The butter had been put back, so that couldn't be the horrible smell, and there was no food left, so nothing was rotting.

He went to his bedroom to fetch the rest of his clothes. That was, if they hadn't trashed them as well. He opened the door and gagged, the smell in there the most noxious. Then he stopped, foot in mid-air as he saw a pool of blood on the carpet.

He looked towards the bed, a scene almost like a horror film unfolding.

Then he dropped his bag and screamed.

CHAPTER THIRTY-FOUR

Since the raid on Car Wash City yesterday, Connor hadn't been able to get Scott Milton from his mind. He'd only worked with him for a few months, but so far, he'd been a fair boss. He was always popping out to buy food or cans of pop for the lads, ice creams when it was hot, and he'd be laughing and joking with them whenever Kenny wasn't around.

He hadn't been like that earlier in the year. It was only since Kit Harper had died. Connor had got on with Kit, too. Back then, he'd been wary of Scott, but Scott had changed. He'd made an effort to fit in more rather than being aloof.

Connor remembered when his mum had been taken ill a few weeks ago. His sister had rung to say she'd collapsed and been taken to the hospital by ambulance. If Kenny had been in, Connor knew he would have made him stay at work until the end of his shift, but Scott had told him to go and not come back until the morning. He'd even got his wife to bring in some flowers for her the next day.

Another time, he'd given him a sub when his car had broken down and he'd had no money to fix it until payday. He'd paid him back in full the minute his wages had hit his bank account, wanting to show how much he appreciated it. Not everyone he knew was like that, and in a lot of ways he reminded him of his father.

Which was why he'd always look out for him. Connor was certain Scott had been set up, but he couldn't work out why. If the cops had been watching him, or the business, for any length of time, they'd know Scott was always the first one to arrive. Someone had planted the drugs last night to ensure Scott was caught red-handed. Was there a mole in the gang? Connor needed to air his thoughts.

He didn't want to think anyone was double-crossing Scott, but he was equally worried about someone getting at Kenny. And it wouldn't do any harm to get on Kenny's good side, especially as he was about to pitch for a job, too.

He knocked on the door to Kenny's office, a tad wary of the mood he seemed to have been in since first thing. Kenny had already barked at two of the younger lads for messing about. Everyone was keeping their distance at the moment. But Connor couldn't wait any longer.

'What?' Kenny said, not even glancing up from his computer screen.

Connor tried not to be deterred by the man's demeanour. 'Can I have a quick word?'

'Not really the right time.'

'I won't be long.' Connor closed the door behind him. 'I wanted to let you know that I saw a light on in here on Tuesday evening, and as you asked us all to go home, I thought—'

'What time was this?'

'About eight.'

'Did you notice anyone hanging around? Or a car?'

Connor shook his head. Without waiting to be asked, he sat down on the other side of Kenny's desk. 'Did someone plant that package so that Scott would get caught out?'

'I've been thinking that.' Kenny steepled his hands together. 'Any idea who it might be?'

'No.' He paused. 'You don't think they were after getting you in trouble instead of Scott?'

'It's possible. I'm looking into it.'

'Good, good, yeah.' Connor took a deep breath, shifted a little in his seat. 'While I'm here, I was wondering if you'd thought of anyone to take over from Davy.'

Kenny narrowed his eyes. 'The man hasn't been dead three days and you're already wanting to step into his place?'

'Well, obviously not until you think it's right to recruit. I know how much you thought of him and–'

'I'd stop right there if I were you, before you dig a deeper hole for yourself.' Kenny smirked. 'I like your style, though. You're not afraid to speak out.'

Connor sat on his shaking hands so it wouldn't be obvious to Kenny how nervous he was to be asking for the job. But he could do it, he was certain. Davy had been a pisshead, and although he'd managed pretty well until his death, even when he'd been off his head on drugs, Connor wasn't like that. He was reliable, keen, and young enough to pick up what he needed to learn.

A silence dropped on the room, and he swallowed. 'I'd like a chance to prove myself to you.'

Kenny eyed him for a moment, leaning forward with a shake of his head. 'You're not ready.'

'But you have to admit I'm good at what I do.'

'You're okay for keeping an eye on the wee ones but you're not good enough to be in command of your own team.'

'I disagree,' Connor tried again.

Kenny shook his head. 'Bide your time. For now, keep on doing what you're doing.'

'I can handle a bigger role.'

But Kenny had already gone back to looking at his screen.

'Just give me a month's trial,' Connor insisted. 'I know most of what Davy does and I can learn the rest.'

'Enough!' Kenny held up his hand. 'Now, push off before I lose my temper.'

He was almost at the door when Kenny shouted him back.

'Remember when your old man went missing?'

Connor frowned at the question. 'I'm not likely to forget.'

'Well, think about that. The things we do every day have consequences.'

'What's that supposed to mean?'

'Nothing in particular. But he must have done something wrong to disappear. You don't want anything like that to happen to you, do you?'

Connor couldn't work out if he was being threatened or warned. Either way, he didn't like it. Did that mean Kenny knew something about why his dad had gone missing? Had Kenny had anything to do with it? Or even Terry Ryder?

With resignation, he sloped out of the room, annoyed his plan hadn't worked. He'd assumed Kenny would snap his hands off. Now he didn't know what to think.

But one thing was clear. Kenny had no loyalty to him. Which meant he didn't have to show allegiance to Kenny.

CHAPTER THIRTY-FIVE

Once the team briefing had finished, Allie had grabbed a quick breakfast in the canteen with Perry. They'd been back at their desks less than ten minutes when her phone rang. She picked it up after two rings. It was an officer on duty in reception.

'Allie, there's a man who wants to see you. He's quite agitated.'

'Has he given his name?'

'Andrew Dale.'

Allie sat upright. 'Can you pop him in a room until I get there?'

'I tried talking to him but when I went near him, he screamed. He won't budge until he's seen you.'

'Okay. Tell him I'm on my way.' She raced out of her office, clicking her fingers to catch Perry's attention. 'Need you with me.'

She explained what was going on as they flew down the stairs.

'I wonder what's wrong with him,' Perry said afterwards. 'I hope no one has hurt him.'

'We're about to find out. Can you get a side room ready, please? I'll try and talk to him first.'

Andrew was standing in the middle of the reception area.

'He's dead,' he cried when he saw her, his face contorted in pain. 'I couldn't save him. I'm sorry.'

Allie reached for his arm to stop him, but he stepped away. She cursed inwardly, forgetting momentarily that he didn't like to be touched. But her instinct to help had taken over.

'Who's dead, Andrew?' Allie asked, keeping her voice steady so as not to agitate him further.

'Milo.' Andrew pointed to the floor, almost as if he was reliving what had happened right there. 'He was lying on the floor, dead.'

The reception area was empty, so Allie didn't feel a need to take Andrew to one side just yet. She wanted to keep him as calm as she could until she was ready. She knew Perry would be watching on the monitor so that he chose the right time to show his face.

'Where was this?' she enquired.

'At my flat.'

Andrew paced up and down.

She had to get his attention. 'How did you know he'd died?'

'Because he was so cold, and I couldn't wake him. His face is all bloated, and he smells disgusting.' Andrew stopped. 'I don't know what to do. They'll blame me and they'll kill me, too.' He looked at her, eyes pleading for understanding. 'But I didn't do it! I didn't touch him.'

'It's okay,' Allie tried to appease him. 'Come and sit in the room next door and we can sort this out for you.'

'I can't. I have to get back.'

'We can take it from here.' She held out her hand again.

'No, I have to go.' Andrew moved towards the door.

'Wait, please!' Allie cried. 'Don't be frightened, you're safe here.'

'But I didn't do anything wrong.'

A side door opened, and Perry appeared.

'Andrew, isn't it?' He smiled. 'I've heard all about you from Allie. Why not come and tell us what you know? I'm sure it will be helpful.'

Andrew paused in the exit doorway.

It could go one of two ways.

'Please, Andrew,' Allie urged. She really didn't want to detain him, but she'd have to if he tried to flee.

Finally, Andrew stepped towards her. Allie ushered him into the room, closing the door behind him quickly.

It took a few minutes, and two glasses of water, until Andrew was calm enough to talk to them. Allie only needed the basics as she wanted to set in motion an inquiry and get to the deceased. A patrol car had been sent ahead to check for signs of life.

Allie smiled. 'Can you start at the beginning for me, please, Andrew, so I can understand exactly what's happened?'

'I went to get some things from my flat.'

'Have you been away?'

He shook his head. 'I've been staying with my mum.'

'Was that because of Milo?'

Andrew flinched at his name, then nodded. 'Him and the others.'

Allie didn't need names right now to get the gist of what had been happening. For months, she'd had her suspicions that something was going on at that address, certain it was being used as a base for a gang of teenagers to hang around, deal drugs, and cause a general nuisance of themselves. Back then, she'd asked Andrew about it, but he'd denied it. At her request, Grace had been keeping an eye on him for them. Perhaps this was why he'd stopped contact with her a few weeks ago.

'I-I'm moving out,' Andrew went on. 'It was nice at my mum's, so I thought I'd live with her again. She's good to me, cooks me lots of my favourite food. And I don't have to worry about anything.'

'Can you tell me why you went to your flat this morning?'

Andrew wiped his cheeks with his palm. 'I was going to get the rest of my clothes and a few other small things I could carry. And then I was going to ring my social worker. She would have helped me with everything else. That's when I saw... Milo.'

'In your flat.'

Andrew nodded. 'In my bedroom, on my bed! His skin was grey, and there were bruises, and blood over his face, and...' He shuddered. 'He looked like he'd been dead for a while.'

Allie hoped they could get some kind of timeline from the evidence they'd find on the body, and also the state it was in, as quickly as possible.

'When was the last time you visited the flat before this, Andrew?'

'I went on Tuesday, but I stopped when I saw someone coming out of it.'

'Who was that?'

'I can't tell you.' He shook his head again. 'I'll be in big trouble even talking to you.'

Allie softened her voice purposely. 'We're not the bad guys, fella. We want to help.'

'But don't you see?' Andrew objected. 'That's why I was leaving. They took over my flat.'

'Who did, Andrew?'

'Milo and his friends. I hated being there.'

Someone knocked on the door and came in. It was a uniformed officer.

'I've been told to tell you that everything is set to go, Ma'am,' he said.

'Thanks.' She stood up, Perry, too. 'This is Trevor, Andrew. He's going to sit with you while I visit your flat. Okay?'

Andrew sat upright. 'You won't be long, will you?'

The distress on his face made her heart sink.

'I'll try not to be, but you'll be safe here.'

Outside in the corridor, Allie turned to Perry. 'Thanks for staying quiet in there.'

'He seemed to settle quickly, until we left.'

'He'll be fine with Trevor.' She ran a hand through her hair. 'What the hell is going on at the moment, Perry? Are we in the middle of some turf war that's going to escalate? Every time my phone rings, I'm half expecting someone else to turn up dead.'

'I'd laugh and say someone is doing us a favour by ridding us of the scum, but it's not funny.'

'No, it isn't.' She gave him a faint smile, though. Her phone rang, and she took the call.

'It's been confirmed there's a deceased male in the flat,' she said. 'He has no ID, but his description matches Milo Barker's. I'll call Dave and Christian while we're on the way and get Sam doing the necessary to start a new case.' She rolled her eyes. 'Another fun day of murder and mayhem. Let's grab a car and head over to Redmond Street.'

CHAPTER THIRTY-SIX

Allie made the necessary calls as Perry drove towards the crime scene on blues and twos.

'Do you think Andrew is involved somehow?' Perry asked, flying through a set of traffic lights.

'No.' Even though she had to keep an open mind, she didn't think that was possible. 'Do you?'

'No. I always thought he was a cuckoo. It's a shame he felt he had to leave his flat because a bunch of pricks have been making his life a misery.'

'It's so annoying.' Allie glanced at her phone again to check if there were any immediate updates. 'There's not much you can do for people who are scared to take your help.'

'Let's hope once he moves back to his mum's he can get on with his life again.'

'I doubt that, if what he's saying is true.' Allie shook her head. 'He'll have to testify.'

'But he hasn't seen anything.'

'Which is good. I imagine walking into a room and finding someone murdered is enough to give anyone nightmares. Let's hope Dave and Christian find us some clues. The week has been dire in that regard so far.'

Twenty minutes later, Perry parked outside Andrew's flat. It was just after ten o'clock, and the sky was a mass of incoming dark storm clouds. Crime scene tape had been rolled out across the entrance to the flats, tied to the wing mirror on the patrol car. Curtains were already twitching, residents spotting something going on.

Directly opposite was where Billy Whitmore had been murdered, at the back of the old Red Lion pub. Allie glanced over, almost expecting Milo Barker's killer to be hiding in there, watching them find him. But she knew whoever had done this was long gone if Andrew's description of the body was true.

They walked down several steps to get to the flat. Although the front door was open, a uniformed officer stood in front of it, stopping anyone from going in. Allie recognised him and nodded her greeting.

'Morning, PC Flynn.'

'Morning, Ma'am. It's definitely a DOA, back bedroom. Deceased by a few days, I reckon.'

Allie grimaced. 'Not too gruesome for you, I hope?'

'No, Ma'am. I've kept my breakfast down.'

'We'll take a quick look and then wait for forensics.'

They flicked on gloves, and shoe covers, and covered their mouths with masks and left him guarding the door as they went upstairs.

In the bedroom, Milo Barker was lying on his back, over by the window. His body was bloated, jeans and T-shirt stretched to their limits. His lips were blue, brown eyes open wide with terror.

Just as Andrew had said, there was bruising around the neck and temple. Whoever had done this to Milo might have marks on their hands. Most of it seemed recent, but then again, could it have been from the fight with Davy Lewis, the one Davy had got a black eye from? She couldn't make out how long ago it had happened.

'He suffered before he died,' Allie muttered. 'From the state of the body, he might even have been killed on the same day as Davy and Chantelle Bishop.'

'Someone on the rampage?' Perry stooped down.

'I hope not.' Allie did the same, peering at the bruising.

'Morning, you two,' a voice came from behind.

They turned to see Dave Barnett and Christian Willhorn, the pathologist, who had arrived together. They were dressed in forensic gear, something she knew they'd have to get into quickly.

'Morning, gentleman,' Allie replied. 'We were just declaring life extinct before getting changed.'

'Yeah, yeah.' Dave flicked his hand, and they moved aside. He took their place as he stooped next to Milo. 'This is nasty. A fight gone too far, perhaps?'

'You're the man to tell us that.'

'I was humouring you.'

Perry chuckled.

'I'll know more later, of course,' Dave added.

'I'll be hassling you until then.' Allie grinned and turned to Christian. 'How are you doing, Chris?'

'Good, thanks.'

'Still liking it in Stoke?'

Christian was from Northumberland.

'Aye, you're stuck with me, I'm afraid.'

'There have been worse things.' She smiled and went back to Dave. 'Can you estimate the time of death?'

'A few days ago, at least. Sunday, Monday perhaps.'

'Before the murders in Neville Street, and not because of them?'

'Possibly.'

She nodded at Dave. 'We'll leave you to it.'

The door to the living room was open, and Allie couldn't help but take a sneaky peek inside. When she'd first visited Andrew earlier in the year, his flat had been immaculate. It was clear he'd been telling the truth about the boys making a mess. There were dirty footprints all over the settee as if someone had been jumping on it like a trampoline, empty beer cans discarded on the carpet.

The glass in a picture on a wall had been smashed, the frame hanging skew-whiff. An ominous stain on the rug made her grimace. It looked like a pile of vomit that hadn't been cleaned up.

Through the kitchen doorway, she saw an overflowing rubbish bin, empty takeaway cartons on the table, and several mugs piled high on the draining board waiting to be washed.

What had been going on inside this flat? Allie knew from Billy Whitmore's death there was no CCTV around Redmond Street. It was too far off the main road. House-to-house would be imperative again, intrusive but essential. They needed to find out who had been coming and going, forcing Andrew to leave.

First, she had to go and tell another family that a loved one had been killed. What a week this was turning out to be.

Once outside again, she and Perry went up onto the pavement. The street was getting busier now as more people were coming out to have a gawp. Several units had come to accompany the investigation, too.

'Another murder is going to hit this street bad,' she told Perry. 'They had enough intrusion when Billy Whitmore died. People might be hostile because of that.'

'I've got broad shoulders,' Perry joked.

'It's a good job. They're bound to think we've been doing nothing.' She paused, and then with another thought, continued. 'Can you ring Grace, get her down here, too? She can take a bit of the flack away from the house-to-house team.'

'Will do.'

'I'll leave you to it.' She sighed. 'Milo's mum is going to be devastated. I'll go and break the news to her.'

CHAPTER THIRTY-SEVEN

Frankie had waited for an update on his phone from Allie and been told to talk to Andrew. Even though Andrew had said he wouldn't speak to anyone but her, Frankie hoped he'd be able to break through to him. They were both in their twenties, he'd try and find some common ground if he could. Perhaps talk about *Game of Thrones* or *Stranger Things* to start with.

Andrew had been moved to a soft interview room. He was sitting on the sofa with a cup of tea when Frankie went in.

Frankie sat on the armchair and gave him a reassuring smile. They chatted for several minutes about things in general and luckily found they shared the same tastes in TV shows. When he felt Andrew might be warming to him, Frankie started to pose his questions.

'Andrew, we've been to your flat and can confirm that Milo has died. What we need to work out now is who it was who killed him.'

'It wasn't me!'

Andrew's frightened cry made Frankie wonder if he'd undone everything he'd worked so hard on since entering the room. The man was petrified. Frankie held up a hand.

'I'm not saying it is, but we have to check every possibility.' Even with his gut feeling telling him Andrew wasn't involved, Frankie wouldn't rule him out until the evidence was in.

'Did you notice anything else about your flat?' he wanted to know. 'You say you haven't been there since Friday morning. Was there anything missing or something left behind that you saw?'

'Other than it being a mess?' Andrew thought for a moment and then shook his head. 'I didn't stay for long. I ran out as soon as I saw Milo.'

'Will you tell me now why you went to stay with your mum?'

Andrew shook his head vehemently. 'I'll wait until Allie comes back.'

'Okay, no worries,' Frankie reassured him, still hoping to win him over as they chatted.

'Am I in danger?'

Was he, Frankie wondered? If Andrew went on to tell them everything he knew, then yes, he might well be. It was a tough position to be in.

'You're safe here.' He hoped his smile was reassuring. 'You're not in trouble, Andrew. These are bad people who took advantage of you. What about your social worker? Can I call someone for you?'

'It won't help. They'll never leave me alone.'

'We can make them go away.' He glanced at the clock. 'Would you like some more tea?'

'No, thank you.'

'What do you think about telling me some things that have been happening, maybe give me some names in readiness for Allie's return? I think it would be really helpful for her.'

Andrew looked as if he was a rabbit caught in headlights.

Frankie didn't envy him the choices he had. To either say nothing or get the wrath of the gang for the rest of his days, being known as a grass and having to suffer the consequences.

He was a vulnerable adult. Even if he went to live with his mum again, someone might get to him. Indirectly, they could both be at risk.

But Andrew had Allie on his side. She would talk to the DCI and see what they could do for him. If anyone could pull strings, Frankie knew it would be her.

Frankie's silence as he ran through his thoughts must have helped because Andrew now sat forward and began to talk.

'Milo and his mates used to come around all the time,' he said.

'How many were there?'

'About six, mostly. Sometimes more, but six who came regularly.'

'And Kenny? Was he your friend?'

'No.' Andrew's eye twitched at the mention of his name. 'He used to bring me gifts, though. He bought my TV.'

'For you to play games on?'

'No. I've never played games. I like to watch detective programmes. I like to watch *Vera* and *Line of Duty*.'

'Me, too,' Frankie fibbed so that he could build a rapport with him.

'He bought me some trainers, too, and my watch.' Andrew rolled up his sleeve and showed it to him.

'Nice. So would you say he was a good friend?' Frankie posed his earlier question another way.

'I think he gave me gifts to keep me quiet.'

'Did you ever do any work for him?'

'I didn't want to, but he made me.'

'That's okay. What did you do?'

'Collected and dropped off stuff for him.' Andrew made a circular shape with his finger on the arm of the sofa.

'Money?' Frankie hazard a guess.

Andrew nodded.

'Can you tell me where from?'

'Lots of houses. I didn't like doing it.'

'That's great, Andrew.' Frankie took down a few notes, glad that at least some of the exploitation had stopped. 'Can you remember when Kenny last came to your flat?'

'About two weeks ago. He doesn't call much, only when he wants to know something.'

'Like what's been happening at the flat?'

'Yes, he wants me to tell him what goes on. But if I do, then the boys beat me.' He played with the fingernail on his index finger for a few moments, then went back to making circles. 'I can't win, so I try to keep quiet as much as possible.'

'Why did you want to go and stay with your mum that particular weekend?'

'They'd been playing games all night for ages. They were drunk and so noisy. I couldn't sleep. And they ate my food and hit me when it had all gone.'

Frankie knew it was time to ask him some names. 'Andrew, do you think you can tell me now who's visited your flat over the past month?'

CHAPTER THIRTY-EIGHT

Andrew said nothing for a few seconds, the circles he was drawing with his finger getting bigger and bigger.

'Will I be in trouble if I do tell you?' he asked.

'Not at all.'

'But they might come to find me at my mum's. I don't want her getting involved. It's not fair. It's my mess.'

'None of this is your fault, mate.' Frankie tried to contain his anger, because it wasn't directed at Andrew. It was aimed at the fuckwits who thought it was a game to mess around with people, not realising an iota of the damage they were causing to their mental health. 'You've been chosen by a gang of men to use your flat as their base. They've probably stored things there, and you've not known about it.'

Andrew flinched and Frankie tried to reassure him.

'If we find something today, you won't be in trouble for it. Have you seen anything?'

Andrew leaned forward and whispered, his right eye twitching. 'I think there might be some things behind the bath panel. I saw Milo going in there a lot.'

'Thanks, that's excellent.' Frankie knew the search team

would look there, so that was a good start. Even so, he would alert them so they could go to it immediately. 'Along with Milo, and the odd visit from Kenny Webb, who else visited your flat?'

'Someone called Aiden. Sam. Little Pete. I don't know their full names. Then there was Davy before he was murdered.'

Frankie took a note of them, knowing them all through his work. Aiden Stewart. Sam Mitchell. Peter Phillips.

'Was it always boys and men, never any girls?' he went on.

Andrew shook his head vehemently. 'There were no girls.'

'And you really didn't want to let anyone into your property when they showed up?'

'No.'

Frankie could feel Andrew's barriers coming down.

'Thanks, Andrew, you've been fantastic. I have just a few more questions, and we can take a break until Allie gets back. You said you saw someone coming out of your flat when you went back on Tuesday. Are you able to tell me who it was, now you're here with us?'

Andrew paused and then nodded. 'It was Kenny Webb.'

Frankie tried not to feel too pleased with himself for getting all this out of him. 'What time was this?'

'It was early. I caught the eight-fifteen bus from Mum's, and it takes twenty-five minutes. It's a five-minute walk from the bus stop.'

'So just before nine o'clock then?'

'Yes.'

'I need you to tell me more about the money that you had to collect for him.'

Andrew looked at the carpet, his knee bouncing up and down. 'I don't really know anything.'

'I think you were collecting rent for people who were living in houses that Kenny owned. Am I right?'

Andrew shrugged a shoulder.

'Andrew?' Frankie said when he went quiet. 'Were you doing that? It's okay to tell us. We need to know so we can use it for evidence to put Kenny and his friends away.'

'They had to give Kenny most of their wages, even though they work for him.'

'But that can't be right.'

'I had to collect it because when Billy died, Kenny made me take his place. I hated it. I really did, and I had to do it every Friday. Kenny would call at my flat to get the money, and then I'd have to go again the next week. And the next. And the next.'

'So you've been doing this since Billy died?'

'Until recently. He told me I didn't have to do it anymore, said it was more hassle than it was worth and that he'd get someone else to do it. I was pleased because I had to pay if someone wasn't in, out of my own pocket.'

'What did you mean earlier, when you mentioned giving Kenny money, even though they work for him? What do they do?'

'They work for Stoke-Clean and have their money paid into the bank. They don't get much. It's not fair that he wants everything else, too.'

'Don't worry, you won't have to work for him ever again, and your wages will be your own.' Frankie waited for him to look up briefly and smiled. 'It's over, Andrew.'

'What happens if he comes after me?'

'He won't be able to.'

'What if he sends someone else to hurt me?'

'Then we'll be there to protect you.'

His smile warmed Frankie's heart. It wasn't an easy answer to give, though, knowing that they didn't have the resources to do just that. Andrew could get hurt; someone could be sent to have a go at him. Maim him, kill him even, but they couldn't police everyone.

But Frankie had a feeling Andrew, if anyone, would be cast aside. The other boys, doing the collecting and delivering of the drugs, would be the ones to watch.

Frankie's mind went into overdrive once he was outside in the corridor. This new information was gold. It could mean that Kenny Webb knew about the body on Tuesday and hadn't reported the crime to them. That in itself could mean several things.

Either Kenny knew who'd killed Milo Barker and was leaving them to clear up their own mess. Or he knew who'd done it and was trying to cover up for them.

Or, even more of a possibility, Kenny was the one who'd murdered Milo and was hoping to clean up after himself but had left it too late.

CHAPTER THIRTY-NINE

With a uniformed officer, Allie made her way to Milo Barker's address again. This time, there was someone at home. A young man opened the door. Allie recognised him straightaway. He was the middle of the three children, twenty-three-year-old Philip. She'd sent him down four years ago for a vicious assault on an elderly couple whose home he'd burgled. How time flies: she hadn't even known he'd got out.

Philip was very much like Milo in size and stature, although his skin was pale due to being inside for so long. Beady eyes glared at her, a sneer on his lips. There was a nasty scratch down his right cheek, a couple on his neck, too.

'Staffordshire Police.' Allie held up her warrant card, even though he'd be sure to recognise her. 'I need to speak to your mum, Philip.'

'She's not in.'

'Do you know when she'll be back?'

'Nope.' He caught her looking at his face and folded his arms. 'Rough sex last night. Catching up with what I've missed. That okay with you?'

Allie shuddered inwardly at the thought.

'Who is it, Phil?' a woman's voice shouted out.

Allie frowned. 'You said your mum wasn't in.'

'Oh, so I did. Sorry, I forgot.'

She raised her eyebrows, not sure of his game but too annoyed to figure it out. She pushed past him and into the house, the officer following behind.

'What do you want?' Maureen Barker almost growled at her.

Another welcoming member of the Barker clan, Allie thought. 'I have some bad news, Maureen. It's about Milo. I'm afraid we've found him deceased earlier this morning.'

Maureen's roar was animalistic. 'He can't be dead.' She shook her head.

Philip's hands were down by his side, for a moment frozen, and then he hugged his mum.

'How did it happen?' he asked, his voice void of any reaction.

Allie explained everything, watching Philip's face darken. She'd seen so many men battle their emotions when she'd told them a loved one had died. But Philip wasn't showing grief. She could practically feel the rage emanating from him.

'Do you know who did it?' he asked next.

Allie shook her head. 'We're processing the scene at the moment.'

'I thought he'd gone away,' Maureen said, taking a deep breath between sobs.

'Did he tell you that?'

'No. He often goes missing for a couple of nights here and there. Never this long, though.'

'When did you last see him?'

'Sunday evening. He was going out for a drink with the lads.'

'Did he say who he was meeting?'

'No.' Maureen sobbed. 'Has he been dead all that time?'

'Wait a minute.' Philip scowled at Allie. 'Are you saying you've only just found him since Sunday?'

'The tenant in the flat has been away. He came home and found Milo.'

'You'd better figure out who's done this.' He pointed in her face. 'And quick. Because if you don't, I'll be round this estate banging on everyone's door until I find out the truth.'

'We'll do everything we can.' Allie took a tone of authority as his voice rose.

'What was he doing at the flat?' Maureen queried.

'We're not sure yet.'

'Get out and start asking questions, then,' Philip said.

'I'm sorry?' Allie caught his eye.

'You heard. Get your arse off that settee and go and find his killer.'

Allie stayed where she was. 'I'm sorry for your loss, but I need to discuss some eventualities with you.'

'I said get out! We can handle this. Email or phone. Mum, give her your number. And then she can leave.'

Allie stood up, thinking it best to say nothing else. Philip was in shock; grief could make people act in many different ways. He also might want his privacy to grieve, perhaps holding in tears until she'd gone. Although she didn't like leaving at his remark, she took the phone number Maureen offered her and moved towards the door, the police officer following her.

'I'll be in touch soon. There'll be a family liaison officer with you shortly, too, and I think–'

'Are you deaf?' Philip roared. 'We don't want any police here.'

'It's not a problem to send someone,' she said, unperturbed.

'I said no!'

Allie left them to it. She could have told Philip to calm

down, even arrested him if he continued to be aggressive. But it wasn't her that he was showing dislike to. It was the system. And the grief over the loss of his brother.

Outside, she blew out her breath as she walked back to her car.

'That was intense,' she said to the officer. 'Luckily, Philip has agreed to let the rest of the family know.' It wasn't Allie's job to inform every relative, but she was glad he was going to tell Lily in person.

She hoped Philip didn't do as he'd threatened and try to find out information. He could even get intel before them, which would make matters worse.

They headed back to the station, so she could drop the officer off. Allie wondered if Frankie had found anything else out from Andrew Dale while the team were working the crime scene. It would allow her time to get started on the usual stuff. A press conference needed to be set up for information about Milo Barker, also to include a fresh appeal for the murder of Davy Lewis and Chantelle Bishop. Then a meeting needed to be set up for the locals. She'd get Grace onto that. They had to find out if there was a link between all three.

But first she would go to Car Wash City. After what Shaun was alluding to, she'd be careful, but she wanted to speak to Kenny Webb. She couldn't see how it was a coincidence that it was another one of his workers, and despite what had happened yesterday, another little chat on the side wouldn't go amiss, not now they'd found Milo dead.

The tip-off about Car Wash City on Tuesday had come from a burner phone, so there was no way of tracing who it belonged to. And she couldn't ring it because of whatever DCI Cooper had planned later in the week. It would test her patience, but she needed to sit on her hands and do nothing for the time being. Let the Organised Crime Unit do their work and hope it was in her favour.

If she hadn't known Milo Barker had been dead before the drugs bust yesterday, she'd have wondered if this kill was in retaliation for it. Having said that, it could be in response to the murders on Monday.

It was certainly a huge puzzle, some pieces fitting together and some not. Still, they wouldn't stop digging until they had a conclusion.

CHAPTER FORTY

Allie took a call from Frankie. She wasn't sure if she was surprised or not to hear that Kenny may have been in Andrew Dale's flat on Tuesday, which could mean he'd seen the body and left it there. Had he happened upon it or been thinking of how to clear up his own mess? It was way too early for evidence to suggest he was involved, but she was eager to hear what was found at the crime scene.

Allie *was* pushing her luck, visiting him twice in as many days, but how was she supposed to know that Milo Barker would turn up dead that morning? She wasn't sure if Kenny would be all sweetness and light after riling her up yesterday either. It hadn't been pleasant, especially when he'd put his hands on her and it had taken all her control not to slam him against the wall and cuff him. She hated this treading softly lark, even if it had unnerved her at the time.

But she planted on a smile, knocked, and went into his office.

Kenny groaned. 'Don't you have anything else to do?' He glared at her. 'People will start talking.'

'It's talk I'm after, Kenny,' she said. 'It seems no matter

what I look into these days, it always has something to do with you or the people who work for you. I'm sorry to tell you that Milo Barker was found dead this morning.'

'Really?' Kenny's face contorted with shock. 'God, that's terrible. He was a good kid. What happened to him?'

Allie told him what she could.

'I hope you're not going to try and pin that on me now.' Kenny shook his head. 'Everything you ask me about *these days* always comes down to that, doesn't it? I could have you for harassment.'

'You could try, I suppose. I'm just doing my job, like yesterday, the same as you.'

'I'm trying to do mine without the law interfering.'

'We found drugs on your premises during our last visit.' She tutted. 'Now we have a member of your staff, another one, murdered. When did you last see Milo?'

'I told you. It was on Saturday afternoon, when he finished work for the week.' Kenny sat forward. 'Are you saying he's been in that flat in Redmond Street since then?'

'He hasn't been home, so perhaps so. Have you ever been to Redmond Street?'

'A few times.'

'And why would that be?'

'I got the lad who lives there a cheap deal on a TV. Billy Whitmore told me he was struggling, so I wanted to do a good deed. He's got learning difficulties, and I felt sorry for him.'

Allie laughed inwardly. He really expected her to believe that?

'He's a weirdo, though.'

Ah, there was the real Kenny.

'Have you questioned him about the attack, seeing as it happened inside his flat?' he went on.

Allie ignored his question purposely. 'Milo Barker. Davy Lewis. Both working for you and both dead.'

'And neither was my fault.' Kenny cleared his throat. 'About what happened yesterday. I'm sorry, I overreacted.'

'You did.'

'I shouldn't have grabbed your arm.'

Allie raised her eyebrows in surprise before she disappeared out of the door. She wasn't going to give him the satisfaction of accepting his apology.

Kenny watched as Allie disappeared across the forecourt, his temper rising with every step. What was it with her? Why did she always want to do things her way? No wonder she'd got the better of Terry Ryder. She seemed one step ahead all the time.

He was annoyed that she was at his gaff again. It wasn't good if she was checking on everything that happened. He needed to speak to Martin, see how long it would be before everything was in place.

Once back at the station, Allie was wondering what to do with Andrew Dale. He was still refusing her offer to call his social worker. If his mum wasn't in poor health, she would have got her to come and sit with him. Mrs Dale was sixty-five, having had Andrew when she was forty-two. She had crippling arthritis, hardly ever leaving the house unless her brother picked her up for the day.

Meanwhile, calls were coming in left, right, and centre. The wider team were finishing talking to the remaining people on the list, with fingerprints they'd found in Neville Street, plus the three names they'd been given by Andrew Dale. Most of them had been brought in for questioning, and so far, talking to one after another had proved to be a waste of time. They were keeping tight-lipped. Again, they were in danger of getting nothing.

After grabbing a quick bite to eat, she received a message from Jenny asking to see her for an update. The press release about Milo Barker had gone out an hour ago.

'Where are we at?' Jenny asked as soon as Allie was seated in her office.

'We're waiting on forensics, but so far, it seems as if Milo Barker had a fight with someone and as a result was strangled.'

'With bare hands?'

Allie nodded. 'It's also looking like Kenny Webb went to Andrew Dale's flat after he was murdered. So he's known about the death since Tuesday at least. I visited him today, and he said nothing to me.'

'You're working with the Organised Crime Unit on this?'

'Yes, Ma'am, with DCI Cooper. I'm not going to tread on toes or walk in with big feet. I'm just sorting as many little things out as I can.'

'Those usually have a habit of leading us to the bigger things, Allie.' Jenny halted. 'We'll have to protect Andrew Dale. He'll be a prime target now, and if this ever gets to court. Keep me in the loop, and I'll address the team tomorrow.'

'Yes, Ma'am.'

Allie went back to her own floor. Mention of Shaun and the Organised Crime Unit reminded her of what might be happening later in the week. If it was what she thought, what she'd hoped and wished for, for so long, she might not sleep until it happened.

CHAPTER FORTY-ONE

Leaving the station feeling quite chuffed with himself, Frankie did another check on the properties that Kenny Webb owned. He knocked on the door of nineteen Coral Avenue. With having to keep Andrew occupied, it was the first time he'd been that day. No one had contacted him after he'd called yesterday, and it seemed as if he was going to be unlucky this time, too.

Waiting a few moments before he knocked again, he glanced around. The garden was a disgrace, nothing done to it in months, very much like all the properties he'd visited on the list. He wondered if anyone had even been to see he'd left a card.

He peered through the living room window. The house was the same, too. The mug on the coffee table had been there yesterday, along with a gossip magazine. He looked across to see the door to the kitchen was still closed.

Maybe the tenant was out at work. But although he doubted that, it might explain why no one had contacted him.

After another knock revealed no one was home, he

walked away, making a mental note to get someone on shift to pop round this evening if he didn't get time to do it himself.

He was sitting in his car when he spotted a young woman walking down the street. It was Lily Barker. He put his head down as she passed by him, even though her eyes were on her phone. Then she went into number nineteen.

Quickly, he followed her, waiting until she was at the door, a key in her hand. He jogged up the path again.

'Hi Lily, it's DC Higgins, Frankie. We met the other day.'

Lily glanced up from her phone, eyeing him suspiciously. 'What do you want?'

'I left a card here yesterday for someone to contact me.'

'I never saw it.' She quickly turned to go in.

'Then I'm sure you won't mind if I explain why I left it.' Frankie let her open the door.

Lily went into the house, glaring at him as his foot went over the threshold to stop her from leaving him on the step.

'I'd rather you didn't.'

'It won't take me a moment.'

'If you must.' She removed the key and went into the living room.

'May I ask why you're visiting?' He followed her through.

'You can but I don't have to tell you.' A blush spread over Lily's cheeks.

There was a bang from upstairs.

'What was that?' Frankie asked, automatically glancing at the ceiling.

Lily frowned. 'I didn't hear anything.'

Two more bangs in quick succession.

Frankie frowned. 'Is there someone else here?'

'No.'

Frankie paused, unconvinced. 'I'll take a look, if you don't mind.'

'I do mind,' Lily retorted. 'Don't you need a warrant for that kind of thing?'

'Only if you have something to hide. You don't, do you?'

Lily made a run for the door.

Frankie grabbed her arm. 'Not so quick.'

Lily tried to shrug him off, but he kept a firm grip.

Frankie held on to her and walked her along the narrow hall that led to the stairs.

'Wait, I–' Lily spoke.

'Let's see what's up there before you try to talk your way out of things.' He pushed her gently upstairs, following behind and keeping an eye on her feet in case she tried to kick out at him.

At the top of the stairs, four closed doors to three bedrooms and a bathroom, and no windows, meant they were almost thrown into darkness. But it wasn't long before Frankie's eyes adjusted to the gloom.

He found the light switch and flicked it on. The first thing he noticed was a bolt on the back bedroom door.

His face darkened. 'Open it,' he demanded, losing his cool in an instant.

'This wasn't my idea,' Lily said.

Frankie said nothing. He waited for her to draw it across.

'In,' he ordered. 'I'm not going to harm you. I just want you where I can see you.'

Lily shuffled into the room and Frankie pushed the door wide to ensure no one was hiding behind it.

There was no furniture, bare floorboards, and dirty netting up at the window. Sitting on a mattress in the corner was a young girl.

'Janey?' he asked, his tone now soft.

She nodded vehemently.

'It's okay, I'm Police.' He pointed to Lily. 'Sit down next to her.'

Lily shook her head.

'Do you want me to cuff you?'

With a sigh, Lily did as she was told.

Frankie called it in, asking for backup and an extra car to transport Lily to the station. The fire in her eyes enraged him. He glanced at Janey.

'Are you hurt?'

'No,' she replied.

'Do you know each other?'

'Yes.'

'Let me deal with Lily for a second, and I'll be with you soon.' He turned to Lily, knowing he needed to be lenient. He had to find out if she knew that her brother had died.

'Have you heard from your mum today, or your brother, Philip?'

'If you mean do I know that Milo is dead, then yes, I do.'

Frankie was shocked at her deadpan response. But then Milo wasn't exactly a saint. Maybe he'd been mean to Lily, too. Still, Frankie had at least expected some kind of emotion.

'My mum told me.' Lily pulled her knees up to her chest and rested her chin on them. 'I was going over there now but I had to get some food for Janey. Look in the bag if you don't believe me. I brought more in case I couldn't get back as often. And it was only going to be until Saturday.'

Frankie nodded, showing some compassion. She was only a year or two younger than he was. How their lives were so different.

But there were two sides to every story. It wasn't all about luck. Even though she could have helped herself more, Lily seemed to have been dealt a bad hand.

'What's happening on Saturday?' he queried.

The women glanced at each other, but neither spoke. Finally, Lily piped up.

'Martin Smith was going to take Janey to Stoke station and put her on a train out of here.'

CHAPTER FORTY-TWO

'This is great work, Frankie,' Allie told him when she caught up with everything back at the station.

'Thanks, but I didn't do much, boss. Lily Barker must have known she was there all the time.'

'We'll find out shortly. Let's go and see what Janey knows. Do you want to join me in the interview?'

'Yes, thanks.'

Allie laughed to herself. Frankie still had that eager beaver work ethic. She loved seeing it. 'Anything else I need to know?'

'Yes, I found out some information from Andrew.' Frankie told her about Stoke-Clean. 'I've passed the details to Sam. She said she'd have a dig around.'

'Good stuff. Well done, Frankie.'

They went downstairs. In the soft interview room, Janey Matthews had been reassured that she was safe, and a uniformed officer had been sitting with her. It was obvious the girl had suffered trauma. Her blonde hair hung limp and greasy, her skin smeared with dirt. Eyes that had no doubt cried buckets of tears while she sat alone, wondering about her fate, flicked around the room. She looked painfully thin, even after a few days.

'Hi, Janey.' Allie smiled. 'My name is Allie, and I'm a Detective Inspector. You've met Frankie earlier. He's a detective, too. Now, there's nothing to worry about. I just need to ask you a few questions. Is that okay?'

Janey nodded slightly.

Allie took it as a cue to sit down. Frankie pulled out a chair from the table, turned it round, and sat, too.

'Have you had a warm drink? And something to eat?'

'Yes, thanks.'

'Frankie found you in Coral Avenue today,' Allie went on. 'We know you were in Neville Street on Sunday evening. Can you tell us what happened?'

'I can't believe Chantelle is dead.' Janey burst into tears.

'We're so sorry.'

They let her cry before resuming.

Allie moved to sit next to her, resting a hand on her arm, enough to comfort not intimidate. 'Did you know that Davy Lewis died at the same time?'

'I thought he had, but Lily wouldn't tell me.'

'Were you there when it happened?'

'Yes.'

'Was it you who attacked him because he was hurting Chantelle?'

'No! It wasn't me.'

Her scared cries assured Allie she was probably telling the truth.

'It's okay,' she soothed. 'We have to cover every eventuality. What was Davy doing there?'

'He'd come to collect his rent. Everyone has to pay to stay there. Chantelle gave him some money, but he said she owed him more than that. He said that if she didn't have enough, then she'd have to pay in a different way.'

Allie tried not to show her disgust. Sexual favours with him would be *any* woman's nightmare, never mind entirely wrong.

'They started arguing, and I didn't know what to do.' Janey shivered involuntarily.

'Did you stay in the room?'

'Davy told me to leave. I said I was going nowhere, but he hit out at me and shoved me back onto the settee. Then he pulled Chantelle up by her hair. She punched out at his hands, and they started to fight. I shouted at them to stop. That's when Davy punched her, and she hit her head on the coffee table as she fell. It made an awful sound.'

Allie gave a reassuring noise. 'And then what happened?'

'I shouted Chantelle's name, and Davy started swearing. I could see blood on the corner of the coffee table. I told him he'd killed her, and he said it was an accident. Davy nudged her arm with his foot, but she didn't move.' Janey glanced up at them. 'We'd just been eating chips, and then she was dead. Davy said she'd passed out, but I knew it was worse than that. And then... then Davy seemed as if he was going to hurt me, too, so I ran to the door to try and get out of the house. But it opened before I got there.'

'Who opened it?'

'Kenny Webb.'

Allie glanced surreptitiously at Frankie. 'You're sure it was Kenny, Janey? I just need to be certain.'

'It was Kenny. He was with Martin Smith. When Kenny saw what had happened, he lost it. He started shouting at Davy and then he... he stabbed him. It happened so fast. I screamed; I couldn't help it. Kenny pushed me down to my knees. He told me to look at Chantelle and then Davy. He said if I told anyone what had happened, I would get what Davy had got.'

Allie reached for the girl's hand as she burst into tears

again, her temper rising at the thought of all she'd been through. How could Kenny Webb have done this?

'You're safe here, duck. There's not much more to go through.' Allie was eager to learn why, and how, Janey had ended up in Coral Avenue.

'I told him that I wouldn't dare, but he didn't trust me to stay quiet,' Janey continued. 'He grabbed my arm and said I had to go with him. I tried to get away, but he kept hold of me. He told me to be quiet and not to make a fuss as he took me to his car.'

'And no one saw you?'

'I don't think so. I couldn't see anyone, and I didn't dare scream.'

Where were the bloody nosy neighbours when you needed them, Allie mused. 'And what about Martin Smith?'

'Kenny told him to stay behind to clean up. Then he drove me to Coral Avenue and locked me in the bedroom. He said he needed to think about what to do about me. I thought I was going to die there.'

Janey started to cry again, and Allie realised she'd had enough. Besides, she would have to speak to Jenny next, about all the people who might be in danger if things were going to escalate.

They left Janey with another officer. Allie shook her head in disbelief and she and Frankie went back upstairs.

'Well, I wasn't expecting *that* plot twist today,' she admitted. 'I'll say it again – well done, you.'

'Thanks, boss,' Frankie beamed. 'All it takes is one little nugget of information, that's what you tell me.'

'I do, because I'm always right.' She grinned at him, going through as he held open the door. 'What I can't understand is why Janey was being kept in that house. She couldn't be held there forever, and surely Kenny couldn't expect her to be so traumatised that she'd keep her mouth shut. Or that she wouldn't speak out indefinitely.' She checked her watch. 'Let's talk to Lily Barker so we can get her back to her family. Then I'll have a word with the DCI to see what to do about Kenny Webb.'

'You're not bringing him in on suspicion of murder?'

Allie sighed. 'I have orders at the moment, but I can't tell you about them.'

'Gotcha.'

'I want to find out about Martin Smith, though. And why he was going to get Janey Webster out of Stoke this weekend.'

CHAPTER FORTY-THREE

They took a quick break, and then Allie went into the interview room with Frankie. Maybe he'd be able to stop Allie from reaching across the table and giving Lily Barker a good shake.

Yet, for all her faults, Lily didn't seem the kind of person who'd be dictated to by Kenny Webb, not after what she'd said about him. Equally, they all knew Kenny had a mean streak and would always act upon his threats.

She wondered if Lily had been paid to watch over Janey. Surely she hadn't tied her up and was keeping her prisoner? Unless Janey had something to do with Milo's death that she wasn't letting them know about. Either way, this would be an interesting interview, providing Lily would speak to them.

Lily glared at them in defiance. But when Allie set up the recording and said the requirements necessary to ensure she knew she was under caution before speaking to her, she almost folded into herself. Was she finally realising how much trouble she was in and what might happen to her children if she was sent to prison?

'Lily,' Allie began. 'I'm surprised to see you here, especially after our chat the other day. Can you tell me why Janey Webster was locked in a room in a house that you visited?'

'I don't know anything about that.'

'So you didn't visit nineteen Coral Avenue to check on Janey?'

'No, because I didn't know she was there.'

'That's not what you told DC Higgins. And, according to your phone, there are numerous texts to the same number, where you blatantly say when you've checked on the girl, and how often. We're also waiting on details of who was receiving those calls.'

'It was code.' Lily squirmed in her seat. 'I went to check if there was any mail, that's all.'

'And do you usually do that, arriving with a bag of sandwiches and soft drinks?'

'They were for me.'

'Again, not what you told DC Higgins.' Allie nodded. 'Who were you collecting the post for?'

'What?'

'The post, Lily. Why were you collecting it from an empty house? Were you going to forward it to someone or give it to them directly?'

Lily gulped, remaining silent.

'Whose name was on the letters you would pick up?'

'Okay, I didn't go for that. But if I tell you what I do know, I'm going to be in trouble, and I have my kids to think about.'

'Ah, the ones you conveniently forget about?' It was a harsh thing to say, using her children as bait, but it had the desired effect.

'I take care of them very well, thank you very much,' Lily retorted. 'The baby's with my mum, and the rest are at school. So don't you threaten me with taking them away.'

'No one's going to do that if you co-operate with us.' Allie brought the conversation onto an even keel again. 'But you need to tell us the truth. Was someone paying you to take care of Janey and to keep an eye on the house before that?'

Lily blushed, giving herself away.

'Come on, Lily. Play ball. We know you're keeping things from us, and my next step will be to arrest you for it.'

'It was Martin Smith.'

Allie did her best not to seem astonished.

'Just to be clear, you were paid by Martin Smith to keep an eye on Janey Webster, who was locked in a room at nineteen Coral Avenue?'

Lily nodded. 'He rang me on Monday asking for a favour. He said he'd pay me fifty quid a day to check in on Janey, bring her some food and drink.'

'Why couldn't he do that?'

'He said he could only visit when it was dark as he didn't want anyone to see him.' She looked at them both, pleading with them to understand. 'I can't turn that kind of money down, not on the pittance I get from the social. I'm already behind with the electric bill and—'

'How long was he planning on keeping her there?' Allie interrupted, not at all bothered about Lily's predicament. Janey Webster had plainly seen too much on the day that Chantelle Bishop and Davy Lewis had been killed. But hiding her at the house would only solve the problem of her not being able to tell anyone about it until she was let go. Janey would be able to identify the killer then, which she'd done.

'Martin said he was going to get her out of Stoke on Saturday.'

'Do you know why Janey needed to be kept there until then?'

'He said there'd been an accident, that Davy had killed Chantelle after she'd stabbed him and then he'd died, too.'

That was different from what Janey was telling them. So who was lying? Was it Lily? Janey? Or even Martin?

'Why do you think Martin would want to keep Janey locked in a room?' Allie was curious to know.

'I don't know. I just did what I was paid to.'

'And you didn't wonder why?'

'Well, I did after I'd heard that Davy and Chantelle were dead, but Janey wouldn't tell me anything when I asked.'

'When she was locked up in that room?'

'It was only to keep her safe.'

'I'm sure she felt very protected in there! Did she have access to a phone, or did you take that from her?'

Lily shrugged. 'I don't know what happened to that.'

'And you did this for money?'

'You clearly mustn't have kids.' Lily's voice was agitated. 'Because if you did, you'd know you'd do anything to feed and keep them warm. I'm not a bad mum but I have to do things I don't like doing just to get by. There's only me, and the cost of everything now is so expensive. I thought Davy would look after me, but he was worse than any of the men I've been with. He wasted more on drugs than he earned.' She sat forward, clasping her hands in front of her on the table. 'All I wanted was to keep my kids safe, clean, and fed.'

'There was an innocent girl locked in a room. You don't see any harm in that?'

'She was only going to be there for a couple more days. It was a warning for her to keep her mouth shut when she got let out.'

'You sure about that?'

'That's what Martin said.'

'And you believed him?'

'I had no reason not to.'

Allie groaned. 'You blow hot and cold, and I don't know

why. One minute you're playing the victim, and the next you're being the hard woman. Which is it?'

'Depends on what day it is.'

'Come again?'

'It was a joke.' Lily rolled her eyes.

'This is not a laughing matter.' The tiny ounce of sympathy she'd had left for Lily evaporated in a second.

Back at her desk, Allie held her head in her hands for a moment. She was annoyed she'd lost her temper with Lily, yet she realised it was the only way she could get through to her. Sure, there was more than one way to skin a cat, but she didn't want to come across as bolshie. It did no one any favours.

Yet the interview with Lily had been maddening. She didn't seem in the slightest bothered about the trouble she was in. It was as if because she had four kids, she thought the courts would be lenient and let her off with a caution. Sometimes it wasn't like that.

And the mention of Martin Smith again was something Allie would be chasing up once she'd had a breather. He was involved in something, she was certain. Perhaps he was the key to it all, pretending that he was sweet and innocent. She'd have a word with Perry. Maybe he'd know more as Martin was his informant.

They'd bailed Lily Barker pending further enquiries. For the evidence they had, in a court of law, for all they knew she *could* have been there just to pick up the post and have no idea Janey was upstairs. Just like Scott Milton could have had no idea about the drugs they found at Car Wash City. They needed more, of everything. Where was the secret sauce?

Her phone pinged a message from an unknown number.

Check out Car Wash City, Longton. You'll find the missing knife used to kill Davy Lewis, and his and the girl's phones. They're hidden behind the filing cabinet in the main office.

Allie sat upright. The message was from someone who knew the number to her work's mobile, although she gave out so many contact cards it could be hard to tell who it would be. But if what the message said was true, someone must have planted the items after the raid on Wednesday morning because the place had been thoroughly searched.

Aware that she'd have to check before acting, Allie raced out of the room and up to see her DCI.

CHAPTER FORTY-FOUR

'I'll need to speak with DCI Cooper first,' Jenny told Allie after she'd updated her on the situation with Janey Webster and showed her the message she'd received on her phone. 'I'll get him to do that, via his unit if necessary.'

'But it's part of our investigation, Ma'am,' Allie spoke out. She couldn't let this go to another team. If Kenny Webb was involved, she wanted to nail him herself. And as most of the evidence coming in at the moment was ruling people out rather than in, it was imperative they looked into the matter quickly. 'If–'

'I need you focused on the job in hand.'

'I thought I had been doing that?' Allie was confused. 'The murders are part of my work.'

Jenny put up a hand when Allie was about to protest further. 'I know this is to do with Car Wash City employees, but you've been wanting to get something on Terry Ryder for over a decade. The man is Teflon unless we gather what we need first.'

'And what about Kenny Webb?'

'We'll bring him in when we can.'

'And Martin Smith?'

'Him, too. He isn't known to us so maybe he'll crack, give us what we need.'

'He'll be scared of repercussions.'

'Enough to get sent down for saying nothing?' Jenny shook her head. 'I doubt that very much.'

'I'd do a deal if I were in his shoes.'

'Precisely. So play softly-softly and, when you're given the go-ahead, get as much as you can out of him in exchange for his and his family's safety.'

Allie nodded, seeing the direction things were heading in. Jenny wanted her to get Martin to squeal. He was the weakest link in this.

'What about the witnesses we have?' Allie said. 'How do we protect them?'

'Who do you have?'

'Andrew Dale, but he doesn't have anything on Kenny Webb, really. He's just ripe for follow-on violence from the gang of kids who accosted him.'

'You say he's moving out of his flat?'

'Yes, I doubt he'll ever go back there.'

'And his mum lives where?'

'A couple of miles away, in a council house.'

'Will the council move them?'

'Possibly in time, but would she want to go?' Allie ran a hand through her hair. 'I'll see what I can find out. There's Janey Webster, too. She was there at the crime scene, and saw it happen.'

'She'll definitely have to be put somewhere safe. Anyone else?'

'I'm not sure yet. I'll let you know once I've spoken to Webb and Smith – when I can.'

'Okay, Allie.' Jenny sat back. 'I need to have a think about the best way to handle this.'

'Ma'am?'

'Don't do anything until you hear from me. Do you understand?'

'But if someone finds that evidence, Webb and Smith could disappear if they know we're onto them. What if Lily Barker tells one of them? Or Martin Smith calls at the house and finds Janey gone?'

'He might think she's left of her own volition.'

'She was locked in a room.'

'Lily could have let her out.'

'Let's hope she says nothing to them.'

Allie couldn't help but stare at Jenny. First Shaun, and now her DCI. What the hell was going on?

'Leave things with me, Allie. Stay in the station because I'll need to see you shortly. All will become clear then.'

'Yes, Ma'am.'

'I've found some details out about Stoke-Clean you might be interested in,' Sam shouted across to Allie as she came onto the floor. 'I remembered seeing it in one of the notebooks.'

'Great, I'll check it with you later. I have a few things to do first.'

'Okay, I'll save these, too.' Sam pointed to a cake box. 'They jumped into my basket at lunchtime.'

Allie grinned. 'A definite rain check.'

She went into her office and closed the door. It was agony waiting for Jenny to get back to her, thinking about what was going on. They had a witness to say that Kenny Webb had killed Davy Lewis, and yet Allie was being stopped from arresting him on suspicion of murder. But equally, she knew when to pause and wait to see the bigger picture.

Finally, the call came from Jenny. 'I need you to come to the large conference room, Allie,' she said. 'You and Perry.'

'Yes, Ma'am.'

Allie was already on her feet, beckoning Perry over. She closed the door behind him for a moment.

'Something big is going down.' Her breathing was off the chart, adrenaline coursing through her. 'We've been called for a debrief.'

'Oh!' Perry's voice went up an octave. 'Is it what I think it is?'

'I bloody hope so. We've waited years to get that bastard for everything.' She grabbed her jacket from the back of her chair and shrugged it on. 'Let's go and see.'

Including Jenny, there were eight people in the conference room when they arrived. Allie knew them all from the Organised Crime Unit. Shaun had an empty seat beside him, and when he spotted her, he patted it. Perry sat across from them.

'Right, everyone,' Jenny spoke to get their attention. 'Welcome to Operation Dexter. The one, no doubt, a lot of you have been waiting for. Our apologies for keeping everything under wraps until we were able to let you in on what was going to happen tomorrow. It's always delicate timings about who knows what.

'As you all know, Terry Ryder is out of prison next month. The OCU have been building up a case on several individuals who have been working with him before that and looking after things while he's been inside. I'll hand you over to DCI Cooper now to go through the finer details. Shaun?'

CHAPTER FORTY-FIVE

Shaun stood up and walked to the front of the room. He pressed a few buttons on the digital screen on the wall and turned back.

'We've been watching a man in London, thirty-seven-year-old Chris Singleton, known to the Met. He's living in Islington, and he's a drug courier.' Shaun brought up six images of Chris in the driver's seat of a nondescript black Fiesta. 'We've been monitoring this vehicle for several months as it's arrived and left the city, visiting different places each time.

'He makes one drop-off, usually in a supermarket car park or somewhere suitably public.' Shaun brought up more images of their man. 'He goes over to another vehicle, hands the driver a bag, and is then on his way back to London.

'We're working with the Met to find out who his supplier is and, although we're not sure we have enough evidence of where Singleton is getting the gear from, in light of the murders this week, and the girl found in Coral Avenue stating Kenny Webb murdered Davy Lewis, we feel we have no choice but to act now and make our move. If we don't do anything, it could alert the men that we're planning something else, and they could run. However, we do feel we have sufficient evidence here in Stoke, from the foot soldiers up to Kenny Webb.

'There are two possibilities. The first is the money will swap hands and we can swoop in and arrest both Webb and Singleton. The other is Kenny Webb won't do the swap and will take the money and scarper. Either way, we can get them both in possession of something.'

Allie's stomach flipped. Were they about to bring down the whole gang? This was more than she had bargained for, more than she had ever hoped. No wonder Shaun and Jenny had been keen for her to be civil to Kenny Webb, when it felt so wrong to ignore his potential involvement in the recent murders.

'We also know Webb has been supplying to other people in the city,' Shaun went on. 'We have CCTV footage of foot soldiers doing the same, sitting in car parks and then passing on their gear to local dealers who then drive off quickly with their goods.'

'Reloading,' Allie said, giving it the insider term they knew it as.

Shaun nodded. 'We have a list of names at various properties that we're going to raid first thing in the morning. Ideally, we wanted to go further up than the courier but for now we need to get our main man.'

Allie sat forward, a huge grin on her face. She knocked it off quickly, hoping no one had seen it. It was unprofessional to smile, but she couldn't help it. *This* was what she'd been waiting for, hanging back for, since 2011 when Terry Ryder had been sentenced for murder. But there was one thing bothering her.

'How does this link to Ryder?' she asked.

'Chris Singleton is on his books. When Kirstie Ryder got out of prison in twenty nineteen, she continued the family business, taking on a lot more than she'd done before she went inside.'

Allie and Perry groaned at the same time. Kirstie was Ryder's only daughter and had landed herself in prison for a few years in connection with the murder of Jordan Johnson. In 2015, the Johnson brothers were looking after Ryder's empire with her, but Daddy wasn't best pleased with her attempts at being the big woman, causing a nuisance of herself, and had set her up to get her out of the picture. Allie still couldn't believe how ruthless he'd been, to do that to his own daughter.

'She's a feisty character, that one, living in Stafford now,' Shaun added. 'She's been transferring the money made from the drugs from car to car, dishing it out to the higher echelon.'

'So it's only the Ryders and Kenny Webb involved in Stoke?'

'As far as we know. We've been watching the Kennedy family, too, but it seems they're not involved. We had thought that, even though there's rivalry between them, that the two crime gangs would work together while Ryder was inside. But as far as we can see, that's not the case. Kenny Webb seems to be the main contact.'

Allie made a few notes. 'Do you have intel for when it's going down tomorrow?'

'We've had another tip-off that the next exchange will be at ten o'clock tomorrow, at Tesco, Meir.'

'Jeez, they're that blatant?' Allie was shaking her head.

'They really are. At the same time, we'll be after Kirstie Ryder and the foot soldiers. It's a bit riskier than going in the early hours of the morning, but we have to follow their routine. Without that supermarket swap, we only have the little people.'

'And does this mean Ryder might not come out of jail?'

Allie prayed silently that this would be the case. 'Do you have enough evidence linked to him via his daughter and Kenny Webb?'

'Let's not get ahead of ourselves.' Jenny couldn't help but smirk. 'There's a lot of work to be done for the CPS to ensure convictions. But I feel as everyone has done such a tremendous job, I think they'll go for it. We just need tomorrow to go to plan.'

'Also,' Shaun spoke next. 'The reason I had to stop you earlier in the week, Allie, was because we knew that while Scott Milton was taking the rap for the drug sting at the Longton branch of Car Wash City, things were being shifted into another property.'

'One we know about?'

'No, one owned by Kirstie Ryder, in Alexander Place. It's been empty for a while. We suspected that the drugs and money were being stored elsewhere, and because of the heat on Kenny over the murders, they were moved on. Surveillance has been going on around the clock for the past few days. We're certain now that they set Scott Milton up, gave us a tip-off, and then moved the gear from one house to another.'

Allie blew out her breath. 'This is such great work.'

'I agree,' Jenny concurred.

'We're going to sniff Kenny out by raiding his foot soldiers over a period of half an hour. Someone's bound to tell him what's going on. We'll be watching Chris Singleton at the same time. We expect he'll do the exchange and scarper, so we'll nab him when it's in the car and away from the meet-up point.'

They went through a few more details and then the meeting ended.

'So do we go about business as usual tonight?' Allie asked. 'I have a community meeting at seven.'

'Yes.' Shaun nodded. 'Ring me if you find out anything that you feel might be to our advantage.'

'Will do.'

'We also need to be careful because we're picking up a couple of people tonight. There's a regular run from Stoke to Stockport via train that we've been keeping an eye on. We're going to stop the people involved this evening, and hopefully keep Kenny Webb off the scent that we're onto them.'

As everyone began to file out of the room, Allie caught Shaun's eye, and he gave her a nod. She grinned again, not bothering who saw her this time.

This was why she came to work every day. To bring down the people who preyed on the vulnerable. Who made their lives a misery because of the power they had, the money they made. It was deplorable.

And doing her tiny bit to help bring crooks to justice was always worthwhile.

CHAPTER FORTY-SIX

It was half past six. Allie was with Grace at Limekiln Community Centre. Grace had rung around the girls she knew from her youth groups and asked them to come in for a chat, on the premise there would be coffee and cakes and somewhere dry to be for an hour as it had been a dreadful rainy month.

So far, fourteen girls had turned up. As Grace had mentioned there were twenty-one in total, Allie congratulated her on a great turnout, even if it was just for the cake.

They set chairs out, two in front of three rows of five, but spoke to the teenagers freely while they took beverages.

Allie watched Grace question them about what they'd been up to since she'd last spoken to them. She worked the room like a pro. She asked one how her mum was, the other about her puppy, checking out adorable photos. Another was due to be a bridesmaid and was showing Grace the awful pink fluffy creation she had to wear, laughing along with everyone at her disgust. One more asking her if she'd caught up with both series of *Ted Lasso*.

Once they were seated, Allie got down to business.

'Thank you all for coming, I'm so pleased that you're willing to help if you can.'

Immediately, a few gazes hit the floor, most likely in case she pointed to someone for an answer to a question. But this wasn't school, and they weren't in trouble. Like Grace had said, they were just after their help.

In the back row, there were two girls she knew. Kelsey Abbott and Mallory Whittaker were whispering to each other. She refrained from singling them out, but she was intrigued. Were they talking about things for the meeting or something else in general?

No one came forward with anything, which was a shame. Allie handed out contact cards to them, stressing if they were worried about anything, they could call her. Then they all drifted away.

She and Grace were now putting out more chairs in lieu of the residents meeting that was next.

Allie rolled her eyes. 'Well, that didn't go to plan.'

'Give them time,' Grace said. 'Often they'll come back to me when they're on their own, so that no one can see them talking to me.'

'Let's hope so, because from the looks on some of their faces, they knew more than they were letting on.'

Allie went outside to catch up on some calls. She had an email from Dave Barnett saying the blood from the door handle on Andrew Dale's living room door was not Milo's. She sighed: it meant a lot of work for them to cross-reference who it belonged to. Was nothing going to go their way?

She went back inside the hall, unprepared for how many people were now there. They'd put about fifty chairs out, and most of them were full.

She walked through the aisle they'd made in the middle, instantly transported to when she was nine and her school had put on *The Pied Piper of Hamelin*. She'd played the part of a villager who had run when they'd seen the rats appear. As everyone fled from the stage, she'd had to race like the clappers down the corridor and into the back of the hall again, running up through the audience with Steven Prince dressed as a rat following hot on her tail. Ah, the simpler times in life.

The meeting began several minutes later, Allie leading to give an update on everything, and then Grace coming in to answer questions with her.

'It's always the same, isn't it?' a man on the front row said. 'You want us to give you information, but when we do, you do nothing with it.'

'That's not true, sir,' Allie replied. 'We have acted on lots of things that we've found out from friends and neighbours on the estate. We can't be everywhere just in case a crime is committed.'

'You don't seem to be anywhere at the moment. Look at what happened in Redmond Street earlier in the year, and now this!'

Murmurs of agreement went around the room.

Allie held up a hand to speak again, and they quietened down.

'Yes, let's *look* at what happened. Billy Whitmore's killer was apprehended. We were spurred on by information from the public. That's you.' She pointed to the man. 'And you.' She pointed to a woman sitting on the row behind him. 'And lots of people. So, if there's anything you can think of, that you've seen or heard, no matter how small, we'd be very grateful. We need to stop this kind of thing from happening again.'

There was nothing else forthcoming that they didn't already know, and the conversation drifted to things in general that were happening, which was not their remit. Some of the attendees were parents, asking about the welfare of the kids on the estates. Others were complaining about the antisocial behaviour of the gangs. None of them were willing to give any names. It was the same old, same old. People wanted to moan at the police but weren't prepared to co-operate when they were asked.

Except for one woman who waited until after most people had gone. Allie spotted her as she put the chairs back into piles around the outside of the room.

'Are you waiting for someone?' she shouted over to her.

'I'd like a word and I didn't want to say anything in front of so many people. Some of those kids have been running riot, and I don't want my windows to be smashed in if they find out I've been talking.'

'Do you have information for us?'

'I took a few photos of girls and boys I've seen hanging around a house in Lymer Road.'

Allie stopped what she was doing and went across to her.

The woman held out her phone.

Allie scrolled through them, the back of a girl in partic-ular catching her eye. She had long blonde hair and was wearing a red hoodie similar to the one she'd seen in Lymer Road earlier in the week. Could it be the same one?

'Is there anyone you know...?' Allie paused, hoping the woman would come forward with her name.

'Steph,' was all she offered. 'I don't want to say anymore. I just thought you could work out who's who from the photos.'

'Could I copy them?'

Steph nodded.

Allie airdropped them from one phone to another and then handed the mobile back.

'Thanks, I'll check these out. Is there anything else you'd like to tell me? Or show me?'

Steph shook her head. 'Just try and get it sorted out, please. I can't stand anyone being exploited. The gangs around here are getting worse, far more violent.'

Allie nodded. 'We'll always do our best. Thanks, you've been a great help.'

She rejoined Grace who was stacking the last of the chairs.

'Got anything?' Grace asked.

'Photos of people going in and out of Lymer Road. I'll send them through to you now but we can have a good nosy at them tomorrow.'

CHAPTER FORTY-SEVEN

Leanne took a pile of ironing upstairs and popped it on the end of Amy's bed. She hoped she wouldn't find the clothes on the floor in the morning. If she did, Amy would be ironing her own things from now on. She was no one's skivvy.

She smiled as she saw the array of make-up on her daughter's dressing table, recalling the time when she'd been fifteen herself and going out with her friends all the time. It had probably been more fun then, too. There had been none of the pressures to conform that there were nowadays, no social media channels to show yourself in a different light.

Amy was a bright child, so far unaffected by too much falseness. In some ways, she was still a little girl, but in others she was fast growing up. So far Leanne had been able to stop her having her eyebrows tattooed in that ridiculous way that, as a mother she hated, and she told Amy as often as she could not to do the trout pout thing when she was taking selfies. There was a whole generation of teenagers who were going to be embarrassed about that when they were older, she thought. Having said that, she'd had some bad perms and hair dye disasters in her time, so it was only part of growing up.

Turning to leave, she noticed a fork handle sticking out from under the bed. She bent to retrieve it and the plate it was on. She sighed, lowering herself to see if there was anything else festering away that Amy had hidden rather than take downstairs.

There was an envelope pushed into a book, its pages hard to close because it was so full. She reached for the envelope and looked inside. Her hand shot to her mouth. It was stuffed full of cash. Surely it couldn't be Amy's? Had Scott hidden it in there after the police had searched the house?

It was like history repeating itself. After Kit's death, Leanne had found envelopes of cash underneath their bed. There had been drugs, too, locked away in a small safe. She'd gone mad at Scott, telling him to get them out of the house immediately. To her knowledge, he hadn't brought any more home. This was puzzling.

As soon as he got in from work that evening, Leanne challenged him.

'I found this in Amy's bedroom,' she said, handing the envelope to him. 'Have you hidden it there, away from me?'

'No, it's not mine.' His eyes widened when he saw its contents. 'Have you counted it?'

'Four hundred and eighty pounds.'

'Where the hell has she got that from?'

Leanne's voice cracked. 'She must be involved with something to get that kind of money.'

'She could be saving it for someone.'

'Then where did *that* person get it from?'

'I don't know, but she's not like that.'

Tears welled in her eyes. 'I thought you weren't until I found out what had been going on for the past few years.'

Scott bristled. 'You know I have no choice but to do as Kenny says now. But that doesn't mean I'm going to sit back and watch our daughter get embroiled in it, too. Where is she tonight?'

'She's gone out with her friends, Dani and Leah.'

'Well, we'll talk to her about this when she gets in. I want to know what she's been up to.'

Leanne followed him downstairs, trying to put the worry out of her mind. She prayed Amy was saving the money for someone else, because she dreaded to think what their daughter would have been doing to earn that much herself.

A few minutes later, Scott was surprised to get a call from Connor. He raced upstairs and into the bathroom to take it without Leanne hearing.

'What's up?'

'I need to see you. It's about work.'

'What about it?'

'I'd rather not say on the phone.'

'Can't it wait until tomorrow?'

'No. Can you meet me on the car park of the White Lion in ten minutes?'

'I suppose so. But—'

The phone went dead. Scott cursed.

'Where are you going?' Leanne asked when she saw him putting on his jacket.

'The alarm's going off at work,' he lied. 'I have to slip out for half an hour.'

Leanne's shoulders drooped. 'You've only just got in.'

'I won't be long. I'll pick up a bottle of wine on the way back.'

Scott spotted Connor's clapped-out car as soon as he pulled into the car park. Connor got out of it and jumped into the passenger seat of his. He seemed agitated, checking all around him as if he was seeing if they were alone.

'What's going on?' Scott frowned. 'I haven't got all evening.'

'You know I like you, man,' Connor started. 'You're a fair boss and, well, I don't like seeing you set up.'

Scott eyed him warily, wondering what he knew. He kept quiet, and Connor continued to talk.

'I went past Car Wash City on Tuesday night. It was about half eight, and there was someone in there. I couldn't see who, but–'

'How did you know?'

'I saw lights on.'

'You sure?'

'I'm positive.' Connor nodded. 'I think someone set you up to take the rap for those drugs.'

'I'm well aware of that,' Scott snapped. 'It was obvious from the start. Do you have any idea who it would be?'

'Apart from Kenny himself?' He shrugged. 'I'm not sure. But I wanted you to know because we were all sent home for a reason. I just can't figure out why someone would want to get rid of you.'

Scott frowned. 'You think that's happening here?'

'Seems too obvious to me. And now with Davy Lewis and Milo Barker dead, we're falling in numbers. Do you think someone is trying to get rid of us all? I've had a feeling I've been followed for the past few nights.'

Scott laughed. 'You're being paranoid. No one's on your tail.'

'Really? How can you be so certain?'

'Because if they were, they'd be after Kenny, not you. You're too far down the chain.'

'Everyone has to start somewhere,' Connor said, clearly annoyed by his words.

'I didn't mean to put you down. For what it's worth, I

appreciate you looking out for me.' Scott relented. 'It's not too late for you to get out of this, you know.'

'What do you mean?'

'You're young, with no ties. You could leave Stoke, start again before you really get sucked in.'

'Ah, that's cool you should think of me. But I can't. I take care of my mum, with my sister. I don't mind what I do. I earn decent money.'

'You could end up doing time.'

'It's a risk, but I'll be fine. Besides, what else can I do? I screwed up at school, and the only other thing I'm good at is thieving.'

'What about college? Learning a trade? There must be something you can do?'

Connor shrugged. 'I doubt it.'

Once he'd left, Scott sat and thought about the conversation. Something was playing on his mind, almost chilling him to the core. Before Kit had died, had they been recruited as managers of the Longton branch to take the rap for everything that had been going on while Terry Ryder was in prison? It was clear someone was out to get him, but why now? Was it to do with Terry Ryder's pending release?

Scott had better start doing some digging of his own. Because if he had to get out of Stoke quickly, he wanted to know as much as possible about it beforehand.

CHAPTER FORTY-EIGHT

Having had a lift in with Grace that morning, rather than bringing two cars, Simon had been catching up on some work while waiting to get a lift home with her. A few minutes ago, she'd sent him a message to say she was nearly ready.

He let himself out through the side door of the office, coming out onto St John Street. As he crossed the road to walk down to the station, someone shouted to him.

'Excuse me.'

He stopped and turned to see two men walking towards him. When they drew level, the nearest grabbed his arm and marched him into the multi-storey car park.

'Hey!' he cried.

He was pushed forward, managing to stay on his feet. But when he turned to protest, the other man punched him in the face.

Simon staggered backwards, his hand to his mouth. What the hell was going on? Immediately, he sensed the danger he was in, realising he could do nothing about it. The lights were bright, but the woollen hats they were wearing had been rolled down to reveal they were balaclavas. In the split second he took to register this, they both came at him.

Fists rained on his face and then his stomach. He dropped to his knees, wondering if he'd been mistaken for someone else. Unable to ask, he curled in a ball as feet came at him next.

When he thought he could take no more, he blacked out.

He woke seconds later, momentarily unaware of his surroundings. The pain was unbearable, every part of him aching. Some were hurting really bad.

Even though his head was spinning, he pulled himself upright, spitting blood. He gagged at its taste.

He sat for a few moments, catching his breath. Looking up, there was no one around, no one to alert.

Holding on to his ribs, he managed to get his phone from his pocket. The corner of the screen was cracked, but it was still working. Pressing on Siri, he asked it to call Grace.

Grace was getting her coat when she took the call.

'I'm on my way,' she laughed. 'I promise!'

'Grace.'

The blood rushed to her brain when she heard the panic in his voice.

'Simon? What's wrong?'

'Some guys jumped me. I'm in the multi-storey car park, ground floor.'

'What? Stay there. I'm on my way!' She kept the line connected as she ran out of the room and down the stairs, almost bowling an officer into the wall on her rush to get past him.

'Emergency, Dan,' she shouted to him.

'Do you need help?'

'Yes, thanks!'

He followed behind her.

'It's my husband.' She dashed out of the building. 'He's been attacked in the multi-storey car park.'

The building was only a few hundred metres away, and they were soon with him. Simon was sitting up, leaning against the wall. She spotted a young couple at his side. The man stood up as she and Dan approached.

'Are you Grace?'

'Yes.' Grace dropped to the floor. 'Did you see what happened?'

'No. We found him lying here when we came back to our car. He told us he'd called you. I think he needs an ambulance.'

'I'll sort that out.' Dan got out his phone.

'Thanks.' Grace didn't take her eyes from Simon, blood trickling from his nose into his mouth. His right eye had already started to swell, bruising appearing elsewhere.

'Grace,' Simon muttered, upset when he heard her voice.

She reached for his hand, unsure whether to hug him until he'd been checked over. 'I'm here. You're safe now. We'll get you sorted.'

His head flopped to the side, and she helped him to lie down. Tears welled as she checked out the cameras to see if any would have caught the attack. But Simon seemed to be in a blind spot. The men who had jumped him knew exactly where they should target him.

The question was who, and why? And was it a random attack or something more sinister?

On Leek Road, DCI Cooper was behind Connor Lightwood in a marked car. They'd been waiting for him outside Stoke Station, and once he'd picked up the girl who had come off the train, they'd tailed him.

Shaun didn't think he'd noticed them until suddenly Connor sped off. He'd had no choice but to activate the lights and sirens.

There were two vehicles in pursuit, a marked car behind him. It took them both advanced driving skills to keep up with Connor and adhere to the public's safety. The lad flew across a main roundabout, but they stayed behind him.

Shaun floored it along Leek Road, hoping to get to him before he hit the main set of lights ahead.

The road divided into four lanes of traffic. Connor took the right lane, the lights ahead changing from amber to red, but still his speed increased.

Shaun slammed his brakes on as a lorry crashed into the side of Connor's car ahead. The crunch of metal on metal was deafening, and then silence. He removed his seatbelt and got out.

'Call it in,' he barked at a uniformed officer and rushed to the scene of the accident.

The car had spun and come to a halt facing the opposite way to the traffic. The driver's door had been crumpled by the truck, but Connor had managed to get out somehow. He ran for a few yards, then collapsed to the ground, turning on his back.

'Stay where you are,' Shaun shouted to a young girl who was in the passenger seat. She was sitting forwards, her hair shielding her face and the red hoodie she was wearing covering up any potential injuries.

'Are you okay?' he asked.

'I think so.'

'Try not to move. Help will be here soon. We'll get you out of there.' Shaun went to check on Connor who was out cold. He radioed through, requesting the ETA of the ambulance.

Another officer had gone to see if the truck driver was okay.

'He's distraught and in shock, but he's walking wounded, sir,' he told him on his return.

'Which is more than I can say for these two.' He pointed to the ground. 'He has a nasty gash on his head.'

Limekiln traffic lights was a major junction, several lanes of traffic in each direction. The area was carnage, and they needed to get at least some of the roads on the junction open again.

'Can you cordon off these two lanes here?' he added. 'Get the traffic from these four lanes to go across the road towards the Abbey. No one turns right. And get someone to turn off the traffic lights.'

The officer nodded and ran to his vehicle. Within minutes, everything was set up. It was busy, organised chaos, but things were moving. Emergency vehicles would be able to reach them quicker, too.

Noticing the girl was trying to get out of the car, Shaun went back to her.

'Please stay still until the paramedics have assessed you,' he urged.

But the girl didn't listen, and he had to restrain her gently.

'Connor?' she screamed. 'Connor.' She looked at Shaun.

'You're okay, duck.' Shaun smiled. 'You've been in an accident. The ambulance is on its way. Can you tell me your name?'

'It's Amy. Amy Milton.'

CHAPTER FORTY-NINE

Allie had barely sat down at home when her phone rang.

'Hi, Grace,' she said, immediately wondering if something was wrong having only left her half an hour ago.

She sat forward while Grace explained what had happened.

'I'm coming to you,' she said. 'I'll be as quick as I can.'

'What is it?' Mark was staring at her with concern.

'Simon's been beaten up in the car park across from the station.'

'What?' He dropped his feet from the coffee table. 'Is he okay?'

'He's going to the Royal Stoke. Sorry, I have to go out again.'

'I'm coming with you.' Mark reached for the jumper he'd discarded on the chair and tugged it on. 'He's my friend, too. I'll drive.'

Allie gave him a faint smile of appreciation. She stood, finishing her coffee in one long gulp. They were out of the house in minutes.

'Did she say what had happened?' Mark asked, reversing the car out of the drive.

'He was jumped by two men as he came out of work. They pulled him into the car park and attacked him.'

'Were they after his money?'

'She didn't say. Apparently, he's not making much sense at the moment.'

The twenty minutes it took them to get to the hospital, park up, and rush to A&E seemed to take forever. Grace's eyes were red raw when they found her in a side room, an empty place for a trolley bed beside her. She rushed into Allie's arms and hugged her tightly.

'How is he?' Allie asked.

'He's gone for a CT scan. He passed out a couple of times before he got here, although he's been conscious since.' She sniffed. 'I knew he shouldn't have got too involved. He's always been so careful, but I think everything was getting under his skin.' Her eyes filled with fresh tears. 'Do you think this was a warning from Martin Smith?'

'I'm sure that isn't what's happened.'

'I'll go and get some drinks,' Mark said. 'There must be a machine around here.'

Allie and Grace sat down.

Allie reached for Grace's hands. 'You need to tell me what you know.'

'He said he'd work late and come home with me when I was done. He's been working on a big feature which will be spread over a week, about the effect of crime in the city. Just as I was about to leave, I got a call from him. He sounded slurred, like he was drunk. He only said my name, and I knew he was hurt. I ran out... I bumped into Dan Macintyre, and he helped me.' Tears poured down her face. 'You don't think he's in any danger now, do you? What if someone comes back to finish off the job?'

'Then he has you to look after him.' Allie smiled, hoping to soothe her.

Grace wiped at her eyes. 'What if he'd died? I can't go through losing someone again.'

Grace's first husband had passed away of leukaemia in his early thirties. Grace had nursed him until his death and had taken years to get through her grief. Meeting Simon had brought her such happiness. It was as if her life had started again.

'Hey, he'll be fine,' Allie tried to reassure her. 'He's made of strong stuff, especially that thick head of his.' She glanced at the clock to see it was nearing nine o'clock. 'It's too late to call anyone back in now, but rest assured, we'll be on to it as soon as we can.'

'I wouldn't want anyone in until the morning anyway, but thanks.'

'Are you kidding? Frankie and Perry will go berserk if we don't include them. I'll get Sam on the CCTV. We'll find whoever did this.'

Mark returned with the drinks while they waited for Simon. Twenty minutes went past, and he was back from having his scan. Allie and Mark stepped out into the corridor while the consultant spoke to him and Grace.

'Have you found out anything else?' Mark asked, reaching for her hand.

'Not a lot. I'll fill you in on the way home.'

A few minutes later, the curtain was pulled back and the consultant appeared, smiling at them before he left. They were shocked to see what state Simon was in.

Allie grimaced. 'Ouch, that looks painful, Mr Cole.'

'That's nothing to what I'm going to do when I get him home again,' Grace muttered, although she was smiling with relief. 'His scan is clear.'

Allie smiled as Grace held on to Simon's hand.

'At least I might get a box of chocolates or a magazine out of you, Shenton,' Simon joked, then groaned. 'Ouch indeed.'

'Really, how are you?' Mark asked. 'You look like you've done twelve rounds in a boxing ring and lost.'

'Cuts and bruises, a broken rib, and my eye, as you can see, is still swelling. They're keeping me in overnight for observation, probably here on this trolley, but I think I'll be able to go home tomorrow.'

'That's good news. Shame it didn't knock any sense into you,' Allie teased. 'Have you remembered anything about what happened?'

'Switch off, Allie,' Mark chided. 'It can wait until tomorrow.'

'No, it's fine.' Simon pulled himself up the bed a little more, grimacing in pain. 'I'd like to talk while I remember it all.'

As Allie listened to Simon telling her about his ordeal, she couldn't help but wonder if this *was* to do with him following Martin Smith. If Smith had told Kenny, it could be a warning for Simon to stay away, or even be careful what he printed in the *Stoke News*.

'How many people knew you were working tonight?' she asked.

'There were a couple of us in the office.'

'People you trust?'

'You're not suggesting—'

'Unless someone was sitting in their car for several hours waiting for you to finish, they knew you were still at work. We'll check all the vehicles and streets in the vicinity.'

'It won't be anyone from my office.'

'Probably not, but it means *someone* could have been following you for a while,' Grace remarked. 'And could know where we live.'

'I'm so sorry.' Simon turned to Grace, his face etched in pain. 'I didn't think.'

'You could have put us both in danger.'

'Not necessarily,' Allie pacified. 'If every officer who was followed home had to move, our houses would be up for sale all the time.' She was trying to appease them the only way she knew how. Humour.

It wasn't working, even though Grace gave her a faint smile.

'We need to work out who attacked you now, and why.' Allie stood up, checking her watch. 'It's late. Get some rest, and I'll deal with this in the morning. I'm not sure we have the manpower for it at the moment, but we'll be giving it top propriety as soon as we can.'

'It's fine. There's no need—'

'No one assaults my friend and gets away with it.' She smiled faintly, too. 'See you both soon, and take care, Simon.'

'I'll be in as quick as I can tomorrow,' Grace replied.

'Like hell you will.'

'But—'

'See you next week, at the earliest.'

'Thanks, Allie.'

Just then, a couple rushing into a cubicle at the end of the corridor caught Allie's eye, and she frowned. If she wasn't mistaken, that was Leanne and Scott Milton.

What were they doing at A&E?

CHAPTER FIFTY

Friday

Riley disconnected her phone and sat down on the bed with a thump. The call she'd received was about a car crash the night before. She couldn't believe what had happened. She'd known Connor for years, quite liked him really. He wasn't as cocky as some of the lads she worked with. She hoped he was okay.

And was the girl he'd been caught with, Amy, the one she'd met a few times? If it was, Riley knew she hadn't been working with them long. Having said that, this was all hearsay until the police confirmed everything. But she had no reason not to believe it wasn't true.

It had thrown her, the police catching up with Connor. They could be watching her, too. She had to talk to her mum.

Stepping out of her bedroom onto the landing, she heard her sister singing quietly in the bathroom, the water from the shower running. Quickly, she tiptoed downstairs. She didn't want Kelsey to hear their conversation.

Fiona took one look at her and baulked. 'You're as white as a sheet. Are you okay?'

'Not really.' Riley told her what she knew.

'It sounds like he was trying to get away from the feds,' she finished. 'He went through Limekiln lights on red, and a lorry slammed into him.'

'Oh no.' Fiona sat down.

'There was a girl with him, too.' Riley sat near to her on the settee. 'She's in hospital as well.'

'Do you know her?'

Riley nodded. 'She's been working for Connor for a few months.'

'Were they waiting for them at the station, after a drop-off?'

'I think so.' Riley glanced at her mum. 'What are we going to do now? They've lost Connor *and* a runner. What happens if they want Kelsey to take her place? You can't let them do that.'

'You know I won't have any say in the matter.'

'Of course you will. I-I'm going to speak to Allie.'

'No.'

'She said she'd help us and—'

'That was a long time ago. You can't say anything. Kenny will find out, and you know how angry he can get. He'll hurt you.'

'This wasn't Kenny running Connor off the road. It was the police.'

'You don't know that for certain. Kenny is sneaky. He could have set it up.'

Riley glared at her. Sometimes she could be so stupid.

'So you think Kenny got someone waiting in a lorry to ram into Connor the exact minute he goes through a red light at Limekiln Bank, after a car chase he didn't know was happening? I don't think so.'

Fiona looked on sheepishly. 'If he isn't behind it, it won't matter to Kenny. He doesn't care who gets hurt, or caught, as long as nothing leads back to him.'

Riley leaned forward. 'If we don't do something, he's going to run our lives forever.'

'If we *don't* do as he says, he'll come after us. You know what he did to me earlier in the year. He beat me up so badly that I ended up in hospital.'

'I can't do this anymore, Mum,' Riley sobbed. 'I want out.'

'It's not your choice. You have to do what Kenny says. If you don't, I'll be in trouble then, as well as you.'

'But I promised Kelsey that I'd take care of her. She's a good kid, and I want what's best for her. I don't want her to get involved!'

'Kelsey needs a mother *and* a sister,' Fiona cried. 'She'll have neither of us if you open your mouth.'

'I have to.'

'No! You need to think this through, and see how it affects us all.'

After a moment's deliberation, Riley shook her head. 'I'm calling Allie right now. She'll know what to do.'

Kelsey burst into the room. 'Please don't call Allie.'

Riley and Fiona physically jumped.

'What's going on?' Fiona's brow furrowed.

'Because... I should have gone to Stockport with Amy last night.'

'No, no, no.' Fiona ran her hands over her face. 'Please don't say you've been doing runs on the train.'

Kelsey dropped her eyes momentarily.

'I told you not to!'

'I didn't get caught.'

'Maybe not now, but if the police have been watching Connor, they might have seen you at the station with Amy.' Riley paused. 'Did you ever go alone to do any runs?'

'A few times.'

'I told you to keep out of anything like this,' Fiona snapped. 'Why wouldn't you listen?'

'Because Connor said it would be okay.'

'Connor Lightwood?'

'Yes, why? Wait. How do you know his name?'

'Is he just a friend?' Fiona asked, gently, throwing Riley a warning scowl not to say anything.

Kelsey shook her head.

'Dear God.'

'I haven't slept with him, if that's what you mean,' Kelsey protested. 'He's just nice to me.'

'He's using you!' Riley cried. 'I bet he has a lot of other girls he does the same thing to.'

'He wouldn't do that to me.'

'What about Mallory? Does she do runs as well?'

'Yes, but he isn't her boyfriend. He doesn't really like her that much.'

'Have you done any runs recently?' Fiona asked

Kelsey nodded. 'Mallory has done three. We both went with Amy the first time.'

'Oh, Kelsey.' Fiona's shoulders sagged. 'We warned you not to get involved.'

'It was your fault! I was threatened. "If you don't help, I'll get your mother and your sister in trouble." They said it'd only take a phone call to the police and either of you could end up in prison.'

'Who said that?' Fiona asked.

'Connor told me.'

'He threatened you?' Riley glared at Kelsey.

'No, not him. He told me what Kenny had said, and I believed him.' Kelsey's bottom lip trembled. 'I thought if I helped out, neither of you would get in trouble.'

Kelsey was crying now. Riley went to her, pulling her down to sit on the settee next to her.

'It's okay,' she soothed. 'We can sort this.'

'It wasn't fair that they pressured you,' Fiona added.

'But I swore to you that I would never have anything to do with Kenny Webb,' Kelsey sobbed.

'So did I,' Riley admitted. 'Sometimes we have to keep each other safe.'

And sometimes, you have to do the right thing despite the consequences, she said to herself. She would go and speak to Allie Shenton. But first, Kelsey had a right to know what had happened to Connor.

'Kelsey, there's been an accident,' she said.

CHAPTER FIFTY-ONE

Leanne sat by her daughter's bedside. It was half past eight. Scott had gone to get coffee for them both, having been there since the night before. In the early hours of the morning, Amy had been transferred to the children's ward. She was in a small bay off the main nurses' station.

Leanne tried to keep her tears at bay, hoping Amy wouldn't hear her crying. The call from the police on Amy's mobile had shocked her to the core. She and Scott had raced to the hospital, praying that Amy would be okay.

When they saw her, she was confused, crying out for Connor, and asking where she was. Amy didn't seem to remember anything about the accident. Leanne didn't know if that was a good thing or not.

Then she'd started to find out details of what had been happening. There had been a police chase. Connor had gone through Limekiln lights, across four lanes of traffic, but he hadn't made it to the other side. Leanne had wanted to know more but knew that conversation was for today, rather than last night.

She looked at her child, an ache in her heart as she knew

she had let her down. Amy had broken her arm as she'd hung on to the door handle. She had a gash on her head that they were monitoring for concussion, but she was going to be okay.

Today Leanne was blaming herself. If she hadn't let Scott continue to work at Car Wash City, if she had been stronger and warned him not to stay involved with Kenny Webb, none of this would have happened.

They should have left Stoke-on-Trent after Kit's death. There was nothing to stay here for. Amy could have done her last year of school somewhere else, and they might have been safe. Now, what a mess they were all in.

Yet, even as she thought it, she knew it was impossible. Kenny Webb was never going to leave their family alone.

Amy's eyes flickered before opening properly. She glanced around, confused by her surroundings. For a moment, panic set in, and then her gaze landed on her mum's face.

'Hey, darling. It's okay.' Leanne sensed Amy's panic.

'Where am I?'

'You're in hospital, but you're all right.'

Actually, that might not be the case, Leanne surmised. Amy had been told about the accident. Had something happened to her memory, or could it be shock?

But then Leanne watched, as it all seemed to come rushing back to her.

'Connor.' Amy tried to sit up. 'What happened to him? Is he okay?'

'The doctor is with him at the moment.' She hoped that would appease her for now, until she could tell her how badly he'd been injured. 'How are you feeling? Do you hurt anywhere?'

Amy seemed to shrink into herself.

'It's okay. We know about the police. All that can wait until later.'

Amy swallowed. 'I'm in so much trouble.'

'Try not to think about that.' Leanne stroked her cheek. 'Just rest for now. Everything will be okay.'

'Where's Dad?'

'He's gone to fetch a newspaper and something to eat. We've been here all night.'

Leanne had so many questions, and she didn't want to exhaust Amy. But she needed answers. Had her little girl been groomed? Was that where the money she'd found in her bedroom had come from? What had she been doing with Connor Lightwood?

This morning, she and Scott had had a blazing row outside in the car park. Amy could have only met Connor through Scott, she'd said, accusing him of getting their daughter into trouble. Scott had said he hadn't introduced them. They could have met through Amy's friends. They'd calmed down now, it had been a way of letting off steam, although they were still quiet with each other.

But Leanne didn't want to face anything else yet, and she knew the police would be here again soon. She wasn't even sure she could cope with this on top of everything else. Her family had been through enough during the past six months.

She gritted her teeth: of course she would cope. Like any mother, she would protect her child, comfort her, even when she was in the wrong.

'Mum, is Connor okay?' Amy spoke in a tiny voice.

'He's unconscious at the moment. He took a bang to his head, so they've put him in an induced coma to ease the pressure.'

'But he's going to be okay, isn't he?'

'We'll know more later, sweetheart.'

Scott came bustling into the room, his hands full of coffee and brown paper bags.

'I managed to get us a bacon buttie,' he said, the newspaper that was in the crook of his arm falling onto the foot of the bed. 'Hey, munchkin, how are you doing?' He smiled at Amy.

Amy burst into tears again, unable to get any words out.

Leanne held her while she cried, tears of her own pouring down her face. How she hated this place. She was tired of seeing so much of it. First when Kit had died, then when an attempt on Scott's life had left him battered and bruised. And now, Amy, her little girl, was lying injured.

Leanne wondered how Amy would cope mentally. How they all would, really. This was going to have a massive impact on them, as a family but also individually, too. If Connor didn't survive, Amy would be devastated. If he did survive, Scott would blame himself for being involved with Kenny. If things got worse because of this, they'd start blaming each other. She didn't want all that again. She'd had enough arguing earlier in the year to last a lifetime. All she wanted was a bit of peace and quiet.

Sadly, she had the feeling that things were going to get a whole lot worse before they got better. She wasn't looking forward to that at all.

CHAPTER FIFTY-TWO

As soon as she got into work that morning, Allie had let the team know what had happened to Simon. Everyone was shocked, to say the least.

'Did he give any descriptions?' Perry asked.

'He got a brief glimpse of both men, but they had balaclavas on rolled up as hats and then pulled them down once they got out of sight. It all happened so fast he can't recall anything now.'

'So it was planned. That's a whole new level of scary.'

'It seems that way. Someone was waiting for him.' Allie turned to Sam. 'Can I leave you with the CCTV footage to go through, please? I know it's not top priority for now, but we can get the ball rolling so when we have time, we can look at it in more detail.'

'Yes, of course. I'm glad he's going to be okay.'

'It's bloody typical that it happens this morning, when everything is about to kick off.' Allie's mobile rang. 'Speaking of the devil. Hi, Shaun.'

'Hey, Allie. There's been a development I think you

should be aware of. Scott Milton's daughter, Amy, was involved in a car accident last night.'

Allie frowned, remembering seeing the Miltons the night before. 'I know her. Well, I know her parents. How is she?'

'She's going to be fine, but she was with Connor Lightwood who came off far worse. It seems like she's been a runner for him, on the Stockport run, via train. We found two thousand pounds in a bag in the glove compartment.'

'Christ. Are the whole bloody Milton family involved in this racket?'

'It's possible.'

'Was she admitted, do you know?'

'Yeah, I've just checked. Connor was, too. His head's taken a bashing. He's in ICU.'

'Thanks for letting me know.' Allie pinched the bridge of her nose in dismay. 'Are you okay with me going up now, talking to Amy and her family? I know it's not my remit, but I do know them and might possibly be able to get some intel from them now.'

'Yes, that's fine.'

'Thanks. Oh, did you know Simon Cole was attacked last night, too?'

'I heard. I reckon everything that's gone on this week is connected in some way.'

Allie had cause to think the same.

'And you'll keep me in the loop about everything this morning?' she queried.

'With pleasure.'

She grabbed her car keys and headed to the hospital. She had to see what had been going on. This had gone too far. And, if nothing else, she might get some useful information for the Organised Crime Unit.

. . .

Allie was shown to Amy Milton's bay, and a curtain was drawn around them. The next bed was empty, giving them enough privacy for a chat.

Despite only knowing the family briefly, Allie recognised Scott and Leanne were hurting. Leanne's eyes were red and swollen, and Scott looked as if he hadn't slept in a month. She was sure they wouldn't be best pleased to see her again, but she had to try and make them understand the trouble they might find themselves in.

'How are you, Amy?' Allie asked first.

'Hurting,' Amy replied. 'But I want to see Connor.'

'He's stable, that's all I can tell you for now. He seems to have had a good night. You might be able to see him once he's been assessed again, if you're able to get out of bed yourself.'

Amy frowned. 'So why is he in a coma?'

'Mainly because his brain has suffered a trauma and it might swell too much for his body to work on its own, causing other problems.' Allie held up a hand seeing Amy's bottom lip trembling. 'I'd rather tell you straight. He's quite sick at the moment and he'll need to be monitored, but did you know we have an excellent trauma team here? You might have seen them on TV.'

Allie smiled at Scott as he offered her a chair. She sat down next to Amy, on the opposite side to her parents. Both seemed distraught, worry etched in every atom of their bodies. She'd have to tread carefully not to cause them any more worry, but equally she needed the truth.

'Shall I leave you to it?' Scott said, almost at the door in his eagerness to get away.

'No, I'd like you both here, please,' Allie said. 'I think as a family you all need to know what's been going on.' She turned to Amy. 'I know you're frightened, but you have terrific parents who will be by your side. We all make mistakes when we're young. It's about what happens afterwards that makes us stronger. Are you able to answer a few questions for me?'

Amy glanced at Leanne who urged her to speak with a nod.

'Okay,' Amy replied.

'Thank you. I'm going to record it on my phone. Then, once you're feeling better, I'll get this typed up for you and we can run through it again. Can you tell me where you'd been before you got into Connor's car?'

Amy gasped, her eyes widening in fear.

'It's okay.' Leanne tried to calm her. 'We know you've been catching the train to Stockport to drop off a parcel and collect another.'

'Please, let me do the talking,' Allie said to Leanne.

Leanne stared at her wide-eyed, a little put out, but then she nodded.

'I'm in big trouble, aren't I?' Amy whispered.

'The more you can tell us the better it will be,' Allie said. 'You don't have to be afraid. Your mum and dad are here for you.'

Allie glanced at Scott.

'It's true, Amy,' he encouraged. 'It doesn't matter what you've done. We love you.'

'We'll always love you,' Leanne added. 'We'll get you through this mess, and hopefully put it all behind you.'

'So, Amy?' Allie urged, before Leanne became too emotional. 'Can you tell me what happened last night?'

CHAPTER FIFTY-THREE

'I got back from Stockport, and Connor was waiting to pick me up outside the station,' Amy said. 'When we pulled off, he was okay at first, but as he drove along Leek Road, he said there was someone following us.'

'Was that a police car?'

'It was just a black car to me. I didn't understand what he was worrying about. But then lights started to flash, and I heard sirens.'

Allie watched as Leanne gave Amy's hand a squeeze, at the same time wiping a tear from her face with the other. Despite her frustration, and her warnings to the family, she couldn't help but feel pained at how everything had worked out for them.

'I told Connor to pull over, but he said he didn't want to get caught,' Amy went on. 'He said if they'd been waiting for him, they would have seen me on the train, following me to see who I delivered to at the other end. I told him we *had* to stop, and that's when he put his foot down.'

Scott cursed under his breath and paced the room.

'I'm sorry!' Amy cried.

'It's okay, Amy. Your dad is just worried about you, that's all.' Leanne shot him a warning look, and he flopped down in his seat again.

'Connor said he was going to lose them, and if not, we'd have to bail out and do a runner. He said it would be easier not to catch us if we went in different directions. I was so scared; I didn't want him to leave me. And then he was flying along Leek Road towards Limekiln lights.'

'This is good, Amy,' Allie encouraged. 'What happened next?'

'Connor said if he could get through the lights, he could lose the police.'

Tears poured down Amy's face. Leanne was glaring at Allie, imploring her to stop without saying so, but Allie had no intention of doing that yet.

'He almost ran into the back of a car, and I was screaming,' Amy said. 'I could see the police were still behind us. And then... Connor went through the lights on red. That's when... when... Is he really going to be okay?'

'We'll know more later.' Allie wanted to keep the conversation going. 'There was an envelope of money in the car, Amy. Do you know where that had come from?'

'I-I went to Stockport to pick it up.'

'Tell me about that, please.'

Amy glanced at Leanne, who nodded reassuringly to her.

'I take packages to Stockport on the train. When I get there, I meet a man called Eddie. Sometimes I see him in his car, sometimes we go to the café in the station. A few times, I've met him in the Rose and Crown, next to the station.'

'You're fifteen!' Scott cried. 'You shouldn't really be in a pub.'

'Scott,' Allie heeded. 'Amy?'

'We swap envelopes, then I come back to Stoke and give the new one to Connor.'

'Do you know what's inside either of them?' Allie probed.

Amy nodded, tears in her eyes.

'So why did you get involved?' Leanne asked.

'Again, I need to ask the questions, Leanne,' Allie said, turning back to Amy.

'Everyone was doing it, not just me.'

'Everyone?'

Amy clammed up.

'How often did you do that journey?' Allie prompted.

'Once or twice a fortnight.'

'And how long in total have you been visiting Stockport?'

'Three months.'

Scott groaned, running his hand over his chin.

'Did Connor take you to the station and then collect you on your return every time?'

'Yes.'

'Did he drop you off somewhere or did he go anywhere first?'

'I just gave him the envelope and then he'd take me home.'

'Did you do any day trips?' Allie asked.

'No.'

'Has Connor ever mistreated you, to get you to do jobs for him?'

'No, he's lovely to me! He's really nice.'

Allie spotted Scott's fists clenching and unclenching. A nurse came in to see to Amy, and Allie took the opportunity to ask both parents if she could speak to them away from the ward.

In the corridor, they stood to the side. Allie was aware that she'd need to caution them if the conversation brought up anything interesting.

'I know there's more to this than what Amy is telling me. If you knew she was involved, then—'

'We didn't know,' Leanne insisted. 'Do you think we'd be happy about it if we had?'

'You don't understand what it's like,' Scott reiterated.

'So tell me,' Allie implored. 'I can't help until you do.'

Scott said nothing else.

'I'm tired of living my life like this, Scott.' Leanne rested her hand on his arm. 'We need to talk to someone.'

'We *can't* say anything. It will be more than our lives are worth.' Scott shrugged his wife's hand off and stormed away.

'Scott!' Allie went to follow him but decided against it. Instead, she turned back to Leanne. 'Talk to Amy, see what she will tell you when I'm not there. Any information she gives you about what's been going on, I need to know.'

'It's too dangerous.'

Allie pointed back to the entrance of the ward. 'Your little girl in there is suffering because of what you and Scott are doing. Do you want her to get embroiled any more than she is? Because, believe me, Kenny Webb and his merry men won't think anything of hurting a child to get to Mum and Dad.'

Leanne gasped.

'I won't sugar-coat this. Just talk to me. This mess needs sorting out, once and for all.'

Leanne said nothing.

A text message came in on Allie's phone. 'I'll get an officer to take a statement from you, and then maybe I could speak with you both after that?'

Leanne glanced Allie's way and then gave her the briefest of nods.

It was a start.

CHAPTER FIFTY-FOUR

The text message was from the ICU staff nurse, saying that she could come to them now. Allie quickly walked over. At the door, she buzzed to be let in and sterilised her hands while she waited.

ICU was always so quiet compared to the hustle and bustle of everyday wards. A nurse informed her that Connor's mum and sister were in the relatives' room. Going in, Allie introduced herself and sat down across from them both.

Connor's mum was in a wheelchair, her hands in her lap. She was in her mid-fifties, perhaps. It was hard to tell because she was hunched up so much and in a lot of pain. The young girl beside her seemed to be the same age as Connor and was the image of her brother, enough for Allie to wonder if they were twins. But as she drew closer, she could see she was a little younger than she'd first assumed. She was dressed for work, in a green outfit of trousers and sweatshirt. A badge with a firm's logo on it named her, trainee written underneath it.

'How is he?' Allie asked, a sense of déjà vu taking over as

she'd said that same thing for the third time over the past few hours.

'He's critical but stable,' the older woman said. 'I'm his mother, Sandra. This is his sister, Claire.'

'And you're aware of everything that happened last night?'

'He was run off the road because he was scared of you,' Claire replied. 'You did this to him.'

'Come on now, duck,' Sandra said. 'This is no one's fault but your brother's. How is the girl who was with him?'

'She's okay, mostly cuts and bruises.' And a tad scared of what's going to happen to her, Allie kept to herself. 'Is there anything you can tell me?'

'Connor has been mixed up in a bad crowd since that Davy Lewis, you know, the one who's been murdered, started hanging around. I knew he'd get Connor in trouble, but no matter how many times I told him to be careful, he just laughed it off. He said he was smarter than Davy.' She looked at Allie. 'What could I do to stop him in my condition?'

'I'm sorry.' Allie was being genuine. How indeed could she stop him doing anything?

'Please find out why my boy was involved in something that nearly cost him his life, then jail the bastard who's leading him astray.'

If only it were that simple. Allie's thoughts strayed to Operation Dexter. The raids should be happening now, her stomach flipping as her nerves got the better of her.

'Do you know either Kenny Webb or Martin Smith? Milo Barker? Or anyone named Eddie?' she finished.

'I've heard Connor mention them all at one time or another,' Claire spoke out.

'Any recently?' Allie asked her.

'He told me he was trying to get in with Kenny Webb now that Davy Lewis had been wiped out.' Claire shook her head. 'He was almost proud when he said that.'

'I can't believe what my son has been up to.' Sandra shook her head in embarrassment. 'One minute he's loving, caring for his sick mother, and helping his sister, and the next he's involved in some dodgy dealing with despicable people. He hasn't been the same since his dad disappeared.'

Allie was familiar with the case of Derek Lightwood. Now a cold one, she hoped it would be solved one day. People often skipped town, came back, and stayed or left again, throughout the years. A few never came home. Yet, for someone to go off the grid completely, with no cash withdrawals, no bank cards used since, was highly suspicious. Unfortunately, the officers working the case had drawn a blank with no hard evidence.

'I don't have anything to tell you that will help, I'm afraid,' Sandra went on. 'I'm really sorry about what he's done.'

'It's not your fault, Mum,' Claire spoke out in her defence.

'Sure it is.'

'No, it really isn't,' Allie said. 'As a parent you can only do so much.'

Allie's stomach gave an involuntary flip at what might come in her life soon. Would she ever get to the stage where she thought she'd failed a foster child? She hoped not but knew it was entirely likely.

'You take care,' she added. 'Connor's going to need someone strong to rely on. I hope he makes a swift recovery.'

Allie didn't mention they would be talking to Connor as soon as he was able to respond. She'd do that when she was sure he'd survive. There was no point in causing any more pain to the family until then. Connor was young. Hopefully he would fight to stay alive, whatever had happened to him.

And then they'd talk.

Another text message came in from Dave Barnett asking her to ring him when she was free. The corridors outside the ward were busy, so she took the call in her car.

'Please say you have something for me,' she said.

'I do, as a matter of fact.'

'At last!' Allie couldn't help but laugh. 'From which case, though? I have so many coming at me.'

'Well, the information I have might make things easier.'

'Sounds good. Go on.'

'We have a match on our system to the blood samples we found on Milo Barker's body, in particular from beneath his fingernails. They belong to Philip Barker. We also have his fingerprints on the inside of the bedroom door and on the handle.'

'You're kidding!' Allie gasped, recalling the scratches on Philip's face and neck when she'd told him and his mother of Milo's death. 'Well, I know you're not, but really?'

'Yes. That's his brother, isn't it?'

'I'm afraid so. His mum is going to be distraught.'

'I dislike families attacking each other even more than druggies killing one another.'

'Me, too, but nice work. I assume you have enough for us to charge him with?'

'I'm sure we have.'

'Great stuff. We'll bring him in.' She was about to add when they could but stopped just in time. Besides, as far as they were concerned, Philip Barker wasn't involved with Car Wash City. There was time to be proved wrong yet, though.

Allie drove away from the hospital, thankful for the change of scenery. She couldn't wait to get back to the station and share the news. There were so many things she needed to catch up with, tell people about, and points to action. She also had to talk to Jenny about the forensics found on Milo Barker's body.

That was without the raids.

It was going to be a busy day, and it had barely started.

CHAPTER FIFTY-FIVE

Kenny hadn't slept much the night before. All he wanted was to do the exchange that morning and he was leaving. Stuff everything else. He'd already started packing a few things to take with him that weekend, so it wasn't any trouble bringing his plans forward.

Now, it was just after nine. He'd barely got out of the shower when he heard his phone ringing. He rushed to answer it, expecting a meet-up time and place. It was then he saw several messages, too.

The call was from Eddie, one of the men in Stockport.

'Something's going down,' he said. 'Two of my guys have been pulled out of bed by the cops this morning.'

'Fuck!' Kenny gasped. 'Was it a dawn raid?'

'Yeah, took them all by surprise. Luckily, I wasn't in when they got to mine. I was staying over at my mate's house after a skinful last night. My missus is pissed off, but I can't go home.'

'Are you bailing?'

'I might have to. I'll keep my head down and wait it out a

bit. Just wanted to give you the heads-up. They might come to Stoke, too.'

'Yeah, cheers, Ed. I'll check out what's going on at this end and get back to you when I can. Look after yourself.'

Kenny disconnected the call and quickly skimmed the messages he'd been left. As well as the time for his exchange that morning, he found out that some of his crew had been arrested, too. He'd better get a move on in case the police came knocking on his door.

He stopped for a moment. There was one hundred grand in a bag, waiting to give to Chris at this morning's swap. He could leave with that, without going to meet him. That would be ample to tide him over, plus the money of his own that he had. Once Terry knew he was gone, he'd be on the run anyway. But was it really too risky to get the rest of his money from the house in Alexander Place?

Quickly, he gathered together his stuff, shoving a few more clothes into a suitcase as well as an overnight bag. It might be a while before he came back home, if at all.

His phone rang again. The caller ID flashed up Martin. He ignored it while he zipped up his case. There was no time for him right now.

Downstairs, he took the luggage out to his car and put it in the boot. Then he collected his laptop, emptied his safe of the three grand petty cash he kept in there, and his passport. He would stop for breakfast when he was well away.

Before he left, he checked his phone once more. Martin had called five times, and there were several messages from him, too. He pressed his number.

'What the fuck's going on?' he said, not giving the man time to speak when he answered.

'We're being hunted, left, right, and centre. I don't know what to do!'

'Where are you?'

'At home, but I don't feel safe. I keep thinking the police are going to knock on the door.'

'I'd get out if I were you. Grab some things and lie low.' He sniggered. 'Head to Manchester. You have something set up there, don't you?'

'No, I—'

'Don't bullshit me. I know you're up to something.' Kenny picked up the bag with the money in it and opened the front door.

'Wait! You have to help me. I don't know what to do!'

'That's your problem, not mine. Don't think I haven't guessed what you've been up to behind my back.'

'What do you mean? I haven't done anything.'

'Don't lie to me! You've been working with Terry for a while now. But you're not getting the better of me. You and me, we're done. You're on your own.'

Despite Martin's protests, Kenny disconnected the call. He couldn't be arsed to listen to his whinging. He'd known what he was getting himself into from the minute he'd come to work for Ryder.

Kenny had never trusted Martin. There was something too perfect about him, too well turned out. He'd found out ages ago that he was on Ryder's payroll, but Kenny had thought he could stay one step ahead. It seemed he'd failed.

He got in the car, popped the bag in the well of the passenger seat, and started the engine.

At the end of the road, he paused at the junction. If he was going on the run, it really would be stupid to leave behind the money in Alexander Place. He should suss it out before going, see if the police had found it. If not, he could be in, out, and on his way again in less than five minutes.

. . .

Twenty minutes later, Kenny parked his car. He walked the length of Alexander Place and back, glancing in vehicles as he went past, checking for movement in windows of the houses.

Satisfied that it was worth chancing it, he went to the back of the house and climbed over the fence. He only had a front door key, but it wouldn't take him long to get in.

He trod carefully along the side of the house and glanced around again. He could see nothing, so he stepped forward. Within seconds, he was inside with the door shut. He tore upstairs.

In the rear bedroom, he rooted out the bag that he'd pushed underneath the wardrobe. He pulled it out and looked inside, his elation turning to dismay. The bag was full of something, but it wasn't the cash he'd put in there. A pile of household rubbish and waste food had been tipped inside it, and it stank.

He threw it to the floor and glanced around the room in a panic. Had someone hidden it somewhere else? Or had someone taken it with them?

He couldn't risk any more time.

Cursing loudly, he went outside and over the fence into the field. When he was back in his car, he wondered who could have taken it. The list was too long to think about now.

He got to the end of the road, waiting to turn right, and banged a fist on the steering wheel. Some bastard had double-crossed him, and there was no way of getting revenge. The hundred grand he had now was definitely his pay-off.

He drove steadily, constantly checking his rear-view mirror, knowing he would only relax once he was on the open road. After a few minutes, it seemed as if he was in the clear. If so, he'd be in Manchester in an hour and on his way to the airport.

If he got out of the country quickly, there might not be time to put out an alert on his name. He'd have to take a risk and hide the money inside his clothes the best he could and hope his luggage didn't get searched. But it was a gamble he was willing to take.

He was almost at the A500, which would take him to the motorway, when he heard sirens. He checked through the rear-view mirror to see flashing lights. A police car was behind him. To his side, an unmarked vehicle appeared, with armed officers.

There was nowhere for him to go.

'No, no, no!' he yelled.

Within seconds, they'd boxed him in. He tried to squeeze past the car in front but got embedded on its bumper.

A plain-clothes officer wearing a stab vest tried the door handle as his colleagues surrounded Kenny, their guns up and ready.

'Open the door!' he shouted, pulling on the handle.

'Okay, okay!' Kenny put his hands up where they could see them.

They dragged him out of the car and onto the ground.

'Kenny Webb, I'm arresting you for conspiracy to supply and deal class A drugs and money laundering.'

'Wait!' Kenny cried. 'You can't do this!'

'You do not have to say anything. But it may harm your defence if you do not mention when questioned something which you later rely on in court.'

'I haven't done—' Kenny tried to struggle, but the officers kept a firm hold on him.

'Anything you do say may be given in evidence.'

Kenny didn't say another word. He wasn't going to waste his time.

CHAPTER FIFTY-SIX

Even though she had so much to do, Allie was on pins waiting to hear if they'd caught Kenny Webb red-handed. Really, she'd wanted to be there when they'd picked him up, but it wasn't her remit. And she couldn't wait to question him about the things she wanted to know more about.

Perry and Frankie had been to Car Wash City, Longton branch, to retrieve the phones and knife. She'd get them fast tracked for evidence immediately.

Her phone rang, and she put it on loud speaker.

'Give me good news, Shaun,' she cried.

'We have both Webb and Singleton in custody.'

'Yes!' Allie punched the air, her team crying out in excitement, too.

'We also have Kirstie Ryder, held in Stafford, along with Martin Smith and a few of the foot soldiers.'

'It just gets better.'

'There was no swap with Chris Singleton, though. We saw him talking on the phone, looking pretty concerned, so we got him with the drugs as he tried to leave.'

'Today has been a very good day,' she told him.

'Kenny left his home and then went to Alexander Place.'

'The greedy bastard. He wanted more cash?'

'He did. And it turns out the bag from there was full of household rubbish. Not sure where the money went, but it wasn't with Kenny.'

Allie laughed. 'I wish I'd been there to see that!'

'I'll be back shortly. Do you want to interview him with me once he's booked into custody?'

Allie could think of nothing better.

Perry was waving for her attention as she finished the call. 'What's up?'

'Riley Abbott is downstairs, wanting to see you. I asked if I could help, but she won't speak to anyone but you.'

'Well, aren't I Mrs Popular this morning?' Allie chuckled.

She couldn't help it. This could turn out to be one of the most important days of her career, and here she was, being pulled from pillar to post with people she either needed to speak to or who wanted to speak to her. 'Can you put her in a side room, tell her she'll have to wait a while? I have to update DCI Brindley, but I'll go afterwards.'

'Will do. I'll make her a brew.'

'Thanks. I won't be long.'

Twenty minutes later, Allie was downstairs. Riley had been shown into a soft interview room. She stood up when Allie entered.

'You told me I could speak to you anytime, about anything,' Riley said, anxiety clear on her face.

'I did, but that was a while ago.' Allie's tone was curt. She was done helping that family.

But then her compassionate side won as Riley sat down, deflated.

'Depending on what you're going to say, I must warn you that I might have to caution you first,' she added.'

'I don't care. I have to tell you what's been going on.'

Allie closed her eyes momentarily. 'You're going to tell me Kelsey is involved with the county lines, aren't you?'

For a moment, Riley looked startled that she'd guessed, but then she nodded.

'How long?'

Riley told her what she'd learned that morning. Then she paused for a moment. 'I've been doing it, too.'

Allie rolled her eyes in annoyance. 'And Fiona?'

Riley shook her head truthfully.

'Has she been dealing instead?'

Riley nodded.

Allie held up a hand. 'I need to stop you there. I'm cautioning you on suspicion of intent to supply an illegal substance.'

As Allie continued, Riley's chin sank into her chest.

'I need to book you into custody,' Allie finished.

'Please don't charge Kelsey with anything,' Riley pleaded. 'I'll say it was me, but I need to keep her safe.'

Allie was surprised that she was calling out the friend card now. After all the times she'd warned the Abbott family not to get involved, how could she help them now?

Then again, they were most likely too scared of Kenny Webb to do anything.

If they got Kenny out of the picture this afternoon, lots of this would go away. She might be able to give the family a bit of time. Although it wouldn't be her call as to what happened to her, she'd make Riley stew first. Perhaps a short, sharp shock would be good for her. A couple of hours on her own in a cell might give her a wake-up call.

'That's not up to me, I'm afraid,' she said. 'From there you'll be taken to a cell and–'

'*Please!* Don't do this to me.'

'Believe me, you'll thank me for it later.' Allie glared at her. 'There are things that are going on right now that I can't talk to you about, but I think you'd be better staying here with us at the moment.'

'I've never been in a cell before.'

'Well, then, I really hope it's your first and last time.'

Allie left a tearful Riley, praying she'd heed her words, if only for her younger sister's sake. Kelsey deserved so much better.

Back upstairs again, before going in to interview Martin Smith, Allie caught up with her team. Alongside the raids and her hospital visits, so much had been coming in that morning. Sam had done some cracking detective work on the notebooks, Frankie had followed up on the car seen in Redmond Street, and worked on going through the list of fingerprints, now cross-referenced in full, and Perry had checked out the photos from Lymer Road, putting some faces to names. It meant a lot more work moving forward, but finally pieces of the jigsaw were fitting into place.

'Time to get the show on the road,' she said, spotting Shaun coming across the floor.

'Smith is refusing legal aid,' Shaun said as he drew level.

'Really?' Allie was surprised to hear that. 'So we don't have the displeasure of seeing Charles Dinnen yet?'

'Not until we interview Kenny, I suppose.'

'Ugh, you can have too much Dinnen. Still, I think Smith will spill, don't you?'

'I think he'll squeal like a pig.'

Allie stood up. Eager to get going, she was finding it hard to contain her excitement.

But she couldn't wait to convict the two of them. If it was up to her, both Smith and Webb were going down today.

CHAPTER FIFTY-SEVEN

Now downstairs, Allie was sitting opposite Martin Smith. She gave him a curt nod as she settled into her chair.

'This is DCI Shaun Cooper from the Organised Crime Unit,' she said. 'I hear you've refused legal advice. Are you sure?'

'Yes, I want to speak to you without Dinnen hearing,' Martin replied.

'You could wait for the duty solicitor to see you?'

Martin shook his head. 'I need protection, for me and my family.'

'In return for?'

'I tell you everything I know.'

Shaun paused for a moment, to let Smith think they were pondering his proposal, Allie assumed, rather than them having the upper hand. It was up to the DCI to make that decision. Eventually, he nodded, then proceeded to run through the necessary to set up the interview.

They waited for Martin to speak. He cleared his throat a couple of times, then sat forward, his hands on the desk.

'It's all part of Terry Ryder's masterplan.'

Allie tried to keep her face impassive. She hadn't been expecting him to say that, not so soon. She'd assumed there would have to be some teasing out, some slipping up, questioning that would aim to get the truth from the lies.

'I've been trying to get away for months, but it's hard once you're in,' Martin said. 'They get something on you, and they keep at it until you're in too deep. But I've had enough. I'm worried for my safety, my family's safety, and I just want it over.'

'Had you any idea what you were getting into?' Shaun asked. 'Surely you knew who you were dealing with?'

'I was in debt, and the money offered was good. My job was to keep everyone sweet by telling them what they wanted to hear straight from the horse's mouth.'

'You mean Terry Ryder?'

'Yes. He told me what to say. I'd tell Kenny what Terry wanted him to hear. I'd tell Steve Kennedy what he wanted him to hear.' A pause. 'And I told Perry Wright what Terry wanted him to hear.' Martin held his head in his hands. 'But I wasn't keeping what Terry told me to myself. I was telling Kenny things I shouldn't have, too. I thought I could play one against the other. I was a fool.'

'You were informing to all of them?'

He nodded.

'Did Steve Kennedy pay you?'

'A little.'

'What about Kenny Webb?'

'No, he never. I just had to keep him sweet. But it was harder and harder. I wasn't certain but I had my suspicions he was on to me. I admit, I was scared.'

Shaun took a few notes and then looked up again. 'How did you get your information?'

'I had to report back to Terry what was happening. He would call me every Friday, and I'd tell him what I knew – or sometimes what I needed him to know. And then he'd tell me what to do next.'

'He'd ring you on a prison phone?'

'Burners, different ones.'

'And Kenny, did he do the same?'

'Yes, but it was all show. Ryder knew he'd always be loyal to Steve Kennedy. He just couldn't work out why he'd changed sides once he'd gone to prison. But it was always about money with Kenny. Terry paid more than Steve. It was that simple.'

'Did you ring in the tip-offs, too?' Shaun asked next.

'Yes. Ryder wanted a clean slate when he came out of prison. That's why we set Scott Milton up to take the rap for the drugs. I told Kenny it was to see if he was a grass, even though I knew he wasn't. Ryder wanted to be sure when he came out that he could go right back into what he'd been doing, what he'd been planning inside ready for his release.'

'Which is?'

'A drugs empire to rival anyone else's. Right under your nose. He wants to get rid of you, too.' Martin looked directly at Allie, who had been sitting quietly listening until then. 'I think you'll be in danger when he comes out. Make sure your family is safe. You know how dangerous he can be.'

'I have that covered,' Allie replied without emotion. She didn't want to think about that.

'Can you tell me about the murders earlier in the week?' she went on, her time to ask the questions. 'Were you there when Davy Lewis was killed?'

'Yes, it was Kenny who attacked him. I was there, too. He just went mad when he saw Chantelle on the floor. But why he put Janey under house arrest was beyond me. I think he panicked. I took care of her as good as I could.'

'Really? She was locked in a room.'

'We had to make it seem as if she was being held against

her will. I was going to split to Manchester tomorrow and take her with me if she was still in that house. It was barbaric that Kenny took her there. It made me think he'd kill her if I didn't do something.'

'You didn't think to inform us? We could have protected Janey.'

'You know I couldn't have done that.'

'On the contrary. You could have used a burner phone or given us a call on the national hotline, telling us where she was and the danger she was in. Kidnap is a very serious offence.' Allie would come back to that. She had more to figure out yet and also wanted to be clear about what he was alluding to.

'So you're saying that you saw Kenny Webb stab Davy Lewis, and yet you left him to die. Why didn't you help him?'

'I... I panicked. It all happened so quickly. That's why I wanted to help Janey instead. Chantelle didn't deserve to die like that. If Davy hadn't been so high, none of this would have happened.'

'How did Janey Webster end up at Coral Avenue? Did you take her there?'

CHAPTER FIFTY-EIGHT

There was a pause, and Allie thought she might lose him. But then Martin shook his head.

'Kenny took her there.'

Allie listened, making notes as he went through something similar to what Janey Webster had told her earlier. 'Why didn't you come forward with this before now?'

He raised his eyebrows in surprise.

'For the benefit of the recording,' she prompted.

'Oh, right. I was worried what Kenny would do. I'd seen him beat men with his fists, but I'd never seen him that violent. He told me afterwards he'd been waiting for an excuse to waste Davy. Terry had said to get rid of him, too. It was just a matter of time.' He rubbed his hands over his face. 'I remember Kenny laughing at one point, saying it had saved him a job. He said it would look like they'd killed each other anyway.'

'But without a murder weapon? One wasn't found on scene?'

'He's not the cleverest tool in the box. I don't think he

thought about that at the time. It was a spur-of-the-moment thing.'

'You mentioned ringing the hotline telephone number with a tip-off. Did you also ring me on my direct line, telling me about the whereabouts of the knife and two mobile phones that were missing?'

'Yes.'

'Who gave you my number?'

'Lots of people had your card. It wasn't hard to find.'

He was right there, but it could have come from Terry Ryder, she assumed. She hadn't changed her number since she'd started working in the major crimes team.

'Why had you called at Neville Place at that particular time on Sunday evening?'

'I was with Kenny when he had a call from Chantelle. Davy had been mouthing off at her and said he was calling to see her. She was really scared. She said what time he was due to arrive, but Davy was a little early. When Kenny saw what had happened, he was furious. He couldn't believe Davy had killed the girl. So he took him out.' Martin struggled with his emotions as he recalled everything. 'That's when I realised how dangerous Kenny was, and how much trouble I'd got myself in.'

'What did you do then?'

'On the outside, I was cool and reserved, as if it was a natural thing to see a murder every day. I had to convince Kenny I wasn't fazed by it. But inwardly, I was a wreck. I knew there and then that when I next rang Terry this week, which would have been tonight, I wanted out. No matter what the consequences would be, it had gone too far for me.'

'Did it cross your mind that they might be setting you up to take the rap?'

'Of course it did. But Terry told me to take any murder weapons I was ever handed and store them for future use.'

Martin rubbed his hands on his jeans. 'That's why I called you about the knife and phones. I was told to get rid of them, but I kept them for insurance purposes.'

Allie laughed inwardly. There was always someone out to double-cross a Ryder. That had happened to him before, the reason he was in prison now. Someone had planted evidence where bodies had been disposed of, all pointing back to Terry.

'So Ryder wants to get Kenny out of the way?'

'Yes.'

'Do you know why?'

'Like I say, the man is weird. He wanted to start again when he came out of prison. Kenny suggested burning each branch of Car Wash City down, but Ryder didn't want that. He said he needed somewhere you could visit so you could... talk unseen.'

Allie shuddered. Shaun glanced at her, and she nodded a little to indicate that she was okay. But she wouldn't be human if it didn't get to her.

Was it all going to start up again the minute Ryder got out of prison? They had to stop him somehow.

She had to stop him.

'Do you want to know what else I know?' Martin went on. 'It was Kenny who killed Milo Barker.'

Allie raised her eyebrows. 'Did you see that, too?'

He nodded. 'Kenny had been getting really volatile these past few weeks. He said Milo had been taking the piss out of the lad who lived in the flat. I was with Kenny when he called to see him. He got some lip off Milo, but he shoved him in the living room and closed the door so I couldn't see. It went from there.'

'What did?'

'He said he beat him, killed him after losing his temper again.'

'When was this?'

'Tuesday.'

'Right.' Allie looked at Shaun, who gave her a nod this time. She took it as approval to continue, showing their hand.

'We have someone else in custody on suspicion of the murder of Milo Barker, so I wonder if that's true. Of course, we'll review all the evidence as it comes in. But this does make me wonder what else you might have been lying about.'

Martin held his head down again. There was nothing more to be said. For now, they drew the interview to a conclusion.

Out in the corridor, Allie held up a hand to high-five Shaun. She didn't care if he was a grade above her. She just needed to celebrate.

'Talk about twisted lives,' she said as he high-fived her back. 'What a bunch of so-called friends.'

'Losers more like.'

'Everyone is working with everyone else, but equally they're all dishing the dirt on each other to stay one step ahead. Madness.'

'That we might have stopped, Allie,' Shaun said. 'We did a brilliant job.'

CHAPTER FIFTY-NINE

The cells were still pretty busy. One by one, they were getting through the many people who'd been brought in as part of Operation Dexter.

Frankie had gone with uniformed officers to collect Philip Barker. The knife he and Perry had picked up earlier had gone for analysis, and Sam was going through the data that had been retrieved from the phones. Scott Milton had left a message saying he wanted to speak to Allie, too. Well, he'd have to join the queue right now. She had a far more important job to do before that.

Allie went first interviewing Kenny Webb. Both she and Shaun had lots to get through, but they were on separate issues, so she took Perry in with her.

Kenny was sitting with his arms folded. He glanced up and glared at them, following their every move until they were seated.

Next to him was Charles Dinnen. Allie reckoned the solicitor must be on a retainer, because he was always at hand whenever needed. There hadn't been a time they'd had to wait for him to turn up. He'd always arrive at the station within half an hour of an arrest. Ryder must pay him well to be at everyone's beck and call, she mused.

'Let's start at the beginning with Davy Lewis,' Allie told Kenny once the interview had been set up. 'We have a lot to get through, as you can imagine. Firstly, we've found a knife we believe was the one used to inflict a fatal stab wound on him. It was located at Car Wash City, in your office, along with two mobile phones. One belonged to him and the other to Chantelle Bishop, the second victim at your property in Neville Street. What can you tell me about that?'

'Are my prints on anything?'

'They're being tested as we speak. I'm sure there'll be some interesting findings if it was a spur-of-the-moment thing.'

Allie took a little pleasure in seeing the look of horror Kenny tried to hide.

'Oops.' She paused. 'Might it have been on Terry Ryder's say-so not to wipe the knife clean this time? We'll have to wait and see.'

The vein in Kenny's temple twitched. All of a sudden he didn't seem as cocky.

'We also have witnesses who say that you stabbed Davy Lewis.'

Kenny sat forward then. 'Hearsay,' he offered. 'I had nothing to do with it.'

'Was it on Terry Ryder's say-so that you killed him?'

Kenny sniggered. 'You're clutching at straws, aren't you?'

'I thought maybe he'd want to get him out of the way before he was released from prison?'

Kenny went to speak, but Charles shook his head.

'No comment,' he said instead.

'Ryder wanted Lewis gone, didn't he?'

'No comment.'

'He told you to kill Lewis and then he set you up to take

the rap by giving us a tip-off about the knife and the phones. You thought you were in the clear, when in actual fact, he wanted to take you out at the same time.'

'Was there a question in there I needed to answer?'

'Let me add one, then. Why was that?'

He sneered at her. 'No comment.'

'Did he pay you to kill Davy Lewis?'

The evil stare he gave Allie would have chilled anyone else, but over the years, she'd got used to the venom directed her way. She didn't care, because she wasn't going to see him for a very long time. Apart from his court case, of course.

When he said nothing, she continued.

'Let's move on to Milo Barker. We have a further witness who puts you and your car at number seven Redmond Street on Tuesday morning at approximately nine a.m.'

Kenny said nothing.

Even the way he folded his arms irked Allie. He was so irritating.

'We have your car on CCTV coming onto the main road a few minutes later.'

'You still can't prove I was in the flat.'

'How did you feel when you saw Milo Barker was dead when you got there?'

'I didn't see him because I wasn't there.'

'Why didn't you contact the police when you found him deceased?'

'Really? I'm not going to repeat myself.'

'We found your prints inside the flat.'

Kenny nodded. 'I look out for Andrew. He's the tenant.'

Allie couldn't help but raise her eyebrows in surprise.

'I've already told you that I visited a few times.'

'Not just to kill Milo Barker, then?' She knew they had Philip Barker in custody, but it wouldn't hurt to pressure Kenny. Maybe he'd slip up about something else.

'Your line of questioning is bordering on intrusive, Detective Inspector,' Charles Dinnen said.

'No, let her continue,' Kenny told him. 'I'm not getting into trouble for something I didn't do. My fingerprints will be there, I expect. But so will a number of folks'.'

'Because the flat was used as a meet-up point for your, I use the term loosely, workers?'

'Not to my knowledge.'

'So why were you in the flat in the first place?'

'I told you, I wasn't there.'

'We're going round in circles now. Just one last thing, before we finish.' Allie stared at Kenny pointedly until he caught her eye. 'We've been doing a little digging and have found a cleaning company that you own, Stoke-Clean. How many employees do you have working for you at the moment?'

'Fifteen or so.'

'And they are independent of you, these employees?'

'Yes.'

'Then can you tell me why the money you receive from the recruiting agency that pays their wages goes straight into your business account and you hardly pass any of it on to them?'

'They pay me board and lodgings. What's left after that belongs to them.'

'And how long have you been running this company?'

'You tell me. You seem to know so much.'

'Okay, then. You set it up in twenty seventeen. That's over five years of board and lodgings that you've taken from them, and yet you claim that money from the city council, too, don't you?'

Kenny squirmed.

'I'd call that benefit fraud.'

'Whatever.'

'You don't agree? Well, how about modern-day slavery then? I think you profited off vulnerable people for your own greed.'

Kenny launched across the table at her.

'Whoa!' Perry pushed him away as Allie ran from her seat. 'Back off.'

'I'm going to get you for this, you bitch,' Kenny snarled. 'For all of this.'

'I said back off!' Perry reiterated.

'Funny how it's always me you want to have a go at, isn't it, Kenny?' Allie snapped. 'Aren't you man enough to do better than that?'

Kenny was about to speak, but Charles Dinnen touched his arm and shook his head. Kenny shirked away his hand and folded his arms.

'The evidence we have will be put to the Crown Prosecution Service. I expect we'll be speaking to you shortly when the forensics come back on the knife.'

Minutes later, Allie and Perry left the room, their work complete for now. Although shaking, Allie was pleased with the outcome so far. She'd done what she'd set out to do.

She had got him.

CHAPTER SIXTY

After the running around and interviewing she'd done all day, Allie felt drained. It was nearly eight p.m., and the team were finishing off with a pizza takeaway. Allie was bringing them up to speed about Philip Barker, who had confessed to killing his brother, Milo.

'He was so calm,' she said. 'Once we said what evidence we had, he just told us what had happened. He and Milo had an argument about Milo not wanting him back at home. Milo had stormed out and was staying over at the flat after going out for a pint. Philip had gone round to have it out with him again. They had a huge row, starting in a fight and ending up with him strangling Milo.' Allie shook her head. 'It was almost clinical, the way he spoke about it, as if he had no feeling either way as to what he'd done. It's sad, but he seems conditioned to stay in prison.'

'He'll be back inside for a longer stretch now.' Sam reached for a can of Coke and opened it, taking a sip. 'It's his mum I feel sorry for.'

'I bet she has more peace when he's inside,' Frankie noted. Sam laughed. 'You're probably right.'

'Well, we've created one hell of a pile of admin work today.' Perry wiped his fingers after devouring a slice of ham and cheese pizza.

'For sure,' Frankie agreed. 'It's a good end to the week, though.'

'It is, and I need a glass of something cold now to celebrate it with.' Allie screwed her napkin up into a ball and threw it into the bin. 'Let's call it a night, team. I'll be in for a few hours tomorrow if anyone wants to join me. Other than that, the weekend is your own. Unless we have anyone else playing up over it.'

'I hope not.' Sam collected the takeaway boxes to throw away. 'I'd like to see my daughter for at least an hour or two.'

Allie smiled. It was tough on them all when there was an active case. The hours were long and, even when they did leave the station to go home for some rest, minds tended to stay on the job in hand. Family time was important to everyone. She couldn't wait to chill out tomorrow evening. Just her, Mark, and a good film.

Driving home down Bucknall New Road, Allie thought of Scott Milton and why he wanted to see her. She would visit him next week to see if he had any information she could use. But for now, she wanted to give him time with his family, too. Amy had been released from hospital and would be cautioned in due course.

Riley had been interviewed by Sam and released pending further enquiries. Allie would visit Fiona Abbott, see if she could catch up with all three women at the same time. She wasn't sure how welcome she'd be, but she wanted to try and put their minds at ease, perhaps get them to see that this could be their chance to move on and not be involved anymore.

There were also things she wanted to iron out, like who had been doing the drug runs and how many times. So far, there was no evidence that any of them had been involved. It could have been so different for them, again. She hoped this final scare would be enough.

Both families had the opportunity to start afresh, either staying here or moving away. It was up to them now. They all had a better future ahead of them.

As she sat at traffic lights at the bottom of Limekiln Bank, on a whim, she went left instead of going straight across towards home. She drove for several minutes, passing through Abbey Hulton, Milton, past the crematorium where her family and sister were buried. On to Baddeley Green, Stockton Brook, and finally Endon.

She turned into Royal Avenue. Twelve individually designed houses, most having new vehicles parked in their long drives. She and Mark had nicknamed it Millionaires Row a long time ago. Now she'd never look at it that way, its reputation tarnished by one family.

She parked across the road from The Gables, glad to see lights on at several windows. Even with her earlier thoughts, it was quite some house. It was good to see another family enjoying it.

The property had haunted her thoughts, and often her sleep, for many years. It had belonged to Terry Ryder.

Husband of a murdered wife.

Father of a daughter who was going back to prison.

A patriarch who Allie wished they could keep behind bars for the rest of his life.

CHAPTER SIXTY-ONE

Monday

Allie sat in the meeting room, the team around her. Jenny was at the head of the table. Over coffee and a box of custard and cream doughnuts, which the DCI had brought in, Allie was updating her on everything that had happened over the weekend.

'I've had an email from the tech team,' she said. 'They kept Martin Smith's phone on all day Friday, but there was no contact from Terry Ryder. He must have heard about the raids through the grapevine.' She grinned. 'Sorry, Ma'am, but I hope he's quivering in his cell.'

'At the very least, I hope he's fuming,' Jenny said.

'I'd love to be a fly on the wall when he realises what's been going on,' Perry agreed. 'He's going to be panicking now about what else we'll find.'

'Martin Smith will be given witness protection,' Jenny added. 'A lot will be riding on his testimony.'

'I know it's not an easy option, but I think he'll be glad of it,' Allie said. 'He's got himself into something too deep to get out of.'

'Can't help thinking it serves him right,' Perry remarked. 'He knew about people's reputations. I'm still annoyed that he played me, too.'

'But did he?' Allie asked. 'You told him what he wanted to hear, and he relayed it back. I think that worked a treat.'

Perry screwed his face up. 'I suppose, but I still feel aggrieved that he didn't trust me.'

'You're a copper!'

'I wouldn't trust you either,' Frankie said, most probably to lighten the mood.

It did the trick because everyone laughed. Perry flicked Frankie's ear, then grinned sheepishly as he looked at the DCI.

Jenny was still smiling. It was nice to see her appreciating them, allowing them to let off steam. Allie could tell that Jenny enjoyed the camaraderie as much as she did. They were a considerate bunch, having been through so much together, and with a great deal to come, no doubt.

She took a moment to glance around the room at her closest friends.

Perry Wright, *her* right-hand man. He'd changed through the years they'd known each other; so, too, had she. But if anything, it had deepened their respect for one another, and together they formed a formidable partnership. She'd been lost without him when she'd worked in the Community Intelligence Team for a spell. Not that she'd ever tell him that. His head would grow too big.

Sam Markham. Without Sam, they would have taken longer to solve a lot of their crimes. She was excellent at her role, and Allie knew her team worked well when they did things they enjoyed. The understanding they had that she acted as the office manager even when the position was vacant, as well as excelling on anything technical or detailed, worked well.

Frankie Higgins. He was being attentive as usual, listening to what Jenny had to say. He was going to make a great inspector one day, should he choose to go that far. He was young, keen, and very affable, always able to wrap people around his little finger to get the result he required. And he was a great team player.

They all knew their patches, and the people, across the city. Stoke-on-Trent, like most urban areas, had its positives and negatives. They worked with troubled families. They liaised with the community groups who were striving to do good things. Luckily, there was far more beauty than neglect, and lots of exciting things happening that would improve the six towns.

Grace had gone back to her team that morning, as their cases had drawn to a close. The news on Simon was getting better by the day. At least he was out of the woods now and was likely to be back at work in a few weeks, once his broken rib had mended. They would start trawling through more camera footage from today to figure out what had happened to him.

It always amazed Allie just how much work colleagues became like family. Spending so much time together meant getting used to each other's foibles; accommodating and learning mood swings; realising when someone was upset and needed to talk, or indeed wanted to be quiet. Being there for each other. Keeping one another safe.

And Allie might get too involved with the public emotionally at times, but it was hard not to. She did detach herself from it mostly. Occasionally, cases made her have nightmares, often spilling over into her downtime, but she wouldn't apologise for being caring and compassionate. Not ever.

And despite being an inspector, she secretly much preferred being a sergeant, even though she did far more hands-on work than she should. One day she'd probably go back to working in the community, especially if things with the foster care team worked out well. She could see herself enjoying something like that, once she'd had enough of all the murder and mayhem.

'Allie?'

She looked up to see them all staring at her. 'Sorry, I was in a daze.'

'I was talking about your favourite man, Mr Ryder,' Jenny said. 'He's out of prison soon. We have a lot to do before then if we are going to keep him in there. We need more evidence.'

Allie frowned. Was Jenny saying what she'd longed to hear? That they were going to put in the time to nail the bastard once and for all?

'Why the long face?' Jenny teased. 'I thought you'd be pleased.'

'I am, Ma'am.' Allie grinned then. 'I also have the best team to work with to get the job done.'

CHAPTER SIXTY-TWO

One month later

Over the past four weeks, everyone involved in Operation Dexter had worked hard to gather as much information as they could on Terry Ryder and his team. Some of the lads who'd worked for him had talked, most hadn't. But it was more to do with the damning evidence they had on Kenny Webb which would lead one man to the other. Surprisingly, Kenny hadn't squealed, choosing to stay quiet about everything he knew.

Fingerprints on the knife used to murder Davy Lewis had come back as a match to Kenny Webb's, along with Davy's blood on the blade, both of which had been key to getting forensic evidence to place Webb at the murder scene.

As well as the tip-offs, Martin Smith's burner phone had been used to stay in touch with Lily Barker with regards to Janey Webster's welfare. Lily Barker had been cautioned, pending further enquiries. There had been no further Friday calls from Terry Ryder.

So far, two men had been tracked back to a white van parked in Huntbach Street in relation to the assault on Simon. But they'd kept their faces covered with their balaclavas, heads down. The vehicle was on false plates belonging to a Mondeo, so it was a question of searching to either find the right number plate or figure out where it had been stored. They wouldn't give up until there were no more leads, and often vans like that came up on a crime further down the line.

Now, Allie was waiting outside HM Prison Long Larton, with Perry and DCI Cooper.

'This is rather satisfactory, don't you think?' she said as she watched the exit door, waiting for a certain man to appear.

'Here comes the cavalry.' Perry nodded in the direction of a black BMW with tinted windows. It stopped a few metres along on the opposite side of the road. 'I wonder who's come all the way to pick him up and will now have to go all the way back to Stoke.'

Shaun laughed. 'I doubt anyone will get out and give us the satisfaction of showing their face.'

'Still, I'm looking forward to this as much as you two.' Perry smirked.

The door on the gate opened. Allie's breath caught in her chest when Terry Ryder stepped out onto the pavement. He was wearing what seemed to be a new suit, modern in its design with a crisp white shirt, undone at the collar.

She hadn't seen him since 2015, when he'd been four years into his sentence. For all his time inside, age might not have mellowed him, but he was certainly still dignified. His short dark hair was almost grey, and he was clean-shaven. Allie imagined he'd smell of something expensive.

She remembered when she'd met him, when he'd tried to

win her over like he'd done with all the women he'd manipulated. It had irked him that he didn't have her under his thumb; couldn't have her in his bed. She liked that now, that she had not succumbed to his charms.

Terry tilted his face towards the sky, the feel of the bright winter sun on his skin, by all accounts, a treat. A smile played on his lips, but when he spotted them, his whole demeanour changed.

They walked across to him, the marked transportation van next to their vehicle giving the game away a little. It was good to see Ryder frown when he noticed it.

'Mr Ryder, we meet again.' Allie smiled, drawing level with him.

'Allie!' Terry's tone was jovial. 'How lovely to see you. To what do I owe this pleasure?'

'There's a small matter we have to clear up, I'm afraid.' She took out her cuffs. 'Hold out your hands, please.'

Terry's face darkened, but for once, Allie had the upper hand. For all his charm and smooth talk, he couldn't outrun the law.

'What's this about?' The strap on the bag dropped down Terry's arm until the bag hit the ground.

'Hands, please,' Allie said again.

With an exaggerated sigh, he held them out, and she cuffed him.

'Oh, Allie, I've missed the aroma of your perfume. How have you been, sweetheart?'

'All the better for not seeing you.' She'd love nothing more than to kick the man in the balls, causing as much pain as she could muster. His sheer arrogance beggared belief.

Instead, she ignored his comment and let Shaun take over. It was mostly his collar anyway.

'Terry Ryder,' Shaun began. 'I'm arresting you on suspicion of intent to supply an illegal substance, money laundering, and conspiracy to commit murder.'

'My, my, my, you have been busy.' He sneered, glancing at each of them in turn. 'I hope you have your facts right, Detectives, along with all your evidence to back it up. It's not easy to prove something like these accusations when I've been out of circulation for so long.'

Shaun read out the rest of his rights before Allie replied to him.

'People have been singing again, and really loud,' she said. 'We've been told a *lot* more than we bargained for.'

They marched with Terry towards the transport van. He didn't put up a fight. Perhaps he believed there wouldn't be enough evidence against him. It was up to the CPS whether Ryder would stay behind bars, or if he would be let out on bail. They were all praying for the former but equally getting ready for the latter.

Shaun opened the door. 'In you go, fella.'

There was no response from Terry. As the door closed, he caught her eye, the stare he gave her intimidating but not successful.

'Gotcha, you bastard,' she said.

Allie glanced at Perry, matching his smile, and shook hands with Shaun.

'Nice work, everyone.'

CHAPTER SIXTY-THREE

Allie was standing in the living room window, watching every car that went past. She was exhausted. She hadn't stopped that morning, making sure everything was in place.

She wanted it all to be perfect, but it was eating her up inside. What if they failed? What if they weren't good enough to be parents? To understand the needs of children who had been torn away from everything they knew and placed with them. To deal with some who would be so traumatised they wouldn't realise they were safe staying somewhere else. It was going to be a steep learning curve.

'Come and sit down, and stop wringing your hands!' Mark protested.

Allie turned to him. He was sitting on the settee, his iPad in his hands, as if nothing monumental in his life was about to happen.

'How can you be so cool about it?' She flopped down beside him. 'I'm so nervous.'

'So am I, but I'm not showing it.'

She wished she could be the same. How she contained herself at work in stressful situations, she didn't know.

Because right now, she was nigh on ready to have a heart attack.

'I'm actually petrified, Allie,' Mark admitted then. 'I might look all cool and collected, but...' He held out his hands to show her how much they were shaking.

'We can do this, right?'

Mark put down the iPad and placed an arm around her shoulder, bringing her near.

'Of course we can.' He nodded profusely. 'It's going to be scary but wonderful. Besides, if we don't, we'll have to eat our weight in lovely food and treats we've brought in for her.'

'Not too much chocolate, for starters.'

'Chocolate for starters?' He chuckled. 'Now, there's an idea.'

'You know what I mean.' She paused. 'Do you think she'll be here for Christmas?'

'Possibly. It's only a few weeks away.'

'I might burst if we can spend Christmas Day with her. It's going to be wonderful to see her face light up. Well, unless she's fed up with us by then.'

A car door slammed outside, and they eyed each other. Allie got up and raced to the window.

'They're here!' She turned again to face Mark, but he was already at her side.

He reached for her hand.

'Here we go,' he said.

They went through to the hall and opened the front door.

'Hi, sorry we're a bit late. The traffic was a nightmare.' Rachel Flint, their allocated social worker, was holding on to the hand of a six-year-old girl. 'It's a bit blustery, isn't it? I thought we were going to be blown into the house!'

Allie smiled, but she wasn't listening. Her heart had melted, all her nerves forgotten as she saw a child, wary of all the adults around her, and the house she was stepping into.

The girl's face was creased with a frown, her button nose red from the cold. She had deep-set blue eyes and the longest of eyelashes. Brown plaits were visible at each side of a striped woollen hat, a white bobble on the top.

She was a tiny thing, Allie noted, holding up a hand in a wave.

'Hi, you must be Amelia,' she said. 'I'm Allie, and this is Mark. We've heard so much about you. Why don't you come on in?'

The little girl paused, looking at Rachel for reassurance. When Rachel nodded eagerly, she stepped inside the house.

Allie closed the door behind her and glanced wide-eyed at Mark to see him grinning like a loon.

'Do you like milkshakes, Amelia?' he asked. 'Because I think we have every flavour you can think of to try out. And wait until you see the garden. It's got a trampoline, just for you. Come on.' Mark held out his hand.

Allie's eyes brimmed with tears to see the little girl's face light up. She watched in awe as Amelia took Mark's hand and followed them through into the kitchen.

She turned to Rachel, almost forgetting she was there in her rush to greet their guest. 'Would you like a coffee?'

'I'd love one, please. Then I'll leave you to it.' She lowered her tone. 'I can see you have everything under control.'

Amelia's eyes were flicking everywhere as she saw her temporary home for the first time. A flicker of a smile appeared as she glanced up shyly at Mark.

Allie breathed a sigh of relief. They had done it. They had started their journey, a new chapter in their life. And for every child they helped along the way, she reckoned it would give them as much pleasure.

Just like her work team, she and Mark would face anything that was thrown at them. It wasn't going to be easy, especially adapting to children on short stays rather than getting to know a child of their own permanently.

But one day, who knew? They might get to adopt one... or two... along the way.

***

First of all, I'd like to say a huge thank you for choosing to read Twisted Lives. I hope you enjoyed my sixth outing with Allie Shenton and the team.

If you did enjoy Twisted Lives, I would be grateful if you would leave a small review or a star rating on your Kindle. I'd love to know what you thought. It's always good to hear from you.

Why not join my reader group? I love to keep in touch with my readers, and send a newsletter every few weeks. I also reveal covers, titles and blurbs exclusively to you first.

Join Team Sherratt

ALL BOOKS BY MEL SHERRATT

These books are continually added to so please
Click here for details about all my books on one page

DS Allie Shenton Trilogy

Taunting the Dead

Follow the Leader

Only the Brave

Broken Promises

Hidden Secrets

Twisted Lives

The Estate Series (4 book series)

Somewhere to Hide

Behind a Closed Door

Fighting for Survival

Written in the Scars

DS Eden Berrisford Series (2 book series)

The Girls Next Door

Don't Look Behind You

DS Grace Allendale Series (4 book series)

Hush Hush

Tick Tock

Liar Liar

Good Girl

Standalone Psychological Thrillers

Watching over You

The Lies You Tell

Ten Days

The Life She Wants

ACKNOWLEDGMENTS

To all my fellow Stokies, my apologies if you don't gel with any of the Stoke references that I've changed throughout the book. Obviously writing about local things such as *The Sentinel* and Hanley Police Station would make it seem a little too close to home, and I wasn't comfortable leaving everything authentic. So, I took a leaf out of Arnold Bennett's 'book' and changed some things slightly. However, there were no oatcakes harmed in the process.

Thanks to my amazing fella, Chris, who looks out for me so that I can do the writing. I wish I could take credit for all the twists in my books but he's actually more devious than I am when it comes down to it – in the nicest possible way. We're a great team – a perfect combination.

Thanks to Alison Niebieszczanski, Caroline Mitchell, Louise Ross, Talli Roland and Sharon Sant, who give me far more friendship, support and encouragement than I deserve.

Thanks to my amazing early reader team - you know who you are! I'm so blessed to have you on board.

Finally, thanks to all my readers who keep in touch with me via Twitter and Facebook. Your kind words always make me smile – and get out my laptop. Long may it continue.

ABOUT THE AUTHOR

Ever since I can remember, I've been a meddler of words. Born and raised in Stoke-on-Trent, Staffordshire, I used the city as a backdrop for my first novel, TAUNTING THE DEAD, and it went on to be a Kindle #1 bestseller. I couldn't believe my eyes when it became the number 8 UK Kindle KDP bestselling books of 2012.

Since then, I've sold over 2 million books. My writing has come under a few different headings - grit-lit, thriller, whydunnit, police procedural, emotional thriller to name a few. I like writing about fear and emotion – the cause and effect of crime – what makes a character do something. I also like to add a mixture of topics to each book. Working as a housing officer for eight years gave me the background to create a fictional estate with good and bad characters, and they are all perfect for murder and mayhem.

But I'm a romantic at heart and have always wanted to write about characters that are not necessarily involved in the darker side of life. Coffee, cakes and friends are three of my favourite things, hence I write women's fiction under the pen name of Marcie Steele.

Printed in Great Britain
by Amazon